"After [...] [...]nces involving a plunger being used as a weapon, I knew I was going to love *Monster in My Closet* complete with all of its cheekiness and quirky characters."
—*All Things Urban Fantasy*

"*Monster in my Closet* has it all, suspense, romance, growth for the character. I couldn't put it down—it sucked me in from the start, which is what I love about a book. I had to know more about Zoey, she was always in the back of my mind when I wasn't reading."
—*The Reading Diaries*

"This first installment in a developing series shines with its originality and playfulness. Ms. Naquin has created an entertaining world of the supernatural with intriguing characters that will have you anticipating the next book."
—*Romancing the Dark Side*

# R.L. NAQUIN

# *Monster*
## in My Closet

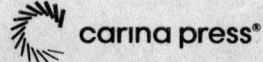

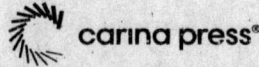
carina press®

ISBN-13: 978-0-373-00261-0

Monster in My Closet

www.CarinaPress.com

**Printed in U.S.A.**

Recycling programs
for this product may
not exist in your area.

Dear Reader,

The two most frequently asked questions every writer gets are these: "Where do you get your ideas?" and "How long have you been writing?"

The initial idea for this book was a whisper of *what if* and a fully formed picture in my head of a closet monster drinking coffee and reading the newspaper at a kitchen table. The opening scene of this book is exactly as I first pictured it—except the protagonist who comes across the monster, Maurice, is not a twelve-year old boy, and *Monster in My Closet* is most definitely not for kids. Also, I un-furred the original version of Maurice because, seriously, nobody wants monster fur baked into their cupcakes. Ew.

The second question is a little more complicated. I've been *writing* since fourth grade. But I only started *finishing* when I wrote this book. *Monster in My Closet* was a turning point in my life. At the ripe age of forty-one, I finally grew up, stopped being too paralyzed by fear of failure to finish what I'd started, and began the career I'd always wanted.

I'd figured out that not finishing what I'd started was the only real failure.

*Monster in My Closet* was as much an adventure into a new life for me as it is for our heroine, Zoey. I'm so excited to be sharing the adventure with you.

Thanks for coming along!

Rachel

For Kevin, who mended what was broken.

# in My Closet

# ONE

O<small>F ALL THE</small> possible weapons I might have grabbed, I chose a toilet brush. The men's boxers and over-sized Hello Kitty T-shirt I wore reinforced my feeling of absolute stupidity. I made a mental note to buy myself a baseball bat, should I live through the next few minutes. And maybe some grownup pajamas.

I choked up on the brush and prepared to leap out at the intruder in my kitchen.

Logic, if I had any that early, might have suggested the unknown guest was my friend Sara, making coffee and waiting to ambush me into going to the gym. I didn't think of that until later. I woke to the smell of coffee and naturally jumped to the conclusion someone had broken in.

And my response was to grab the toilet brush on the way down the hall. I'm not my brightest first thing in the morning.

I craned my neck around the corner and peered into the kitchen. Logic would have been wasted anyway. It wasn't Sara at the table.

The intruder sat with a newspaper tented around his face and torso. He hummed to himself. A cup of coffee disappeared behind the paper. The humming paused for a sip, then resumed its tuneless refrain. The cup reappeared.

I was a bit put out—curious, but also irritated. I suppose I should have been more alarmed, but who breaks into a house with ill intent and stops to make coffee and read the paper? Under the table, a pair of checkered high-tops bounced in near time with the humming. My guest turned the page of the newspaper, and my throat locked in mid-swallow. The chalky, bony fingers holding the edges of the *San Francisco Chronicle* were familiar.

I ducked my head into the hallway and leaned against the wall for support, gulping air. I knew those hands. I clutched the toilet brush against myself as if it had the power to ward off nightmares. In the flash of a forgotten memory, I could see those hands grabbing at my doorframe, reaching to snatch out my eyes. My skin was clammy with terror ripened by over twenty years of repression and denial. I was five again, and monsters were real.

KIDS ARE BORN with self-preservation instincts, and that night those instincts kept me still. The slightest twitch would alert the monster in the closet that I knew he was there.

I lay motionless beneath the sheets and stifling blanket, my fingers clasping the fabric beneath my chin. In the ambient glow of my Care Bear nightlight, the closet door seemed to swing out—not enough to be certain, but enough for me to hold my breath and squeeze the covers tighter. A floorboard wheezed a soft sigh.

I considered pulling the covers over my head for protection, but a sudden move like that would yell "I know you're in there!" which would make the monster fly out and devour me so fast I wouldn't have time to scream for help. Besides, having my head covered meant I'd eventually have to come out for air. If I wasn't watching, what would stop him from creeping beside the bed and waiting for me to peek out to find his warty, drooling face breathing over me?

I held still, limbs locked in place. In my mind I practiced making a run for it. My nightgown was damp with sweat. Between the cotton fabric tangled around my legs and the white socks on my feet, I knew I couldn't break free of the bed and sprint across the room before the monster heard me. I had to cross in front of the closet to get out. I would never make it.

I needed help. It was a huge risk, making sound enough for someone to come, but it was my only option. I had to try.

"Mommy." The timid whisper was hardly enough to be heard from inches away. I tried again, putting more strength and breath into it. "Mommy."

The closet door drifted open a few inches—this time I was sure of it. I could hear the scritchy sound of the wood dragging across the carpet.

"Mommy." My voice sounded steady this time, conversational in tone and volume. No need for panic. Monsters love panic. They slurp panic through a crazy straw and make gross sucking noises.

The closet door moved again, now halfway open. Chalky, bony fingers slid up the doorframe, and yellow eyes blinked in the blackness.

A face moved into the muted light. Pointed ears cupped its head like giant shells, and shadows gathered in the carved-stone valleys around its bulbous nose. As I had known he would be, the monster was grinning. His teeth were ragged, and slobber dripped down his pointed chin.

My paralysis melted. I sat up and slammed my back against the wall. My lungs filled to capacity, and I screamed, holding nothing back. "Mommy!"

A light snapped on in the hall. The grinning, slavering monster winked at me and stepped into the closet, thoughtfully closing the door behind him.

"Zoey, baby, what's wrong?" Mommy was there, and I was safe in her arms, shaking and sobbing. The familiar scent of the ocean blew over me as she stroked my hair and murmured soothing nonsense sounds. We stayed that way until the shaking subsided, and I was capable of releasing my cramped fingers from her sweater.

"He was going to eat me," I said. My eyes flicked to the closet door, and tears threatened to spill down my cheeks in a fresh outburst.

Mommy frowned. "Let me take a look."

She yanked the door open and tugged the string hanging from the bare bulb. From my vantage point on the bed, I couldn't see inside, but Mommy didn't scream. That was a good sign.

She stood in the doorway staring into the space for a few moments, still frowning. In a loud, authoritative voice, she addressed the pile of dirty laundry, the clothes drooping half off their hangers, the toys crammed into boxes and on shelves. "There are *no* monsters allowed in this closet. Go away, monsters! You aren't welcome here!" She shook her finger and made a stern *mom face* for emphasis.

I giggled. My fear faded. I knew there were no monsters and Mommy was putting on a show to make me feel better. It was a trick of the light. It was my mind making things up. There was never anything there.

Mommy thoroughly checked and berated the rest of the room until I was too exhausted from the emotional typhoon to keep my eyes open.

For good measure, I slept with the light on for a few days, but the monster didn't bother me anymore. It was all in my imagination.

Everyone knows there's no such thing as monsters.

HERE I WAS, twenty-three years later, looking at those same panic-inducing fingers clutching my morning paper. Squeezing my eyes tight, I concentrated on breathing. I thought about my mom. She'd been gone since I was eight, and I didn't remember much about her. With the return of the forgotten monster memory, her face came back to me in detail. I could hear her voice commanding the monster away.

"No monsters allowed here," I whispered. "Go away, monsters. Go away."

This was stupid. I was a grownup and a business owner. Monsters were not real, but intruders were. I pulled myself together and put on my stern *mom face*. This newspaper-reading, coffee-sipping, tuneless-humming asshat better have a damn good explanation for waking me up so early and taking over my kitchen. I dropped the impotent toilet brush on the floor next to a pile of shoes I'd meant to put away days ago.

I swung around the corner and glared into the room, fists on my hips, feet planted apart, in my best impression of an angry schoolmarm.

I felt pretty good about it. I was certain I looked formidable. My dark red locks were probably shooting out in every direction, lending me an air of ferocity. I added a little crazy-eye to my expression for good measure.

The effort I put into looking tough didn't matter. The mystery guest was still reading behind the paper, taking sips of coffee and, of course, humming. He was oblivious to me.

I considered clearing my throat to get his attention, but that was trite. In my head, I tried out various threatening, angry, sarcastic, nonchalant and mildly curious remarks, but none struck me as appropriate.

I settled on the ridiculous.

"You better pray you haven't done the crossword, buddy." I focused on amplifying my crazy-eye.

The paper slid down to reveal the same horrific,

grinning face I remembered from childhood—only bigger.

I stood my ground. It was obvious that I was hallucinating, since monsters were fiction. Backing down from an illusion would be embarrassing.

"You're up!" he said. "Sit-sit-sit! I made you orange-strawberry muffins. They'll be ready in a few minutes." He jerked to his feet and waved me to a chair. "I'll get you some coffee." He paused for a long moment, and his smile grew larger as he gazed at me. "Gosh, you grew up pretty, Zoey. Sit-sit-sit."

I felt an odd detachment as I drifted into the room and took a seat at my own table. I watched in silence as the creature moved through my kitchen, banging cupboards with enthusiasm and setting the table. He brought me a cup of coffee and patted my arm. His pale, mottled hand was warm. I'd expected the chill of a dead thing.

On autopilot, I sipped my coffee and found it just as I liked it, overly sweet with artificially flavored creamer. Aside from the seismic activity in the cup I was holding, I probably looked perfectly calm. I tried to breathe through it, expecting the hallucination to pop like a soap bubble or be blurred away by the blare of my alarm clock.

"Zoey, Zoey, my friend, Zoey!" His singing was off-key as he danced around my kitchen, the song apparently made up on the spot. His voice was higher in pitch than one would expect from a closet monster—more like Kermit the Frog than Cookie Monster. "Made her muffins, but they're doughy.

Zoooooeeeey!" He frowned. "That could've been a better rhyme. David Bowie? Do you know anyone named Joey?"

The oven timer buzzed and he pulled out the muffin pan, leaving it to cool on the stovetop. I blinked. No oven mitts. I took a swallow of coffee.

The monster-thing plopped into the chair across the table, his round, yellow eyes fixed on me. "So can I stay? Wait, don't answer that yet. Taste a muffin first. I'm a good cook! I can clean the pool, too. Honest, I won't get in the way."

I blinked again. "What?"

"You're still mad at me, aren't you. I'm really sorry about that. I didn't mean to scare you the last time I was here."

Even for a hallucination, this was surreal. Across the top of the creature's head, a sprinkling of fine hairs sprouted, all combed carefully to one side. I focused on a single, stubborn hair that had sprung up in a show of independence. It jiggled when he talked, bobbing forward and back with each enthusiastic gesture. I wondered if he would be insulted if I offered him a little hair gel. That would tamp it right down.

"…and that's why I came here when she kicked me out. It's the only place I've ever felt safe."

"What?" I knew I'd missed something crucial. I glanced down at the table in an automatic search for the DVR remote. I needed to rewind and replay that last part.

"You're not awake yet." He patted my arm again. "Drink your coffee. We'll try again when you're fed."

MY CLOSET MONSTER (who introduced himself as Maurice) turned out to be more than a good cook; he was an amazing cook. The muffin melted in my mouth before I could chew it. The flavors mixed together on my tongue as if the muffin was made from a magical fruit that grew on an orangeberry tree situated in a vanilla-scented orchard shaded by double rainbows and watered exclusively with unicorn tears. They were enormous, and I ate three.

Somewhere into my second one, the fog lifted, and I was able to focus on what he was telling me. The food made it all more acceptable, almost normal.

"I was only eight, myself, back then," he said. "I had nowhere to go, and your mom took me in. Oh, Zoey, she was so mad at me that night. I was supposed to stay in the hall closet, but yours had all those great toys. Even then I loved to cook, and your Easy-Bake Oven was perfect for trying out your mom's recipes in small batches. The lightbulb inside it gave such a warm, even toast to my shortbread." He reached toward me as if to touch me again, then pulled away, looking down at his hands. "I wasn't trying to scare you. I thought we were playing a game. Didn't you see me smiling?"

I nodded, the memory of that grin still giving me chills. "I thought you were going to eat me."

Maurice wrinkled his fat nose. "That's disgusting, Zoey. Anyway, your mom found me a new family not long after that. I came to visit sometimes while you were at school. I grew up, got married to a beautiful gargoyle, moved around a bit." His face fell, the first crack in his cheerful demeanor. "Pansy kicked me out. I think she's sleeping with a bridge troll. I don't know." He picked at a muffin and watched the crumbs fall to the table.

"I'm really sorry," I said. His sadness caressed me like invisible tentacles wrapping around my chest and squeezing softly. I reached my hand out and stopped short of touching the mottled skin that poked from the sleeve of his green and yellow checked shirt. "Maybe you can patch it up. Sometimes these things work themselves out."

"Maybe." Maurice looked up from his muffin deconstruction. "So, can I stay?"

I ground the heel of my hand into the space between my eyes. Before I was forced to answer such a preposterous question, the phone in my purse jangled out a muffled "Wedding March." I dug for it while it rang, cursing myself for dropping it into my bottomless pit of a handbag. By the time I found it, I was so afraid of missing the call, I answered it without looking.

"Morning, Zoeygirl!"

I groaned and considered crawling back into bed. Any day that started this rough should be ignored until it went away.

"What do you want, Brad?" I was deadpan, trying not to encourage my ex-husband by a show of emotion in either direction.

"Don't be that way, baby. Can't I call and see how you are? Maybe I just missed you."

That was an alarming thought—even more than if he called because he wanted something.

"Having a weird morning here, Brad. Let's pretend we already did the greeting dance and covered the obligatory chitchat so we can cut straight to why you dialed my number."

Maurice stared at me from across the kitchen table, then decided it was necessary to pour all his concentration into cleaning up the muffin crumbs he'd scattered.

There was a deep, melodramatic sigh from the other side of the phone. "Fine. Zoeygirl, I'm a little short on my rent and I was wondering—"

"No."

"It's just a couple hundred and I'll get it right back to—"

"No."

"Come on, Zo. Just this once. I promise—"

"Brad, there are so many reasons for me to hang up right now. I've 'loaned' you more money than I care to tally up—money I know I'll never see again. Also, you live with your parents. My God, it's not like they're going to evict you."

"Actually, they kind of did. I got my own little place now. You'd be so proud. And a job working at a paper company, unloading boxes. Pretty good money, too."

"But not enough to pay your rent." I ran my fingers through my hair and slumped in my chair. Maurice was busy at the sink, washing dishes. I could tell by the set of his thin shoulders he was paying close attention.

"I have most of it. I'm just a little behind until payday. Please, Zo?"

"Did you drink it or gamble it?"

Brad had the testicular fortitude to sound affronted. "I'll have you know I haven't had a drink in four months."

His desperation seeped through the phone and slid down my neck. It was thick and choking, running sticky over my shoulders like hot molasses. We'd only been married for six months, but it had taken a further six months before I was able to get him to move out. That was eight years ago, and I still couldn't dislodge him from my life.

"I'm not giving you any money."

"But—"

"No, listen to me. I won't give it to you, but I will help. Come down to the office at two, and I'll pay you to do some deliveries. We could use a little extra help."

"That's great, Zo, but I have plans this afternoon. Any chance we could move it to a little later?"

"Two. If you want my help, be there. If you're late, you miss out."

I hung up on him before he could say anything else. It gave me enormous satisfaction. In the movies, nobody ever says goodbye.

"If you give a mouse a cookie," Maurice said into the dishwater.

"Oh, you're hilarious. Especially when you're asking for a place to live."

Maurice said nothing, scrubbing at an invisible stain on the counter. I buried my head in my arms, trying to shake off the phone call. The hand on my shoulder was gentle.

"It's not your fault," he said. "It's your gift."

"What? Collecting needy people like gum stuck to the bottom of my shoe?" I winced. "I didn't mean you."

"I know. It's the gift. Your mom had the same problem."

I lifted my head. "What *was* my mom doing harboring a closet monster in our house?"

"She was helping. That's what she did—she helped." He moved to the sink to dry the dishes. "Just like you."

# TWO

---

THE NUMBERS ON the paper mocked me with their inadequacy. I rubbed the spot above the bridge of my nose, feeling the slight twinge from my crazy morning beginning to grow. At this rate a full-on migraine was sure to follow.

"Megan," I said. "You can't afford me. Sweetheart, you can barely afford a wedding at all, let alone a planner."

The girl wasn't even drinking age. I imagined myself leaping across the cherry desktop and taking Megan by the shoulders. A good shake might scare some sense into her. Why, oh why, would someone want to throw away two futures by getting married so young and broke? If I could wobble her head hard enough, some of that fluffy blond hair might clear out of the way, and the kid's brain cells could have a chance to work. It would have saved me a lot of heartache if someone had done the same for me at this age.

Megan's brown eyes puddled.

"I'm sorry," she said. Her voice was barely above a whisper. "I've wasted your time." She gathered up her cheap purse and stood on shaky legs.

I sighed. The girl's disappointment, frustration and embarrassment pressed against my shoulders and neck.

"Megan, sit down." *Sit-sit-sit. If you give a mouse a cookie.* "My partner is going to kill me, and if I help you a little, you are not to tell anyone, okay?"

Megan nodded and slid into the plush love seat reserved for clients.

I took a long look at her, more than the cursory once-over I gave on her way in. Her dress was outrageously modest, a plain, faded-yellow cotton with small blue flowers scattered across the fabric. The neckline cut straight across her collarbones, the sleeves stopped just above the elbow. It screamed *church dress.* Her shoes were slightly scuffed flats with tiny little bows. A gold band with a breath of cubic zirconium ringed her finger, but Megan was more interested in fiddling with the silver ring hanging by a chain around her neck. Her thumb rested against it, smoothing it around and around the chain in a gesture that appeared at once nervous and comforting. As it looped around, I saw the engraved word *Purity* run past.

Ah. So that was the hurry.

I put the pieces together in my head, pursing my lips in disapproval. Religious background, purity vow, two broke kids desperate to be together guilt-free. I wasn't going to win this battle. All I could do was help move it along.

I rose without a word and collected our coffee cups for refills. It bought me time to gather my thoughts and reclaim my professional mask. I set the cup in front of Megan and sat again behind my desk.

"Nate has a job?"

"Yes, he works for his dad at the appliance store."

"You've talked to your pastor about this?"

Megan's cheeks turned pink. "No, not yet."

"That's your first step. You belong to the church, I assume, so the ceremony shouldn't cost much. Also, there's a good chance you can have the reception in the basement for free." I looked her over again. "Baptist?"

"Yes."

"That will save you on music and alcohol if it's at the church."

Having lopped off a considerable amount from Megan's near non-existent budget, I wrote down a series of phone numbers and presented the sheet to her.

"Discount florist, a woman who makes cakes out of her home, a couple places in the city that rent wedding gowns and bridesmaid dresses. You can do this if you work hard. It won't be a big, ostentatious wedding, but it can still be nice."

Nearly an hour (and two tearful breakdowns) later, Megan had a plan, a long list of contacts and a lecture on self esteem.

"Thank you so much, Zoey," she said. Halfway out the door she came back to the desk and threw her arms around me. She was so quick, she didn't give me a chance to stand up. "I'll send you an invitation."

As Sara came through the door, she held it open and eyed Megan on her way out. When the door closed, she swung around and looked at me with one eyebrow arched.

"You just did another freebie," she said.

"How the hell did you pick that up so fast?" I gathered my unused paperwork and made a show of tapping it straight against the desk before filing it away.

"Honey, she's dressed like a pilgrim, her purse is a knock-off of a knock-off, and she looks like she's twelve. Tell me you charged her for the consult and I'll apologize."

I made a face at my old college roommate. We'd known each other too long for me to attempt a defense. It was an old argument, and I knew Sara was right.

"You can't save the world, Zo. There are too many needy people in it. You'll drown."

I wondered what Sara would think of the homeless monster I had squatting at my house. I grimaced. Worse, I was going to have to bring up Brad in a minute, and that was likely to earn me another disapproving lecture. My head throbbed.

Sara never missed anything. That was part of what made her good at her job.

"Migraine again?"

I nodded. "It's coming. Really weird day, and it's only eleven-thirty."

"That's your third one this month. Go home. I've got it covered the rest of the day. No appointments left. It's just phone calls and deliveries. Come back Monday."

"The Miller-Radcliffe wedding is tomorrow.

Gotta make sure everything goes smoothly." I was stalling. Any second I would have to drop the bomb.

"They didn't pay for on-site coordination for tomorrow, so you're done. I'll get Charlie to make the deliveries, put in some last-minute calls so they know we're on it. You're good. Go."

I groaned. "Don't be mad."

Sara's eyebrow went up again. Always a bad sign.

"I told Brad if he got here by two, I'd give him some delivery work."

"Oh, good Lord, Zoey. Stick your shoe in the freezer already. The gum will come right off."

I was silent for a moment, feeling like a five-year-old caught sneaking around after bedtime. "If he's not here by two, call Charlie. I left money in an envelope in my desk. Do *not* give it to him unless he's made all the deliveries."

Sara snorted. It was a strange sound coming from such a petite, immaculately dressed woman.

She wore her blond hair in a short, clean bob with well-placed highlights that looked at once orderly and natural. There wasn't a disobedient strand. Her designer skirt and jacket looked tailored to her tiny frame, and a touch of cleavage flirted from the folds of her peach silk blouse. Somehow, and I couldn't imagine the man-hours involved in the search, Sara's pointed-toe heels were the exact same peach, several shades darker. Her fingernails, a businesslike, squared-off shape, duplicated the color of the shoes as if they had come from the same factory. I glanced down at my own chewed nails and considered painting them an obnoxious chartreuse to yank Sara's chain a little.

For years Sara had tried, with growing exasperation, to counsel me on wardrobe choices. I had agreed to disagree, but Sara was still fighting the good fight.

Gathering my things together, I rose from my desk to head home, hoping I'd slip out without Sara commenting. She was not, however, going to let me go that easily.

"*What* are you wearing?" It wasn't so much a question as a verbal eye-roll.

I had a tendency to choose clothing items one at a time, without thought to how they would look in an outfit. My closet was filled with oddly patterned tights, men's hats, sequined blouses with Disney characters, skirts that were too short, skirts that were too long. When we opened the wedding-planning business, we had come to the agreement that I would be allowed one quirky item per outfit. I tried to comply, since Sara was pressed, powdered and perfect no matter what the occasion.

Today, in my haste to clear out of a monster-invaded house, I hadn't been as careful as usual. The deep purple, button-down blouse had been a gift from Sara, so sitting behind the desk, I had passed muster. When I stood, the jig was up. To be fair, I had attempted to stay within a particular color palette. My black and purple pumps went well with the blouse, and in my opinion, the short, floaty yellow skirt spattered with violets was a nice complement. Perhaps the yellow tights with lavender butterflies had been over-enthusiastic. The gigantic fabric daisy I'd attached around my waist as a belt buckle was probably the kicker.

It was a good thing Sara was my partner and not my boss.

To me, this vast difference in taste between the two of us was an external expression of why we worked so well as a team. Sara had the aura of a capable tyrant who controlled every detail of a client's big day. I came off as creative, whimsical, and in touch with the emotional needs of an anxious bride. The dynamic worked. But my sense of style (or lack thereof) still drove Sara nuts.

From my black leather bag, more traveler's carry-on than purse, I pulled out a lemon-yellow beret. I kept defiant eye contact with Sara as I shoved it over my mass of unruly curls and headed out the door.

The minute I hit the sidewalk, Sausalito at low tide smacked me in the face like a punishment for playing hooky from work. Most stressful days the salty bay breeze blowing in from two streets away was soothing. This, however, brought to mind dead things washed up on the shore and left to rot in the open air. Scrunching up my face in distaste, I took in a huge whiff. I often heard people advise breathing through the mouth to avoid a stench, but I was of the well-considered opinion if I didn't want it in my nostrils, I sure as hell didn't want it in my mouth. With my lips shut tight, I breathed deep, and the scent gradually became more tolerable.

Mercifully, the sun had chosen to hide behind an overcast gray rather than stab my migraine-sensitive eyes with lancing fire. To be safe, I dug through my bag and pulled out my sunglasses, cramming them over my face. Properly safeguarded, I turned to walk up Caledonia Street toward my waiting car.

I made it half a block before the cheerful, muffled tweep of my cell phone alerted me to an incoming text. Dropping my hand into the enormous bag-o-crap, I fumbled blindly and got lucky on the first try. It occurred to me that Sara must have remembered some dire situation that needed attention before I left to make the forty-five-minute commute home. I thumbed the screen and read the message:

> *If it's not too much trouble, could you pick up a wedge of Asiago and maybe a bottle of wine, please? Something white. Thanks.*
> *—Maurice*

I stood planted on the sidewalk, staring at the message, while an ocean of joggers, tourists and suited professionals washed past me. I had pushed the morning's events to the farthest back room of my mind in the hope that if I had enough distance from them, they never happened. Denial was a powerful tool. Unfortunately, this time it hadn't worked. Not only did the problem still exist, it had acquired my phone number.

In a fit of rebellion, I made a decision to ignore the text. Obviously, I hadn't put enough effort into ignoring the problem. Denial takes a concerted effort. As I trudged in the direction of my car, the memory of magical orangeberries melting on my tongue took over and replaced rebellion with culinary curiosity. I made a quick pivot and went back the way I came.

My shoulder collided with a man walking toward me, jarring me out of step. He was oddly dressed (even by my wardrobe standards) for late summer. Marin County attracted the weird and different, but this man stood out. He wore a crimson smoking jacket made from cheap velvet. A white, blousy shirt peeked out from underneath, giving him a pirate-y air. Paired with crisp, creased jeans and black, buckled boots, he looked both dashing and prissy at the same time. His dark hair was clipped short, as was his beard, with the exception of an oiled curl jutting out from his chin.

The focused stare of his green eyes licked at my soul as if I were a tasty morsel meant to be savored.

I stood still, frozen in place until a woman walked too close on the sidewalk and smacked my shin with her shopping bag. I broke eye contact and stepped away from the strange man.

"I'm so sorry. Excuse me," I said, ducking my head. Feeling enormous discomfort and embarrassment, I forced myself into a brisk walk, holding back from letting it turn into a trot or full-out run.

As I retreated, I could feel him still watching me, his attention focused between my shoulder blades and searing me there like a branding iron.

THE LOW LIGHT and near emptiness of the gourmet shop were a welcome reprieve after the crowded, noisy street. I took my time picking out an organic wedge of cheese and a bottle of local-label Pinot Grigio. Ahead of me at the register, a woman was buying an exorbitant number of portobello mushrooms and two containers of soy milk. When the woman proceeded to pay the cashier from a large, clunking bag of quarters, I concentrated everything I had on not tapping my foot with impatience. My headache held in place, neither increasing nor abating. Traffic in the store began to pick up and the door swung open and closed several times. I lowered my sunglasses from the top of my head to my eyes and turned away from the door. Even the weak light of the overcast day was a bit piercing in the store's gloom.

Having gathered her bag of change and what had to be the makings of a very expensive vegan mushroom soup, the customer in front of me left. I placed my items on the counter.

"Paper or plastic?" The tattooed woman behind the register frowned at me. Both were the wrong answer, and I knew it. I was being judged inferior before I'd answered. I could feel the disapproval brushing against me like a cat rubbing against my legs—soft, but with the intent of tripping me the moment I moved.

I had no idea why it mattered, but it did. I was twitchy and shifted from foot to foot. I was cornered. I never got this question right.

Inspiration hit. "Just drop them in my bag." I held out my purse. In my head I punched the sky in triumph. *Not going to get me this time.*

The clerk's face relaxed in approval. "Did you find everything you need?"

I nodded.

"This is a good label," she said. "Myron and I toured the vineyard once."

I nodded again and glanced out the window, not bothered by who Myron was. Thick clouds rolled in, giving the sky a smudged appearance. The drive home would be cool with the windows down.

"...and left me alone with two kids and not a single bottle of wine from the trip."

I was startled back to the conversation by a tightness in my chest. The clerk was near tears, chattering at me.

*Anger.*

*Sadness.*

*Grief.*

*Loneliness.*

They lined up like tin soldiers and pelted me with tiny shots of toy ammo.

I gave the woman a tentative, encouraging smile and touched her wrist. The contact sent ripples up my arm and into my stomach. I glanced at her name tag. "Selma, you-alone are so much more than you-with-him. You're going to be better than fine." I squeezed her hand. "Trust yourself."

Her eyes were a little misty as she considered my words. She straightened her shoulders and her chin lifted. "I am better, aren't I? Yeah. I am. Thanks."

The tightness in my chest let go as Selma's emotions receded. Her anger and sadness floated out like cottonwood seeds, and determination and self confidence blew in to settle over me. Time was the only thing that could truly heal her, but for now, she was stronger and less likely to lose it at the sight of a random wine bottle.

I smiled, paid for my purchases and walked out of the store.

This was not a new or bizarre occurrence for me, though it didn't often turn so quickly. My mind had only wandered for a second and the woman had gone into a full meltdown. People often acted that way around me, and I had no idea why. I was a magnet for the over-emotional. Something about me triggered them into spilling their guts and handing over all their problems like a set of car keys. Often, like this time, I opened my mouth and words came out. I had no intention of speaking, yet whatever I said seemed to be what the person needed.

Maurice's words about my mother echoed in my head. *She was helping. That's what she did—she helped. Just like you.* Is that what I was doing? Helping? I didn't mind helping, but a sick day now and then would be nice.

I had so few memories of my mother, but now I doubted what little I did know. I wondered if helping somehow got her killed. Or maybe she wasn't dead after all, but was out there somewhere, still helping. I shook my head to clear it of thoughts I didn't want to think. The motion rewarded me with a fresh stab of pain.

Whenever I had a migraine (which was way too

often), I imagined a tiny man living inside my head, causing all the trouble. At this point, he was sprawled out with his arms pressed against the back of my skull and his feet firmly planted against my eyeballs. The pressure was building. I needed to get home before he called a few friends over for an impromptu exercise session requiring mats, yoga balls and those giant rubber bands that smell like a mixture of old tire and baby powder. The inside of my head wouldn't tolerate that much activity any more than my body would.

Despite my pained, weakened state, I couldn't miss the paramedic across the street. He stood with one foot propped up against the wall behind him, leaning his back against the bricks and drinking coffee from a paper take-out cup. His sandy hair was scruffy, and his gray eyes smiled at me over his drink.

He winked.

My cheeks burned hot. I gave a nervous smile, and he returned it with a crooked half smile of his own. He stood up straight, and my stomach churned. Was he coming across to talk to me? What was I doing flirting across the street with some strange guy as if I were sixteen?

His eyes, so friendly a moment before, lost interest and flicked to the street corner. I dragged my attention away from his face to see what he was looking at.

Nothing. Traffic moved through the intersection in its normal pattern. Pedestrians crossed with the light on one street, waited for the signal on the other.

Apparently, I wasn't interesting enough to keep his attention.

I pulled my purse higher on my shoulder and prepared for the trek to the car, now five blocks away. And then I saw it.

Time somehow became both frozen and supersonic. It was over in seconds with no room to react, yet it all happened at a sluggish crawl in which every detail was clear and sharp.

On the corner facing me walked an average man wearing an average blue suit. His appearance was neat and trim, with the exception of his unzipped fly. With each step, his pants gaped open, giving the world a peek at his tighty-whities. *Funny. I didn't think anybody wore those anymore. I would have had him pegged as more of a boxer-briefs kind of guy. Good thing he wasn't going commando, or he'd be flashing his sausage at all of Sausalito.*

He appeared frazzled and consumed with the argument he was having on his cell. Without checking for traffic, he stepped off the curb.

Coming up the street past me was a Marin Transit bus. It was double length, attached in the center by a bendy, accordion-like connector. Its cheerful green stripe raced across the intersection en route to the next stop.

Man and bus didn't see each other. I wanted to warn them both, but the slow motion of the scene had caught me, and I couldn't move.

Brakes screeched in high-pitched agony a hair before the thunking crunch of a body being sent airborne. The man was tossed like a softball across the lane and into oncoming traffic. His limp form collided with the windshield of a silver Audi and flew back to the foot of the bus. Glass shattered, people screamed, cars braked and rear-ended the cars in front of them.

Fast and slow met in the middle, and time resumed its normal pace.

I blinked, and the paramedic was there, crouched over the body. Chaos hummed up and down the street as people climbed out of their cars and stepped out of shops, repeating the same questions in an ancient ritual of human emergency.

*What happened? Did you see that? Are you all right?*

The questions and panic washed past me as I watched the gorgeous emergency worker. He moved the back of his hand across the victim's mouth. I had little first-aid knowledge, but I thought this was an odd way to check for a pulse—though judging by the angle of the man's head, no way was there life to be found. The paramedic pressed his ring against the bloody lips of the dead man and gave a slight pull. From across the street I couldn't be certain, but I thought I could see something connecting the body to the ring. And then I couldn't see anything at all as dead guy and hot rescue worker were swallowed up in the crowd.

*Pain. Fear. Panic.*

Emotions slammed into me from all sides.

*Horror. Disgust. Grief.*

My headache exploded, and the faces around me swam in a blurry haze.

*Irritation. Guilt.*

I turned to flee into the shop and walked into the arms of the strange man in the cheap velvet smoking jacket.

*Hunger.*

I had enough time to hope for a soft landing before I fainted.

# THREE

IF A WOMAN faints in the movies, she is often out for hours, usually waking on a comfy settee where someone is tending to her with a cold cloth and a glass of water or brandy. This is not how it played out for me.

When I opened my eyes, less than a minute had passed, and I was still marginally upright. Dark velvet that smelled like too much man-perfume encased me. I struggled to be released and stand on my own.

"Ah, here she is," my captor/rescuer said. His voice was deep and rich like chocolate mousse. He loosened his hold on me, retaining a concerned grip on my elbow. "Are you all right to stand or shall I carry you?" A liberal dose of amusement mixed with his concern.

My head pounded and I was having difficulty stringing his words together into meaningful sentences. "I'm good. Fine," I said, hoping that was the appropriate response.

He lifted my chin with one finger and looked into my eyes, searching. "You don't look well yet. Why don't we get a cup of tea in you to strengthen you up?"

His eyes were the green of freshly mown grass.

His gaze shot into me, stroking me in places that shouldn't be touched out on a sidewalk on a busy street. Flecks of gold danced across the irises, and I licked my lips. *So hungry. Yes. Tea would be nice.* If he wanted me to drink antifreeze, that would be fine too. I nodded my head once and took a step toward him.

"Excellent." He slid his arm around my waist. "I'll take good care of you. I'm Sebastian. May I have your name?"

My brain, caught in a sludge of erotic decadence, was slow to answer. I opened my mouth and the words felt like cotton.

"My name. Oh. I'm—"

"Natalie!" said a voice behind me. "Honey, I've been so worried. You look awful."

A man I was fairly certain I'd never seen before appeared beside me, pulled me free from the smoking-jacket man—*Sebastian, he said his name was Sebastian*—and led me away.

"Thank you for taking care of my sister. She gets sick sometimes. You're very kind. I've got it from here."

Sebastian had no time to protest before this new stranger whipped me into an herb shop next door to the gourmet store. He locked the door behind us and flipped the hanging sign to say Closed.

"Okay, honey," he said. "Let's get you fixed up. That was a little creepy."

This latest addition to my sudden male bombardment had shoulder-length hair close to the color of carrots. His eyebrows were so fair they nearly disappeared into his freckle-spattered face. His blue eyes were kind, though nervous, darting to the windows as if he expected Sebastian to break in. He was kind of short, maybe five-eight, but with a stocky, bulldog build to him. If anybody broke in, my money was on the bulldog.

As this stranger led me to a back room, I tried to protest. Even in my fog-drenched brain I knew enough to equate a back room with danger. My knees buckled, and he tightened his grip on my arm. Apparently protesting anything was beyond me at the moment.

"Whoa, you're okay. Just a few more steps."

My head was now one continuous throb.

"I've never fainted in my life," I said, my voice shaky. "I'm so embarrassed."

I was marginally relieved when our progress halted at the back of the store and not in some dark, bead-curtained room beyond. I was deposited on a caramel sofa with dark brown pillows. He was gentle but insistent in forcing me to lay back with a cushion propped under my feet.

"I've seen you around town," he said. "Mind you, the way you dress, everybody's seen you around town. You look good today, though I'd rethink the big flower on your belt. Sometimes you go overboard, which, really, is half the fun in watching for you. Except for that car wreck of a purse you take everywhere." He winced. "Sorry, 'car wreck' probably isn't the best way to describe anything right now.

But we really do need to find you a purse that doesn't say 'homeless person,' don't you think?"

I clutched my bag to my chest. "What's wrong with my purse? Everything *fits* in it."

He rolled his eyes at me. "It's a tragedy, sweetheart. A damn tragedy."

I closed my eyes and watched the bright colors of my headache dance like a moving Picasso against the backdrop of my eyelids. I heard the banging of lids on jars and quiet shuffling of feet on tile. It was soothing, and for the first time all day I began to relax.

Green, piercing eyes flashed at me through the swirling colors. My skin flushed in a heady mix of fear and desire.

My lids sprang open, erasing the image, which left a residual burning sensation behind. What had I been thinking? The guy gave me a case of the screaming willies, and I'd been about to walk off down the street with him. Willingly. Like a bitch in heat. I shivered.

Something small tugged on the fabric at my hip. Tiny, dull claws gripped me for leverage, yanked twice as if gearing up for a leap, then plopped across my stomach in a heap. I peered down at my belly and two small black eyes peered back. A cat? A dog? Whatever it was, it had the most enormous ears I'd ever seen, each one the size of the animal's head. It was a tawny gold with a fluffy, black-tipped tail, and the intensity with which it stared into my eyes was both endearing and unnerving. The head twitched in a micro-sneeze, then it buried its nose in my neck and flopped flat on my chest. Tiny wheezes tickled my neck as it dozed.

"He doesn't usually do that with strangers." The shop owner carried two steaming mugs of tea over and placed them on the coffee table next to me. "I'm Andrew and I'll be your server. Today we have a delightful blend—an intoxicating mix of homebrewed goodness guaranteed to cure what ails you. At least until we get you sorted out so the migraines stop happening." He helped me dislodge the animal on my chest—was it a deformed Chihuahua?—nudged me upright and placed the mug in my hands.

"Zoey." I blew into the hot liquid to cool it off. "Thank you, Andrew. Really. Thank you."

The odd animal made a squeaking protest at having been moved and leaped back to my lap. He turned twice, wrapping himself in his tail, and went back to snoring.

Andrew looked amused. "That's Milo. Apparently, you now belong to him."

"I feel stupid for asking, but what…?"

"Fennec fox. Exotic, but tame. Though not usually *this* tame with people he doesn't know."

I ran my fingers over the stiff fur. A fox. Of course. Big ears, bushy tail. Now I really felt stupid.

I took a sip of tea. The flavors lined up and came through in groups. It was spicy, like Christmas cookies, then flowery like perfume. A nutty flavor threaded its way through, and the whole thing ended on an aftertaste that made me think of gym socks left over the summer in a high school locker. I pinched my nostrils shut with fingers.

"Yeah," he said. "I can't do anything to disguise the aftertaste. You'll get used to it."

We sat in comfortable silence for a few minutes while I sipped. There was no pressure to talk, and it felt right to hang out quietly. Before long, I noticed my shaking had stopped and my headache was receding. My eyebrows rose in surprise.

"Better?"

Years of doctors and useless prescriptions, and the answer had been tea. "What's in this?"

He shrugged. "Stuff. Stuff for pain, stuff for nerves, stuff for nausea. I assumed your stomach's not doing so hot either."

I nodded, noticing that the tidal motions in my gut were also subsiding.

"I have a knack for knowing what to throw in. I should really write it down in case you run out. You're taking some with you, whether you think you need it or not."

While we drank, my eyes roamed the strange little shop. Bottles, jars, boxes and bins lined the walls and counters. Overstuffed bookcases stood side by side, their shelves weighted and bowed with teetering piles of books. Stacks of empty vials, containers, funnels and eyedroppers shared space with brass bowls and marble mortar and pestle sets. Unfamiliar smells mixed in a heady but not unpleasant incense that permeated everything.

"I suppose that happens all the time to people

like you," Andrew said, motioning to the fluffball in my lap.

"People...like me?"

"Empaths. You know."

"Empaths." Repeating what people said to me was the order of the day, apparently. I really needed to get some of my own material.

He slouched in his chair and became still, staring at me for a few moments. He sat that way long enough for me to become self-conscious. "When you meet people, do you feel what they're feeling? Anger, sadness, that sort of thing?"

"Well, yeah. Doesn't everybody?"

Andrew threw his head back and laughed. "Oh, honey, no wonder you're so mucked up. No, people do not normally feel what everyone else is feeling. You're an empath. It's part of you. And it's a rare gift, not a fact of life. The rest of us only feel our own feelings."

I was certain this nice man was off his rocker. I gave him a blank stare that said everything and nothing. "But how can people communicate? If they don't know what the person next to them is feeling, how do they know what to say? It would be like trying to drive at night with your headlights off."

He considered this. "From our point of view, it's more like driving at night without infrared goggles. We never had them, so we don't miss them."

I quieted while I chewed on the idea. My sense of other people's emotions was mine alone. Nobody around me had any clue what I was feeling, what was happening in my head.

No *wonder* communication broke down so often. How could people possibly understand each other? This explained a great deal about cruelty in the world. How easy would it be to dole out emotional damage if you didn't get any backlash yourself? The more I considered the notion, the more it rang true.

I shook my head. "This is crazy."

He smiled and gave me a cheerful bob of his head. "Yep. Crazy. Also true."

I wondered how I could have gone my entire life without realizing that nobody else was *feeling* everybody else. It was like I'd lived with a third arm and only realized now that everyone else had two. It was an embarrassing—and lonely—thought.

All the times I'd stepped in when two people had a misunderstanding, I didn't understand why they couldn't see the problem as clearly as I did. I remembered the quizzical looks Sara gave me when I told her a bride *felt* like a breakdown was imminent.

Sara must've thought I was nuts. But that's what best friends did—they honored each other's quirks as personality traits rather than flaws. For ten years, we'd talked about the people in our lives, from the nerdy R.A. running our dorm back in college to the dumbass who cut me off in traffic last week. I assumed we'd been using the same language to describe a new boyfriend, my father's death or the divorce of Sara's parents. She never once told me I was weird or that she didn't understand.

But apparently not everyone would label this insane deformity of mine as me simply being a lovable weirdo with an odd vocabulary. This guy had called me an empath. My brow creased in suspicion.

"Andrew, how did you know I was in trouble out there?"

"Zoey, there are lots of ways to be different. I heard the crash and went outside to see what had happened. You were standing there, brightly lit, with an aura the size of Wisconsin, and that guy was, well, he was bad. I could see how bad. His aura was the blackest, emptiest thing I've ever seen. And his aura was eating your aura. It scared me half to death."

"You see auras." I reached down and rubbed Milo's ear. His bushy tail thumped against my leg in rhythm with his panting breaths. "Like those weird photographs they take at psychic fairs?"

"Something like that. I see them, and I can read them. And what I read in him had a badness level through the roof."

Auras. Empaths. Closet monsters. Okay. I was game. Enough weirdness had hit me in one day that discounting anything was pretty much an exercise in self-deception.

"What was he?" I asked in a quiet voice.

Andrew looked serious. "I have no idea. Nothing good. We need to work on making you less…tasty. This is going to take more tea."

He took my cup and moved to the counter where he kept hot water steaming in a coffeepot.

Despite the circumstances, I felt safe in this tiny, odd-smelling place. Andrew felt safe. For once, here was someone who didn't feel like any of his own problems. In fact, I felt nothing from him but a low echo of self-assurance. I wasn't being either bombarded or drained.

"Andrew?"

He craned his neck over his shoulder and smiled. "Yeah?"

"What do you know about closet monsters?"

"Not a thing, my darling. But the world is full of strangeness for anyone who cares to look."

OVER A SECOND and third cup of Christmas-flavored sweat socks, Andrew led me through a series of guided meditations. He taught me first to flush out the unwanted collection of borrowed emotions I'd been picking up all over town.

"Every night before you go to bed," he said, "remind yourself as you're meditating that these emotions are not your crap. They don't belong to you, and you don't have to own them."

I had to admit I felt better than I had in a very long time. The tea had worked well, but the meditation felt like I'd opened all the doors and windows in a musty house. The cool breeze blowing through my mind made everything fresh, and my own thoughts were no longer dulled. I was ready to run outside and jog to my car.

Andrew stopped me before I could throw the door open and stare back at my old enemy, the sun.

"If you go out there right now it would be like sunbathing naked on the equator. All you've done so far is clear out all the crap that's been cluttering up your head for ages. In a way, it was keeping things out. You can only cram so much into a full box. But now the space is empty, so you're more vulnerable than before. You need to shield yourself like I do. Think of it as psychic sunscreen."

Andrew spent the next hour teaching me to build an enclosure around myself. We'd started with bricks, but my visualization abilities were too vivid, and I fought. "I can't see anything around me," I said. "And how can I breathe in this tiny room?"

We changed tactics. My imagination formed a rock-hard wall of crystal encircling me, forming a bubble. Because I could see through it, I didn't feel like it was closing in.

I felt invincible.

Invincible, but not without some niggling worries. What if I couldn't sustain my wall? Did I have to think about it all the time to keep it going? How would I know if the protection wasn't working?

What if everything Andrew was saying was a wheelbarrow full of manure from a flying circus elephant?

His explanation for my problems felt right, though. The changes in me felt true, deep in my gut, and not a result of suggestion or positive thinking. So much of the strangeness in my life fell into place.

"Practice, Zoey," Andrew said. "Don't walk out the door in the morning until you put your wall up. Believe it'll stay put. And fortify it from time to time—take a moment to think about it, feel for flaws, smooth them out. Maintenance will be second nature eventually." He pressed a plastic bag of herbs in my hand as I gathered my things to go. "Just in case," he said. "Some days might be hard. I have a feeling you've got shit coming your way."

More good news.

He stood with Milo in his arms, looking worried. Milo made a mewling squeak. I gave the fox's gigantic ears a rub and hugged them both. "Stop worrying, guys. I'll be fine. I'll be by in a few days. With closet-monster baked goods, if he's still around. Thank you."

I left the store a little apprehensive, but feeling like a brand-new Zoey. I'd been inside long enough that traffic from the accident had cleared, the sun had burned through the haze in the sky, and high tide had rolled in, washing the air clean. I yanked my yellow beret over my hair and had to hold myself back from skipping to my car.

THE COMMUTE FROM Sausalito to the small beach town of Bolinas gave me time to calm my euphoria to a more natural level. I found myself inspecting my newly constructed, imaginary bubble for cracks and soft spots. I reinforced it wherever I felt the need, feeling both giddy with new knowledge and silly for believing in it.

My cheerful outlook wavered when Maurice met me at the front door. The look of him was still startling, even with foreknowledge. He'd changed to a bright yellow dress shirt and lime-green slacks. The black and white checkered sneakers remained the same. His brow-less, mottled forehead was pulled down in a scowl.

"Thank Betty Crocker you're home. I've been worried sick. Didn't you get my messages?"

I could feel fault lines forming in my carefully constructed barrier, and his concern seeped through the cracks. *Breathe, Zoey. Patch it up before the dam breaks.* I inhaled through my nose and out through my mouth while being ushered into the kitchen. Maurice muttered to himself while he pushed me into a chair and poured me a glass of pink lemonade.

"I got the cheese and wine," I said, feeling like a naughty child as I pulled it out of my purse and put it on the table. The cheese was a little sweaty. After digging around for a moment, I located my phone. Five text messages and two voicemails, not all from Maurice.

One text message and two hysterical phone calls were from Sara. The timing of my departure in conjunction with the accident had not gone unnoticed.

I made a quick call to Sara letting her know she could stop worrying. No, I wasn't in the accident. Yes, I was fine. Sorry I didn't get the call earlier. I hung up and realized Sara was the easier of the two to placate.

Maurice was staring at me.

"Something else happened, didn't it," he said. The certainty in his voice and the fear on his face brought a flash of green eyes, causing me to shiver.

I took a sip of lemonade through a bright orange and green bendy straw. My mouth made a pleased pucker. Not pink lemonade, strawberry lemonade. I held up my glass and peered through the frosty condensation. Chunks of fresh strawberry winked at me.

I sighed. "Yes, something happened. But I'm fine now. Better than fine, I'm great."

His yellow eyes stared at me across the linoleum table without blinking. He wasn't going to let it go.

I gave it up like a homecoming queen on prom night. Once I started the story, it burbled out of me until it lay between us on the table, heavy and full of dark omens.

Maurice was agitated and ran a gnarled hand through the few spiky hairs on his head. "Zoey, my gods, that was an incubus. You could have been sucked dry right there on the street."

He rose from his chair and paced across the tile floor, his shoes squeaking as he walked. I glanced down.

"Did you mop the floor? It's all...clean."

"Don't change the subject, you're in deep shit."

I watched him make two more circuits of the kitchen before I grabbed his wrist and yanked him into the chair next to me. The warmth of his pale skin still surprised me. I wondered how long it would take to get used to that.

"He's gone. I'm fine. Stop pacing, you're making me queasy."

Maurice appeared to gather himself for another onslaught, then smoothed his face into a mask of calm. "Incubi are demons, Zo. Very bad. They feed off the emotions, the *energy,* of their victims. They seduce their victims into compliance and drain them until the brain is a shell filled with a gooey center. You're a helper—an empath. You draw other people's emotions to you, even with your bubble in place. For an incubus, you're like an all-you-can-eat buffet with no sneeze guard.

"And now he's had a taste."

# FOUR

FRIDAY'S INSANITY MELTED into Saturday, which dawned a fresh kind of crazy. I took a few minutes to rebuild and examine my bubble shield for cracks and chips before poking my toes out from under the duvet. All secure. With an unfamiliar spring in my step and clad in a knee-length, retro Hong Kong Phooey nightshirt, I skipped outside and down my porch steps to get the paper at the end of the drive. Halfway across the lawn I whacked my shin against a protruding growth.

Overnight, a mushroom with a cap the size of a cantaloupe had sprung up out of nowhere. I leaned forward to examine it and was thumped on the side of the head by a rogue dragonfly. The insect chittered at me and grabbed a hank of my hair, yanking me in the direction of the house.

I flapped my hands over my head without effect and took a step backward. The bug let go and flew off.

I blinked. My mind refused to put together what I had observed, and I glanced at the mushroom. It was not alone. A row of fungi grew across my lawn and stretched around the corner of the house. I padded on bare feet, following the curved line. I tracked it until I circled my way back to the front walkway. *No, no, no. I am not seeing what I'm seeing.*

I darted my eyes left and right, then took an experimental step across the mushrooms.

Three creatures bombed me, scolding in indecipherable, high-pitched voices. They yanked at my sleeve, my hair, and one made a grab for my lower lip. *No, definitely not dragonflies,* I thought. *I'm on lockdown by fairies.*

Waving my arms to shoo them away, I pivoted and stomped up the steps, slamming the door both open and closed. I stood in the living room seething.

Maurice popped his head out of the kitchen. "Zoey! Good morning! Perfect timing. Sit-sit-sit! Breakfast is almost ready. Come have coffee."

It was difficult to maintain a high level of outrage in the face of such overwhelming cheer. But I tried. I stalked into the kitchen and threw myself in my chair, hoping to have achieved at least a small show of defiance and ire.

"I'm on house arrest. I can't even get my paper."

Maurice looked unconcerned. "Paper's right there, Zo." He slid a cup of coffee under my nose and pulled the folded newspaper toward me.

"*Fairies* are in my front yard!"

He ignored me. I took a sip of coffee and wondered why everyone always gave me something to drink when I was upset. "Fairy rings, closet monsters, incubi. I quit going to my shrink too soon."

Maurice snorted and kept working at the stove. So he *was* listening to me; he refused to answer.

I sulked and stared out the window. Mushrooms jiggled on their thick stalks, taunting me. Maurice put a plate of food in front of me, and the smell of something incredible blew into my face. I took a bite and tried not to show my pleasure.

"I'm not going to stay locked up here," I said with my mouth full. "You can't—oh my God, did you make these croissants from scratch?" I closed my eyes, savoring the buttery flakes dissolving in my mouth before I swallowed. I opened them again and glared. "I'm not hiding in here, so you can forget it."

Maurice grinned in the way good cooks do when someone enjoys their food.

"It's not forever, Zoey. Give it a little while for the ring to set. Then you can come and go as you please."

"How long?"

He shrugged. "A couple hours. The mushrooms will disappear. If you leave now, the ring won't know you belong. Trust me. It's a good alarm system. People won't be able to wander in and out without us knowing about it once it's set."

I had the overwhelming feeling that I was being handled. It did not sit well with me. Over the last twenty-four hours I'd been dragged, pushed, guided and manipulated by an incubus, an aura-reading herbalist, a closet monster and several fairies.

"Then what? Bells ring every time a neighbor crosses into the yard for a chat? Sirens go off at three a.m. when a raccoon tries to break into the garbage can?" The food on my plate wasn't so appealing anymore. I shoved it away and threw my crumpled napkin into the dish. "I can't live like this. Whatever that guy was, he's gone. I'm safe. You can't take over my house like this." I scraped my chair back and stood up, glaring at Maurice. His calm grated at me and served to piss me off further.

"Zoey, nobody's taking anything over. You won't notice the change. Trust me on this. It's necessary."

How was I supposed to trust a monster I met yesterday? A monster who couldn't keep his own marriage together? I opened my mouth to say so, a thing I would have instantly regretted. Hurting people was not in my nature.

The phone rang.

I snatched it up and snarled a greeting. "What?"

"Zoey, baby. How's my girl this morning?"

"Brad, what the hell do you want?"

"You always were grumpy first thing in the morning. Have some coffee."

"Not the time, Brad. Spit it out or hang up." In a small back room in my head, I felt a tiny bit of shock. I didn't talk to people like this, not even Brad. *Whoa, girl. Ease up. You're dangerously close to being hateful. Somebody's feelings could get hurt.*

"Ok, I gotcha. You're on the rag. I'll speed it up," he said.

"Hanging up, Brad."

"No, wait. I wanted to thank you for getting me the extra work yesterday. So, thank you."

"You're welcome. What else?"

"Nothing much." There was a pause. I could hear him breathing while he gathered his nerve to ask me for God only knew what this time. "Well, it wasn't quite enough to get me through, so maybe, I thought, well, have you got anything else?"

"No."

"Nothing?"

"No. Goodbye, Brad."

"Wait! Could you maybe float me a couple hundred, just for the week?"

My anger level reached the boiling point and the lid blew off. "Get a goddamn job, Brad. Work like the rest of us. Or go bother your parents. Sell your body to science, for all I care. I am not your wife, your girlfriend or your banker. Piss off." I jammed my finger on the disconnect button, wishing for an old-fashioned receiver to slam.

I dropped my phone on the table and covered my face with shaking hands. *What the hell is wrong with me?*

I SPENT THE next two hours locked in my room—crying, pouting, throwing pillows at the dresser and staring out the window. I made a brief trip to the bathroom to shower, but it didn't help my mood. At intervals I peeked out the window and saw the mushrooms circling the house gradually diminish until I looked out and saw no sign of them.

I walked through the house and found Maurice on his knobby knees, scrubbing an old stain on the Egyptian throw rug in the living room.

"I'm going out," I said in a cool voice.

Maurice said nothing. He nodded once and returned to dabbing at the carpet with a damp rag.

I loved my blue convertible VW Bug. Not only was it a sassy fashion statement, but it got great gas mileage. A long drive would help me think, sort through my crowded brain, in peace. I closed the car door and fumbled with the keys. *What is that obnoxious smell? Did something die in here?*

I searched between and under the seats for the offender and came up empty. When I opened the glove compartment, the stench of putrefaction and decay assailed my sinuses. My hands flew to my face in a futile attempt to block it out. A small, burlap bag tied with twine sat nestled amidst my collection of extra fast-food napkins, leaving grease stains where it touched the paper. Using as little contact as possible, I pinched the rough fabric between my fingers and lifted it out, dangling it in the air. The reek was unbearable. Surely breathing it in close quarters was unhealthy. It gave off an oily, ominous feel that made me shudder. I couldn't decide if I should toss it out the window, burn it or scream for help.

A knock on the window made me jump, causing the offensive mystery item to swing against my wrist and brush my skin. I yelped and straightened my arm. At least I hadn't screamed.

"Son of a bitch," I said and looked out the window. Maurice's yellow eyes stared back at me.

I screamed.

I felt like an idiot.

He motioned for me to roll down the window. I ignored him and opened the car door, pushing him out of the way.

"What the hell?" I said.

Maurice grinned down at me. "You have to put that back, Zoey. Aggie made it for you. It'll ward off bad stuff."

"It *stinks*."

"That'll dissipate. Please put it back, Zo. You need protection whether you think so or not."

Resigned, I made a face and tossed the thing inside, then slammed the glove compartment shut. As if I didn't have enough going on, now I'd have to make an appointment to get my car detailed.

I pulled myself out of the car and glared up at the six-foot-tall monster smiling back at me.

"Do I want to know who Aggie is?"

Maurice shrugged. "Just a hag who lives on the other side of the woods. Your mom took care of her when she was sick sometimes. Aggie was glad to help."

My mother had been a very busy lady.

"I'm going for a walk. No more surprises. I can't take it." I turned and stomped away, refusing to look back over my shoulder.

I PLODDED THROUGH the half mile or so of woods that separated my house from the ocean. I dragged my feet through the leaves and pine needles.

"Buying me off with food. Stinking up my car. Monsters and fairies." I kicked a rock and watched it roll under a bush. "Hag? Really? Not even a witch. No, I have freakin' Baba Yaga living down the street."

I wallowed in my own petulance. I wasn't in the

habit of feeling sorry for myself, but dammit, I deserved a little pity party at this point.

"I'll suck *you* dry. Stupid incubus."

Once I stopped grousing and turned my attention to my surroundings, I realized how quiet it was. It could be I'd frightened the wildlife with my stomping and mumbling, but the silence was deeper than anything I could have caused. No birds scolded each other or flew overhead. Squirrels didn't skip between the trees, tails twitching in Morse code. The breeze was slight and didn't rustle the leaves as it passed.

My skin grew clammy and I quickened my pace. To the right, I thought I glimpsed something moving in the shadows, and I whipped my head around to catch it. To my left, something large but silent kept pace with me.

I hurried.

Behind me a twig cracked, breaking the silence. Of their own accord, my feet stopped moving and planted themselves in the dirt path. My ears twitched, and I rolled my eyes to view my surroundings without moving my head. Nothing. The forest was still quiet. The only sounds came from the surf in the distance. I took a careful step, my senses alert for the slightest noise or movement as I walked.

*And now my imagination has run off and stolen what's left of my mind.*

Two minutes of paranoia later, I broke through the thick stand of conifer and eucalyptus. Dirt and pine needles under my feet gave way to hard-packed earth with sparse, gnarly growths, then dark, pebbly sand. I looked over my shoulder and saw only trees and shadow. No eyes stared at me from the brush. No talons reached to claw off my face. There was no smell of putrid, rotted flesh or wobbly zombies moaning their lust for my brains.

My shoulders loosened, and I turned my back to the empty wood.

The mixture of scents struck me first; the fresh, almost medicinal smell of the eucalyptus trees behind me merged with the salty tang of the bay before me. A powerful, instant spirit-lifter, no matter how many times I walked down this way. I bent and hiked up my green gypsy skirt so I could unlace my purple Doc Martens. I took the opportunity to peer under my arm to the woods behind me. All clear. I really was losing my mind.

I shoved the boots and socks into my bag and made my way down the beach to my favorite rock. My purse made a dull thud as it hit the sand. I gave it a critical eye. I supposed it *did* lack style. Surely it wasn't that bad. I stepped over it toward the water and faced the Bay. The wind outside the tree cover was much stronger, whipping spray into my face and through my tangling hair. I stood like that, enjoying the emptiness and freedom for several minutes before I felt eyes watching me.

I whipped around and scanned the woods, not sure if I wanted vindication of my suspicions or more proof of my impending insanity. Off to the right, a large shadow moved and stepped into the light. For the first time in my life, I wished I were a badass chick with a crossbow or wicked knife instead of being an emotion-magnet with a fabulous sense of style.

The something from the woods was mostly furry, probably seven feet tall, and grinning at me. Bigfoot? Wendigo? Wolf Man? I bent to the side, eyes still on the creature, and felt around for my purse.

Because that's how badass chicks take out big hairy monsters. They wallop them with their purses.

The thing took another step forward, still smiling, gave me a big, furry thumbs-up, and disappeared into the trees.

I groaned and buried my face in my hands. I was going to have to kill Maurice, plain and simple. Apparently, he thought I needed a bodyguard in addition to Fairyland home security and voodoo car fresheners.

I slumped on my rock, lost in images of fairy fly-swatters and closet-monster strangulation. I picked up a pebble and hurled it at the water, watching in frustration as it fell three feet short of the water and clunked in the sand. What the hell was wrong with me? I wasn't a violent person. I couldn't even throw a rock without it looking like a lame, half-hearted toss.

I'd been taking care of myself (and everybody else who came along) for most of my life. After my mom disappeared, Dad had been useless. I'd been eight, but filled the gap as well as I could. My dad wilted after that. I kept him fed and going to work. He loved me, I knew that. But he wasn't equipped to take care of himself, let alone a motherless daughter. It wasn't easy on me either, but I was more adaptable.

And now I had a better understanding of why. I'd

taken my dad's grief and loneliness into myself. I
understood it better than he did, and I tried to pour
love into him. Over the years he became stronger,
and the light in his eyes returned for short bursts,
but the loss was a permanent scar. His death when I
was nineteen had been hard, but I would never forget the relief on his face when he finally stopped
fighting and let go.

Without my father to care for anymore, I attracted
an army of needy boyfriends. They marched in and
out of my life while I nursed them, helped them
pass their college courses, counseled them on family problems. My wallet was emptied both willingly
and behind my back when I was in the shower. I fed
the ones who were hungry and helped others detox.

And I'd still had time to stay up all night with
crying girlfriends with broken hearts.

The exception had been Sara. She never asked
for anything, really, except for my friendship. She
was easy to be around, made no emotional demands,
and I never felt exhausted or drained from her company. Now that I understood what being an empath
meant, it gave me insight into our friendship. Sara
kept her emotions in check the same way she controlled her appearance. She had all her hair appointments strategically booked six months in advance,
and if she needed to cry, she'd schedule a half hour in
the afternoon, preferably coinciding with her lunch
break. She was an ideal best friend for an uncon-
trolled empath.

She'd tried to save me from myself on a number

of occasions. If she judged an all-night crying jag from one of the girls in our dorm had gone on long enough, Sara would come to collect me and drag me back to our room. If I had a bad breakup—and let's face it, nearly all of them were bad—she'd stop me from drowning myself in cheap beer and frat boys. A lot of my college experience was highlighted by Sara running interference between me and my own self-destruction.

I snorted and let fly another wobbly rock. It all made so much sense now. This empath thing had been running my life for as far back as I could remember. Hindsight is a worthless bitch.

I thought about the phone conversation with Brad and my heart sank. I'd never been so mean before. Sure, he irritated the hell out of me, but I'd been horrible to him.

I took a breath and held it, then let it out slowly the way Andrew had taught me. Something wasn't right. I probed the walls of my make-believe barrier to check for cracks. It seemed fine. I took several more breaths and went deeper, examining the emotions imprisoned inside my bubble. Anger, frustration, fear. I tasted each one, explored them like a loose tooth. They were familiar, yet new.

*My God. These are* my *emotions.*

After so many years of harboring the runaway emotions of other people, my own had taken a backseat. Now all I had were what belonged to me, and I was ill prepared to deal with them. It was a terrifying thought.

Could I squash them down like I used to? Probably not the healthiest approach. Could I send them out into the world the way I had learned to do with other people's garbage? No. I was going to have to deal with them, one by one, just like any other well-adjusted adult. I could see this was going to take some time.

I spent several hours out there, poking and prodding at my emotional self. By the time I was done I had examined my fear and anger with a microscope, turned them over in my mind like shiny stones. I became thoroughly acquainted with them so I could differentiate between what was mine and what was borrowed from somebody else.

Then I put them away on a shelf in my head, brushed the sand off my skirt and went home.

"Wolf man?" I asked Maurice when I came through the door.

"Skunk-ape," he said. He had a face like a bunny about to bolt.

I sighed. Maybe I didn't want to know after all. "What's for dinner? I haven't eaten since breakfast."

His face brightened, and he darted into the kitchen babbling about tarragon and coriander. I had no idea what I ate that night, but it was delicious.

Meeting my own feelings for the first time in years had restored my emotional stability. I didn't once feel like gutting anyone with my dessert spoon.

I WAS SMUG that evening, sitting in front of the TV with a belly full of food I hadn't cooked. My kitchen was clean without my lifting a finger, and the weird wine stain shaped like Phyllis Diller had been magically erased from my living room rug after five years of residence. Best of all, I was confident that I was mostly getting the hang of this emotional rodeo thing.

Things were looking up.

The news drifted over me as white noise. A shark attacked a local surfer off Muir Beach. Somebody's sweet old granny robbed a San Rafael convenience store. A clerk at a Sausalito grocery was found dead in the storage room.

I sat up.

I'd been in that store the day before. It was next door to Andrew's herb shop. And I knew the tattooed face of the woman in the photo.

They cut to video footage of the scene. Police and paramedics scurried across the screen like worker ants. An officer brushed aside a microphone when a reporter shoved it up under his nose.

The camera crossed to the ambulance as an EMT slammed the back door shut. I shivered. I had spoken to the dead clerk yesterday. Apparently, I'd been wrong. Selma hadn't been "better than fine" after all. She was zipped into a body bag and buckled in for a trip to the morgue.

The paramedic turned to face the camera before he realized it was there, and I sat up straighter. The winking, coffee-drinking guy from across the street. And wow, he was really hot. I'm not usually big on uniforms, but he filled his out nicely.

So focused on how edible the emergency guy looked, it wasn't until ten minutes later that I thought to wonder how the clerk had died.

# FIVE

SUNDAY WAS A much-needed day of calm and normalcy until I decided to give myself a manicure.

Storage space was at a premium in my bathroom, so I stored many of my girly items in the hallway linen closet. I had a metric crap-ton of face creams I didn't follow through on, bath salts I had no time for, hair removers, hair thickeners, self tanners, skin lighteners and, of course, seven thousand shades of nail polish—many with unused matching lipsticks. Seriously, this was not the '60s. While I might've found a use for orange nail polish, nobody ever looked good with orange lips, no matter what the decade. I had no memory of purchasing it.

On Monday, I had a meeting scheduled with a client, a Goth girl named Spider. Spider's daddy was footing the bill for a mega wedding the size of Argentina. In the spirit of solidarity, and in the hopes of snagging a bigger share of daddy's expenses, I decided to darken up a little before I met her. I had black nail polish, but that would be too obvious. I didn't want to look like a wannabe or a kiss ass. But a nice rich chocolate would be somber enough. I wondered if my spider-web tights would be too much. Probably. Might as well powder my face and draw an ankh on my cheek in eyeliner. Better to undersell it.

I opened the linen closet, shrieked like a little girl and slammed it shut.

In that brief peek into my towels and toiletries, I saw several tiny people scuttling for cover. Had I not recently been attacked by fairies I'd mistaken for dragonflies, I might have thought my closet denizens were mice or rats. My self-preservation skills, however, were waning. Reality, no matter how bizarre, was no longer allowing me to take the easy way out.

I took a deep breath. I took a second deep breath for good measure. Gripping the doorknob, I turned it as quietly as I could, then pulled the door open, peering into the crack. Three—no, four—miniature people huddled in the corner, lit by the shaft of light I let in. A woman stood with one arm wrapped around a little boy, and her hand rested on the head of a smaller girl. A taller boy, I'd say about twelve if he were human, stood in front of them, chest puffed out and one hand on his hip in defiance. His other arm was folded against his chest.

They all looked terrified.

I let the door swing open the rest of the way and regarded the small family in my linen closet. They all had tiny pointed ears and skin the color of milky hot cocoa. The little girl clung to her mother's skirts, tiny black pigtails bobbing as she hid her face. The younger boy looked frightened, but ready to break out of mom's headlock if big brother needed an assist. The mom broke my heart.

Her face was beautiful, a miniature, darker version of Audrey Hepburn. There was so much dignity in the way she held herself. However, Audrey Hepburn hadn't sported a shiner like that. The woman's eye was swollen nearly shut, and dried blood crusted one side of her perfect face. My eyes moved to the older son and noted again the way he nursed his arm against his body. This family had been through hell.

"Brownies," Maurice said, making me jump.

"Gah! Would you *please* stop sneaking up on me?"

"Sorry. Zoey, this is Molly Wheatstalk. Molly, this is Zoey."

She nodded her head once and gave me a smile that was far too weak for my liking.

"It's nice to meet you, Molly," I said. I had a passing thought that a brownie family in my linen closet was a preposterous notion and that I was probably lying on a sidewalk somewhere, bleeding after a piano had dropped on my head.

But denial was a luxury I couldn't indulge. These little people were too real to deny, and I'd never turned anyone away when they needed help. Somewhere in the back of my mind, I also knew I hadn't bothered to bolster my newly created walls of defense for the day, but I didn't care. Molly and her children were hurting, sad, frightened, desperate—I felt it all. But I also felt something else. *Love.* It was so thick I could almost see it twisting around them and binding them together, spreading outward into the hallway. There was so much love in my linen closet I wanted to curl up in a pile of fluffy towels and bask in the glow.

This empath thing isn't all bad.

The smile I gave them was the one I reserved for

nervous brides about to bolt—filled with kindness and understanding. "You have a beautiful family, Molly."

Her smile brightened a bit, and the older son relaxed his defensive stance. The little girl lifted her face and gave me a shy grin, dimples puckering. She popped her thumb in her mouth and stared up at me with round eyes.

The younger son squeezed out from under his mother's arm and took a bold step toward me. "I'm Aaron," he said. Just as Maurice's voice was not low and gravelly as I would expect, Aaron's voice was not high-pitched and squeaky. His chest was puffed out in imitation of his older brother. "That's Fred, and my little sister is Abby."

I cocked my head to the side. "It's a pleasure to meet you all. If you'll excuse me for a few minutes, I'll see what I can do to make you all more comfortable." I grabbed Maurice by the wrist and yanked him with me as I turned to go to the kitchen. As an afterthought, I let him go and walked back to the closet.

"And Molly," I said, bending low to look her in the eye. "Nothing will hurt you here. You and your family are safe and welcome in my home."

I strode to where Maurice stood waiting. "You," I said. "Kitchen. Now."

In the kitchen, I went to the fridge and pulled out the pitcher of strawberry lemonade.

"Zoey, I know how this looks," Maurice said.

"Sit." I admit, my tone was a little sharp.

"I was going to tell you."

"Sit-sit-sit." He sat, and for one blessed minute was silent. I poured two glasses and brought them to the table. I knew there was more going on than what I was seeing, and I was trying to form the words needed to get him to come clean.

Questions banged against each other in my head. The clues had been coming at me since I'd woken up to find a closet monster in my kitchen several days earlier. Brownies. Skunk-ape. Hag. Fairies. *Helping. She was helping, just like you.* All the questions swirled into one single, simple sentence.

"Maurice, what was my mother doing before she disappeared?"

It was obvious this was not where he expected me to go. He looked startled and slightly pale, even for him.

"She helped."

"Yeah, I get that. Helped who? And how?"

"She helped the Hidden, mostly."

"The hidden what?" I frowned, not understanding.

He spread his hands and waved his arms around. "Non-humans. The Hidden. Though I'm pretty sure she helped humans, too. She couldn't help herself. If someone was in trouble, they came to her, and she never turned them down."

"Closet monsters and fairies are called the Hidden?"

"And brownies. Really, anything humans aren't supposed to see. Hidden, get it?"

It was good to know there was a group name for all this nonsense. It was less of a mouthful than "monsters, mythical creatures and urban legends."

"What was she doing for you, exactly?"

"A house fire took my parents and left me an orphan, so she took me in until she could find me a family. She also made sure meals were sent to Aggie the Hag when she was sick."

"The fairies?"

He nodded. "Their clearing was being bulldozed for a new Denny's, so your mom brought them here and planted a garden for them. They were here for years before they found a patch of forest they liked."

Despite my growing suspicions, I was stunned. With the exception of one terrifying night with Maurice, I'd never seen anything unusual while I was growing up. And even that I'd forgotten until he appeared in my kitchen twenty years later.

"So, all these 'favors' you called in to protect me, they were owed to my mother."

"Everybody loved her, Zo. We all did."

I thought about the crazy grin and thumbs-up I'd been given by my skunk-ape bodyguard. I couldn't begin to fathom what she might have done for him, but at least it made sense now.

"I miss her."

"Me too." His shoulders slumped. "She taught me to cook, you know. She could turn anything into a pie or a casserole."

"I don't remember much about her." It made me sad that someone who'd only recently come into my life had so many more memories of my mother than I did. I wasn't jealous, exactly. More like I'd discovered a gaping hole where I hadn't realized there was one.

He reached his hand out and squeezed my hand. "You know, after she left, I still came back sometimes to visit. I had to honor your mom's wishes to leave you be, but there were a few times I almost came out of the closet to sit with you. You were so sad. It broke my heart."

"You watched me?"

"You snore, you know."

"Creeper."

"I owed it to your mom to keep an eye on you."

I took a deep breath, steadying myself for the real question. "Where did she go, Maurice?"

He shook his head. "I have no idea. Sometimes a few months would go by between my visits. When I came back to see her that last time, she was already long gone. Did the police have any clues?"

That was a good question. "I don't remember any police. There must have been, right? I don't remember her leaving, and I don't remember anyone searching for her, but they had to have looked. I only remember after. Months after. Dad didn't talk about it, but then, we never talked about her much. It hurt him too much to remember."

We sat in silence for a few minutes, each regarding the ice in our drinks.

"So," I said. "Molly. What's the story?"

Maurice frowned into his glass. "Her husband is a drunken asshole."

"Ah." That explained everything. "And what was your plan?"

He shrugged. "She knocked on the door just after dawn this morning, and I stashed them in the cupboard. All I could think was to get them inside for safety. The fairies won't let him in through the ring. They're okay in here."

"Safety is good. They also need a better living space and long-term goals. If I've got a supernatural halfway house going here, we have to help them get their lives together. Otherwise, I have a feeling folks are going to start stacking up." I was already making lists in my head, figuring out what I'd need and how to make it happen. After all, that's what wedding planners do. It's my livelihood.

"You're not mad?"

"I'm mad you didn't tell me. And I really could have used the heads-up on what my mom was up to, especially once it started again behind my back. No secrets, Maurice. Obviously, word is getting around. I can't help if I don't know. I probably traumatized that poor woman screaming like that. Quit springing shit on me. One of these days I'll keel over with a heart attack and then who will you cook for?"

I WAS IN my element, drawing up a plan of action and multiple to-do lists. I could hear Sara's voice in my head informing me that I was, once again, avoiding my own problems by focusing on the problems of others, but I brushed the criticism aside. I had no real problems. I had a pretty good life. Okay, maybe I was a little lonely banging around this big house by myself, but hey, now I had plenty of company.

The first thing I did was send Maurice to the linen closet to see about getting them some food. They'd been stuck in the dark, terrified, for hours. The kids, at least, must be starving.

I had to admit, he'd stashed them in a good spot. But I wanted to make it homier and less like, well, like a closet. I'm sure Maurice had seen it as perfect. To him, a closet was ideal. I didn't know much about brownies, but a family needed more than shelf space and linens. Fortunately, I thought I might have a solution out in the garage.

My father had been a packrat, and I really wasn't much better. My little Bug was parked in the driveway because the garage was too full for a vehicle, even one that small. I rarely ventured inside. A few times I'd tried to go through some of the boxes to clean it all out, but the memories were too hard. My childhood was packed away in there. My parents' lives were stored in plastic containers and cardboard boxes.

The door complained when I pulled it open. Cobwebs grabbed at me on the way in, as if attempting to talk me out of wading through all my precious junk. I pushed on. At the back wall, I found several boxes marked "Barbie" and pulled them free.

I had been a complete Barbie junkie when I was little. Every Christmas and birthday brought a new glamorous location for Barbie to spend her time. She had a pool with a cabana, a ballet studio, the dream house, a beauty salon.

I dug through the boxes, shoving past semi-clothed and fully naked dolls with ratty hair. Why is it, the more you brush a Barbie's hair, the grosser it ends up getting? I pulled out her van and her airplane and set them out of the way. Near the bottom of the second box, I found what I needed. Sofas, chairs, beds, tables—they were all there, and all as close to the right size as I was going to get. In a shoe box tucked under a wardrobe of moldering doll clothes was a collection of cups and dishes. There was also some tiny silverware, only a little bent from years of chubby fingers stabbing at invisible pancakes. Barbies love pancakes.

I piled it all into an empty box and folded the flaps down. Satisfied and more than a little pleased with myself, I turned to go.

Behind me, something sneezed.

I looked over my shoulder, squinting into the shadows. I didn't see anything. The second sneeze gave me a better idea of where it was coming from, and I moved my gaze to the corner. An animal— small for a dog, but gigantic for a rat—shifted. I moved closer and peered down.

Not a rodent, so that was good news. Not a dog, either. It looked more *reptilian*. At this point, panic probably should have set in. But the sniffly guy didn't *feel* hostile. In fact, it seemed pretty damn miserable.

And it was pink.

It looked up at me with doe eyes and sneezed again. Tiny sparks shot out of its nostrils.

Though I may have been past the point of doubting my own sanity, surprise was still in my repertoire.

"Hey, buddy," I said in as soothing a voice as I

could muster. "You don't look so good." What does a person do for a sick baby dragon? I squatted down next to it and stuck out my hand to be sniffed, hoping it wouldn't sneeze again and give me third-degree burns. Or lop off my well-intentioned hand.

It smelled the offered fingers, then stuck out a forked tongue and licked me, leaving my skin feeling hot and oddly dry. I patted its head, which radiated heat. The unhappy little thing tilted its head to the side and closed its eyes while I scratched the ridge between its ears. The purring sound it made was much like a cat's, until it was interrupted by another sneeze that scorched a hole right through my favorite comfy sweats.

I patted its head again and stood up. "Okay, buddy. You stay here and rest. We'll get you all fixed up." Empty promise, that. I had no idea what I was doing.

Maurice met me at the door. I shoved the box of furniture at him. "These are kind of dirty from being in storage, but they should clean up fine. Did you know about the dragon?"

"Dragon?" He shifted the box in his arms and looked confused.

Ha! Finally, I was one up on him. "There is what appears to be a small, pink dragon in the garage. Sneezing. And spraying snot sparks. Probably a fire hazard. Are dragons supposed to be hot?"

"Dragon?" His expression had gone from confused to blank.

"Maurice, I need you to focus here. If you don't know anything about dragons, find somebody who does. I have to make a phone call. Could you maybe get him some water or something? Please?"

I left him standing in the open doorway juggling a dusty box and looking out the door toward the garage. In the kitchen, I dug through my bag-o-crap and found my phone and a scrap of paper with a number on it. I needed help.

On the second ring, a cheery voice answered.

"Andrew, this is Zoey."

"Zoey, hey. How's the head?"

"Perfect. You're a miracle man."

"Glad I could help. What's up?"

"I need more miracles." I felt bad calling him for help, but he was the only one I knew who not only had mad herbal skills, but wasn't as likely to think I was out of my mind. I ran through my morning, beginning with the surprising brownie family and ending with the unbelievable dragon. To his credit, he didn't laugh at all. In fact, he was all business.

"I'll pack up some supplies and we'll be right there. Find out what you can about dragons and we'll see what we've got. Milo's been pining for you ever since you left the store."

I thanked him profusely and gave him directions. I had a strong suspicion a psychic herbalist on retainer was going to make my life a lot easier in the future.

As it turned out, brownies know a whole lot about dragons.

While I waited for Andrew and Milo, I helped Maurice clean up the Barbie furniture and move it into the closet. I padded the beds with fabric samples and washcloths, set up a table and chairs, and ran an extension cord into the closet to give them a light. The setup was pink, and it was mostly plastic, but it worked. Molly put Abby down for a nap and came to the edge of the shelf to talk to me.

"You are too kind to us," she said.

"I'm sorry it's not more." I looked at the cut on her head and her swollen eye. "I have a friend coming who can help with that. You can trust him. If you don't mind, I'd like him to look at Fred's arm, too."

Poor Molly's good eye filmed over with tears. "Again, thank you."

We spoke in low voices so Abby could sleep. When I told Molly about the dragon in the garage, her face scrunched up with worry.

"No, they are not supposed to be hot on the outside," she said. "You must cool him off. His furnace must be broken inside. You do not want him to blow up."

# SIX

HALFWAY UP MY driveway, Andrew's battered Pontiac sputtered and died. From my vantage point on the porch, I could hear the starter click-click as he turned the key in the ignition several times. Nothing. He smiled and waved at me from behind the wheel, then reached for the door handle to get out. Again, nothing. He shoved his shoulder against the door a few times, then reached across and tried to open the passenger door. His cheery smile was beginning to fade, and his face had turned an interesting berry shade. From the backseat, Milo's head popped in and out of sight, his excited barking a faint squeal from within the sealed car.

"Maurice!" I yelled into the house.

The monster came flying down the front steps in a rush. "Sorry, sorry!"

He disappeared around the corner of the house, muttering under his breath. A moment later, both of Andrew's doors flew open, and he spilled onto the gravel. Milo exploded through the open door, bounced off Andrew's prone figure, and darted toward me like he'd been shot from a blowgun. The fluffy blur came so fast I didn't have time to do more than hold my arms out before it launched into the air and plowed into my chest, knocking me back a step. My face was promptly covered in foxy kisses. I laughed and let him do his worst.

Andrew pulled himself together and made his way up the steps.

"I am so sorry," I said. "Fairy Homeland Security didn't get your clearance."

"No worries," he said, brushing himself off. "But one of these days maybe I'll be able to say hello to you before doing a supernatural cha-cha first." He gave me a quick hug over a happily squirming Milo. "How are you holding up, sweetheart?"

"I'm good, actually. Maybe shock will set in soon, but I think enough weirdness has happened that I'm getting used to it. You don't seem shaken at all."

"I'm unshakeable, doll. Besides, I get to go home afterwards. You're the one living in Storybook Land."

Maurice came around the corner, saw Andrew and ducked his head. He tried to get past us without drawing attention, but he was a little hard to miss.

"Hey, wait," I said. I waved my hand back and forth between them. "Andrew, Maurice. Maurice, Andrew."

Maurice lifted his head for a second, then ducked down again, mumbling. Undaunted, Andrew stuck his hand out.

"Nice to finally meet you, Maurice."

Maurice stared at the hand for a few ticks before shaking it with a delicate grip. "Nicetomeetyou," he said, the words tumbling over each other in a rush. He released Andrew's hand and disappeared into the house.

I watched him go, my eyebrows raised in curiosity. "Well, that was weird. He's usually so...outgoing."

Andrew's face was thoughtful. "I used to date a guy like that. He was friendly as hell until somebody he didn't know showed up. Then he'd clam up and wouldn't talk to anyone. Maurice will come around. You'll see. I'm too damn charming for him to resist me for long." He winked.

I looked Andrew up and down, a little surprised. I took in the yellow Polo shirt and creased designer jeans, the tone of his voice, the jewelry he was wearing. Ah. Of course. I snickered. "How the hell did you get past my gay-dar?"

He grinned. "You've been a little busy. It's not like I introduce myself that way."

"Well, no, but I'm glad I've been too preoccupied to start checking out your ass or dangling my cleavage at you. That would be humiliating."

"It's okay." He turned around, facing the driveway, hands on his hips. "Go ahead. Check out my ass." He looked over his shoulder at me, waiting.

I shook my head and snorted. "Yes. Very nice. You could bounce a quarter off that baby."

I WAS UNSURPRISED by Andrew's steady hands and gentle treatment of the brownie family. What I didn't expect was how quickly they took to him. He spoke with a slow, calming voice and checked their tiny bodies for bruises and scrapes. Aaron and Abby appeared to have escaped physically unscathed. Molly had cleaned up, and without the dried blood, was in much better shape than I had thought. Fred posed a problem. Not only was Andrew not a doctor, he didn't have a mini X-ray machine on him to determine the extent of Fred's injuries. After scrutinizing the color of Fred's arm and making him move his fingertips and shoulder, Andrew decided to immobilize it with a scrap of cloth as a tiny sling.

"Keep an eye on it, Molly," he said. "If any part of it changes color, or if he doesn't improve, call me and I'll come right back."

Molly looked at her oldest son and frowned in worry. "Tell him to keep it in the sling. If you do not specifically say it, he will forget. On purpose."

Andrew laughed and looked at Fred. "Don't move it until I come back and tell you to take off the sling. Deal?"

"Deal." Fred looked miserable. Injured pride was the emotion I was getting, not self-pity. I had the strong feeling that Fred was accustomed to taking care of his family.

I followed Andrew to the kitchen and watched as he ground up a variety of pungent-smelling, mysterious herbs, liquids and greasy stuff.

He made tea and poured it into a shot glass for them to dip their tiny Barbie cups into, then slathered two kinds of mystery goo on little Pepto-pink plates. I made a face as I helped him pile the smelly load on a small tray.

"I thought Christmas Sweat Sock tea was nasty," I said.

Standing outside the closet, Andrew explained each item. Fred and Molly were to drink the tea for pain and for stress. The goopy stuff was a poultice, though I was clueless as to what that meant. I hadn't seen any chicken parts go into it, so *poultry* and *poultice* must be unrelated. I, apparently, was an idiot. The brownies knew exactly what to do with the gunk.

The one with all the leafiness to it was patted along Fred's possibly-broken arm.

"It should reduce swelling, and if bones are broken, it'll help them knit faster," Andrew said. He tied the tiny sling in place and gave Fred a cheery smile. "Better in no time, Fred."

Molly's goop was a little more delicate to apply. Andrew enlisted Aaron's tiny hands to help smear it over her black eye and along her hairline where she'd been cut.

"Now," Andrew said, "let's take a look at my first dragon."

Without warning, Molly let out a series of yippy barks that bore an eerie similarity to the sound of a fennec fox, then made a flying leap off the ledge of the linen closet shelf. I didn't have time to react. My heart felt like it blew a valve in that single second. She did a little somersault midair and landed neatly on Milo's back at my feet. After grabbing a double handful of fur, she barked once. Milo answered and trotted off toward the front door.

Andrew and I exchanged alarmed expressions and tore after them.

When we reached the back corner of the garage,

I was a little out of breath. Maybe those trips to the gym with Sara shouldn't be such a low priority after this. If I ever had time.

Molly was tsk-tsk-ing from astride her mount.

"You did not say he was pink. This is not good. Who ever heard of a pink dragon?"

Andrew and I agreed that we had not, up until today, seen or heard of a pink dragon.

The brownie woman made a series of snorting sounds which were returned by the miserable dragon, punctuated by sneeze-induced sparklers.

"We must cool him off," she said. "Inside and out. And he is very hungry."

"I'm on it," I said. I ran into the house and yanked bowls out of the kitchen cupboards. "Maurice!" I hadn't seen him since Andrew had arrived. That was odd. Still, whatever his sudden bout of shyness was about, he was at my elbow within seconds.

"I'm here," he said.

"Where did you go? Never mind. I need towels. Will you grab some out of the linen closet and bring them to the sink, please?"

He was gone as quickly as he'd appeared. I dumped every ice cube in my freezer into one of the bowls, congratulating myself for getting a fridge with a size-able ice maker. In another bowl I piled every bit of frozen meat I could find. Chicken, fish, hamburger, steak. I was a little sad about the steaks. They had been on special, and I'd been so pleased with my-self about getting such a good deal on an expensive cut. I shrugged. The universe had given me a deal on dragon feed.

Maurice brought in a stack of towels and set them on the counter.

"The steak, too?" he said. "You have to be kidding me. That was going to be tomorrow night's dinner." He looked pouty.

"I'll get you more steak. Don't be stingy." I sorted the towels, grabbing a few of my favorites and setting them aside. I didn't know if wet towels on a hot dragon would disintegrate on contact.

The rest I threw into the sink and ran under the faucet. Without wringing them out, I dumped them into my monster-sized popcorn bowl.

"We're set. Can you help me get it all out there?"

Maurice looked a little ashen. Well, compared to his normal ashen complexion.

"He won't bite," I said. I shoved the bowl of sopping towels into his arms. "I promise. He saved my life, remember? He's a good guy."

"But." Maurice's bottom lip quivered. "But he's human."

"I'm human. My mother was human. What's the problem?"

"You're special. Regular humans aren't supposed to see the Hidden."

"Trust me. Andrew's special, too." I gave him an encouraging smile and walked out, hoping he'd follow. I did not have time to hold a closet monster's hand. I was terrified a baby dragon was going to spontaneously combust in my garage.

Between the metal bowl of ice cubes and the plastic bowl of frozen, packaged meat, my teeth were

chattering by the time I got back into the garage.
Andrew took the ice from me and knelt down next
to the dragon.

"Hey, handsome. How about something cold to
chomp on with those wicked teeth of yours?" He
held a chunk in the palm of his hand and offered it
like a sugar cube to a horse. The dragon sniffed at
it, slithered out a forked tongue, then grabbed the
ice with his lips, exactly like a horse. He crunched
it once and swallowed. Steam blew out his nostrils
in twin streams.

The sneeze that followed bounced sparks off Andrew's palm. I jumped. Andrew held firm.

While Andrew continued to feed ice to the
dragon, I looked around for Maurice. My foot kicked
the bowl of towels, and water sloshed over the edge,
drenching my new Skechers. I finally spotted Maurice in the corner, his enormous eyes shining from
the shadows. His issues would have to wait. A sick
dragon had to take precedence over a closet monster
with social anxiety disorder. One problem at a time.

I pulled a sopping towel from the bowl and draped
it across the dragon's back. He shivered, and a blanket
of steam rose from the ridge along his spine. Within
minutes, the towel was dry and crisp. If I were the
type to iron my linens, this is the way I would do it. I
pulled the towel off and replaced it with another wet
one. By the third application of wet towel, half the ice
was gone and the dragon was a little less pink than
he had been.

I scratched his head. "Poor baby," I said. "Where's

your mama?" That thought made me nauseous. "Oh
my God. What if his mother comes looking for him?"

Molly laughed. "He is not a baby. Do not be ridiculous."

"But he's so small."

"He is a pygmy dragon. They do not come much
bigger these days. It is hard enough for someone my
size to hide from humanity."

She had a point. There was so much I had to learn.
I was woefully ignorant in the most basic folklore.
And half of what I *had* read was wrong. Probably
more than half. Why was there not an instruction
manual for this? *Mystical Creatures and Urban Legends for Dummies* would come in handy right about
now. Or maybe *Care and Feeding of Your New Hidden Horde*.

"Think he's ready for some food?"

Molly exchanged a few grunts and snorts with the
dragon. "Bruce is ready to eat."

"Bruce?" The mundane aspects of the supernatural floored me more than the crazy stuff.

I clawed at the plastic wrapping on the frozen
chicken and became frustrated quickly. I can never
get them open without a sharp implement, and by
the time I get one, I'm usually so irritated that I do
damage to whatever is inside in my haste to stab at
the problem.

A knife appeared as if I'd wished for it. Maurice
had stepped out of his protective shadows to present it to me.

"Thought you might need this, so I brought it with

me," he said in a stage whisper. Or maybe, for a closet monster, that was a regular whisper. I was sure my missing *Dummies* book would have answered the question.

I poked at the plastic and sliced the package open. Holding a chicken leg between my fingers as delicately as possible, I offered it to Bruce.

"Here you go, buddy. I know it's cold, but you need that right now."

Bruce snarfed down the frozen chunk of flesh so fast I had trouble following it with my eyes. If it weren't for the single, very loud *crunch* coming from his jaws before he swallowed, I might not have believed he'd gotten any of it.

Two packages of chicken, three sea bass (also on special), and all of the ground beef were gone before he started to slow. Maurice and I looked at each other with hopeful relief, but it was not to be. Bruce let out a long, rumbling burp and asked for more. With sadness in our hearts, we unwrapped the steaks and tossed them in with the rest of the contents of my freezer. So much for dinner.

On the bright side, it looked like it worked. Bruce let out a warm sigh, turned on his side so his distended belly would be more comfortable, and dozed off. He didn't snore so much as gurgle in his sleep.

He wasn't exactly cool to the touch, but he wasn't hot either. And the snot-sparkler sneezes had tapered off.

"See?" Molly said. "Broken furnace in his belly. He should be better now. His color is much better."

Bruce was now a brownish green with darker

green spots—apparently the industry standard for adult pygmy dragons.

We all stood there watching him for a few minutes until it started to feel uncomfortable. Maurice resumed his spot in the shadows, and Molly made tiny braids in Milo's hair. Andrew grimaced, still hunkered down on the garage floor.

"Need some help?" I stuck my hand out and helped haul him to his feet.

He brushed himself off and stretched. "That was pretty cool. Not sure you needed an herbalist for it, but I'm happy to be here."

"Glad we could entertain you." I grinned. He had no idea how much I had needed another human around today. If nothing else, I needed confirmation that I wasn't insane.

"I guess the show's over for now. Milo and I should head back."

I was a little worried about getting them out of the driveway, but apparently security wasn't as concerned about who left as they were about who arrived. I watched the tail end of his car disappear down the road, and my stomach sank.

I was on my own again.

# SEVEN

THE BABY RACCOON in the basket by my desk wouldn't eat the Tootsie Roll I was trying to feed him. Frustrated, I wished I had some celery. Raccoons love celery.

I returned to my paperwork and squinted. The words jumbled together and my eyes wouldn't focus. It was as if each letter squirmed out of reach of my direct gaze, making it impossible to string them together into words, phrases and sentences.

Maybe I needed glasses. The light was a little dim, but the wedding was about to start and Maurice hadn't lit all the candles yet.

Sara appeared beside me, looking stern. "What *are* you wearing?" she said, dragging me from my desk. "You look ridiculous. Start the music. Everybody's waiting."

I grabbed my cell phone and punched at it to bring up my ringtones. A synthesized version of "The Wedding March" rang out, and Sara pushed me toward the aisle.

*My* wedding? Crap. I looked down at my clothes. I couldn't get married in a Hello Kitty nightgown. Did I have a wedding dress? The music from my phone ended. Everyone was leaning over the pews looking at me. I tapped buttons and scrolled through the ring-tone list, but I couldn't find the song again to restart it.

Panicked, I darted into the church foyer to rum-mage in my closet. No wedding dress. No, wait, there it was. I ripped the plastic from the frothy black gown and pulled it over my head. The sleeves were too long and the hem was above my ankles. Now ev-eryone would see my bare feet. I should have painted my toenails.

I ran into the church and walked down the aisle as slowly as I could. The groom faced away from me. His sandy hair curled over the collar of his tuxedo. My feet moved faster.

From his seat in a pew ahead, Dad smiled and gave me a thumbs-up. I worried for a moment that he wasn't walking me down the aisle, but then I re-membered he had died, so couldn't possibly give me away. When I walked past him, he leaned out and grabbed my hand.

"Your mother's dress suits you," he said. "I hope you kept her chili recipe." He pulled his arm back and faced front.

The groom was gone. I must have taken too long. The candles had blown out, and I was alone.

The darkness was oily and thick. Weak moonlight trickled in through the stained-glass windows causing shadows to flit around me. I tried to leave, but a tree branch snagged at my skirt, pinning me in place. I tugged at it, desperate to press my back against some-thing solid. The open space left me exposed to something moving in the lightless night. A hungry thing. A thing with claws.

I ripped the fabric free and fled, every step impeded, like taffy pulling at my feet. I raced in slow motion, knowing something was coming for me in the dark. The pressure on my legs released and I stumbled forward into soft, velvet arms.

Glowing green eyes bored into me. "My dear, you look lovely. Positively delicious."

Sebastian leaned his head forward to taste me. I opened my mouth to scream and his mouth engulfed mine, tongue darting in to lick at my panic. His eyes remained locked on mine, and waves of fear and pleasure shot through my body. My struggles weakened and my arms went limp.

I loved him. Of course I did. How could I have forgotten? I stroked my hands against his velvet coat and up to his face, then curled my fingers in his hair. I moaned and moved my body tighter against his.

He broke the kiss and chuckled. "Just a taste. Let's not be greedy. I wouldn't want to overfish the lake when the harvest is so bountiful."

He released me, and my legs buckled. A pathetic, mewling protest escaped from me as I watched him go.

I crawled after him through the grass, but I didn't have far to go. He stopped and knelt over the prone figure of a woman covered in tattoos. He glanced at me and winked before pressing his lips against hers.

She stirred and moaned, her body twisting about in a sensuous dance. He stroked his hand along her waist and she bucked, her moans more frantic. Sebastian pressed his mouth harder against hers, and her back arched in the throes of orgasm. His hand moved to her hip, fingers digging into the fabric of her jeans. Her back arched again and she groaned. Her legs kicked out and her arms shoved at him to release her.

He clutched her harder.

The pitch of her muffled cries became higher, more frantic. Another orgasm ripped through her body. Her back arched so hard I thought it might snap. Her arms flapped like caged birds, batting at him with less and less force.

Selma's hips continued to twitch long after her arms and legs fell to the grass, motionless. When he released her from the prison of his kiss, her head fell sideways. Her lips were bruised and swollen, her eyes glassy and empty. The grocery clerk was dead.

Sebastian rose to his feet and looked down at me where I knelt in the grass.

He pulled a delicate handkerchief from his lacy shirt sleeve and dabbed at his mouth. "I must say, you are a fabulous cook. That was superb."

His eyes flashed at me and something tightened between my legs. I reached my hand up toward him, a shameless whimper escaping from my throat.

"No, no," he said. "Thank you, I couldn't eat another bite. I'm stuffed. But I can't wait to see what you'll cook for me next. You are truly an artist."

My throat cramped and a tear slid down my cheek. He walked away and I crumpled, sobbing.

"Zoey."

Someone was shaking me.

"Zoey, wake up."

I opened my eyes to find Maurice standing over my bed, his yellow eyes glowing in the near dark. "Wake up, Zoey."

I sat up and wiped at my wet face. "What time is it?"

"About three-thirty. You were crying. Are you okay?"

I thought about it. "I think so. That was a weird one." I slid out from the sweaty, tangled sheets. "I'm sure as hell not going back to sleep anytime soon."

Maurice dragged me to the kitchen and sat me down at the table. He grumbled while he made hot cocoa from chocolate milk mix.

"Real cocoa, Zoey," he said, shaking a wooden spoon at me. "You have no idea how hard it is to cook in a kitchen so woefully thin on ingredients."

I grinned around a mouthful of caramel-pear pie. "From where I'm sitting, you don't seem to be having any problems." I poked my fork into the flaky crust and gave a suspicious frown. "In fact, I know I didn't have any pears in the house."

In response, he became extra busy at the stove, stirring furiously.

"Maurice, what have you done?"

He pulled his shoulders straighter and faced me with a slow reluctance. "Nothing. I did nothing. They couldn't eat all those pears anyway."

I thought about all the deliciousness of the past

several meals and cringed. Strawberries. Melons. Cabbage. Green beans. "Oh my God. You've been stealing from the neighbors."

"It's not stealing, Zoey. I only take a little, hardly enough for them to notice. Fresh is better. And the hens practically show me where their nests are."

I was stunned. I didn't know any of my neighbors had chickens.

"Eggs, too? Maurice, we can't do that. Please, please, write me a grocery list. I'll go to the farmers' market if you're so set on fresh. But I need you not to harvest my neighbors' produce. We have enough going on here without pitchforked villagers storming the house looking for their missing butternut squash."

He poured the heated cocoa into mugs and brought them to the table. Taking a seat, he sipped at the steaming drink and blinked his yellow eyes without saying a word.

"Maurice, promise me."

He gave me a dramatic sigh. "Fine. No eggs. No gardens. But I reserve the right to pick from trees when the fruit is going to go bad anyway. You really are unreasonable."

I rolled my eyes and speared a chunk of gooey fruit. "Deal. Thank you."

I slid the fork between my lips. I felt bad for being angry. The pie was incredible and far beyond my meager cooking abilities. What harm was he doing if nobody missed the ingredients from their yards?

Neither of us spoke as we ate. Cups clinked, silverware scraped, and bodies shifted. Maurice's eyes flicked to my face from time to time, looking worried. I realized halfway through my second cup of cocoa that he was showing incredible restraint in not asking about the dream that had me sobbing in my sleep.

The truth was that I didn't remember a lot of it.

"It was a crap dream," I said. I wasn't sure which one of us needed the reassuring the most. "It didn't mean anything. Garbled stuff mostly. I was taking out my subconscious trash for the day."

Green eyes flashed in my head, demanding and hungry. I shivered.

"Taking out the trash makes you cry?" Maurice wasn't buying it.

"I don't remember much. A chapel, my wedding dress was wrong, something about a raccoon. It was nothing."

*I can't wait to see what you'll cook for me next.*

The second half of the dream slammed into me, and I choked. I saw Selma's body contorted in pleasure and agony. Emerald eyes danced in my brain and sent my head spinning. I could feel him reaching for me through the dream, engulfing me, tasting my emotions. A tiny whimper trickled through my lips, and I clutched at the table.

"Zoey!" Maurice was up and around to my side of the table in a blur. He grabbed my shoulders and shook me. "Zoey, don't let him in. He can't touch you unless you let him. Push him away, Zoey!"

Through the fog of the remembered dream, I

reached for Maurice's voice and pulled myself back to my warm kitchen. A thin layer of sweat coated my skin. Enormous, unblinking yellow eyes stared into mine, grounding me.

"How is he doing that?" I said. "How can he get into my head?" I was trying my best to hold back panic. "Maurice, what do I do? He got in, despite all the fairies, stinky bags and skunk-apes."

"You can keep him out, Zoey. You have to take back your power. He tasted you on the street, so he's tracking you. But he can't come into your head unless you allow it. Remember what Andrew showed you—you can use that against this demon. Next time, push him out."

I snorted. That sounded simple enough. Just push him out. Of course. I could do that. "I may never sleep again."

He squeezed my shoulder and sat back down. "You're strong, Zoey. And he can't hurt you from a distance, not really. He's messing with you. Don't let him."

"Am I intruding?" Molly popped onto the table, having vaulted from floor to chair.

I smiled. She was disheveled from sleep, her bruised face already looking far better than it had the day before.

"Not at all. There's pie and hot chocolate. I hope we didn't wake you."

"My little one had a bad dream, and I heard voices. I like pie."

Molly joined us, and the conversation turned to

mundane things like turnip crops, babies and high-top sneakers. For all my years of living alone (and cherishing the solitude), I'd never imagined the warmth of having people around me when I needed companionship. It was a new feeling, and I savored every second. I knew Molly was only with us temporarily, but my heart skipped at the thought of Maurice leaving. How long would it be until he could sort out his own life? For having been there for such a short time, he'd managed to fit into my life and my home as if he had always belonged. After only a few days, I didn't think living alone again would sit well with me. He'd have to leave sometime, though. He had a life before he came to stay with me, even without his wife in the picture. As if reading my mind, Molly asked the question I'd been too afraid to ask.

"Maurice," she asked in a gentle voice. "Have you spoken to Pansy since you arrived?"

He swallowed hard and scratched at a dry spot on his wrist. "She won't take my calls or answer my letters."

Molly and I exchanged looks. "What will you do?" she asked.

He shrugged. "Give her time. She'll miss me eventually, right?" He shifted his gaze to my face, pleading.

I had serious doubts that this could be fixed, but that wouldn't do him any good to hear right now. It was too new, too raw. "Give it time, Maurice. However it's going to turn out, today probably isn't the day it does. You've got a home here as long as you want it."

I glanced at the clock over the stove and was stunned to see it was five forty-five. I rubbed my eyes.

"I have two appointments today, one of which is a cake tasting," I said. "This is going to be the longest day ever."

Molly nodded her head in commiseration. "My children will be up soon. We are all going to need naps."

Maurice cleared the plates and cups.

"Maurice, when do *you* sleep?" I asked. I realized I knew hardly anything about him. "And for that matter, *where* do you sleep?"

He laughed. "I'm a closet monster. I'm nocturnal, mostly, but I don't need much sleep. I doze in the guest-room closet when you're at work."

"Do you need anything to make you more comfortable?" I felt terribly guilty for not considering the question before.

"I'm fine, Zoey. I don't need much."

"Nothing? Blankets? Pillows? Can I clear stuff out of there for you? Anything?"

He thought about it. "I could use a radio, if you have a spare. It's awfully quiet around here during the day."

With all the drama throwing itself at me lately, it probably was a great deal quieter when I was gone.

"Okay. And if you think of anything else, tell me," I said. "I'm off to the shower, see if I can beat some magic into myself to give the illusion of presentable."

The hot water and steam engulfed my tired body

like a warm hug. I inhaled the scents of shampoo
and soap and let them work their way inside, lifting
out the disgusting muck that stuck to my consciousness like tar. I used the exercises Andrew taught me
to clean it all out, exhaling it into the air and visual-
izing it swirling down the drain and away from my
vicinity. My skin was pink and glowing when I finished, having scrubbed my outsides as hard as my
metaphysical insides. I stepped onto the thick purple
bathmat feeling cleaner than I had in days.

Sometimes a hot shower can cure a world of ills.

It bothered me that Maurice had done so much for
me, yet I hadn't had one thought for his comfort. Part
of it, I supposed, was his efficiency in running my
house and the visitors we'd had. He slid into the role
so smoothly it seemed he'd always been there. To be
honest, he didn't ask for anything except a roof over
his head. But there was more to it than that. I supposed, as much as any of the rest of us, he wanted a
place in the world where he fit. It made me uncomfortable to think that Maurice saw cooking and cleaning
for me as his place.

I resolved to get him the best little stereo I could
find. And maybe speak privately with Molly about
the care and feeding of closet monsters. There had to
be something more I could do for him.

I dressed carefully. My Goth bride was my first
appointment, but the cake tasting this afternoon was
with a more traditional bride. I chose a simple, knee-
length black skirt, black tights and black heels with
gold buckles. I debated the blouse for some time

before finally choosing a light cotton with red and black horizontal stripes which I topped off with a black suit jacket. Somber, but not ass-kissing for the Goth, professional, but slightly quirky for the traditional.

To me, it was on the boring side and needed brightening up. I'd have to make an effort in the future not to mix my brides on the same day. It limited my wardrobe choices.

Having gorged on pie a few hours before, I tried to slip out of the house without stopping for breakfast. Maurice wasn't having it. I got a very dad-like lecture on good nutrition and starting my day out right.

I tried to argue. "There were fruits, and grains, and milk," I said. "All of these are part of a nutritious, balanced breakfast. Ask any cereal commercial."

He stared at me with his enormous, unblinking eyes. "Sit. Sit. Sit." His tone indicated I was not in charge and would not win this fight.

As I snarfed down a bacon, egg and cheese sandwich on a bagel, I wondered how the hell I'd lost so much control over my life.

On the way out, I stopped in the garage to see Bruce. He'd kept my ice maker working overtime since I found him, but when I'd checked on him before bed last night, his temperature had been normal, as near as I could guess.

I pulled up the door and peered inside. "Bruce? It's just me." I headed into the far dark corner. "How do you feel, buddy?"

At the back of the garage, I stood over his corner, allowing my eyes to adjust to the lack of light. "Bruce?"

The dragon was gone. The corner had been vacated, a rounded spot of clean left on the floor in his place. I looked for him between boxes and under tables. I looked up at the rafters overhead, in case his puny wings had managed to carry him there. Nothing.

I was surprised at how sad I felt at his loss.

"Good luck, buddy," I said to the shadows. "Come back anytime." I went to his spot to double check. Maybe he left a note? Could dragons write notes? Doubtful. His claws were probably too long to hold a writing utensil. And the paper could catch on fire.

Nope. No dragon curled up in the corner of my garage and no note. But there was something. I bent closer to look, and my breath caught in my chest. A gold amulet encrusted with diamonds and rubies lay in his place. A shiny gold chain coiled around the pendant. I lifted it from the cold cement and brushed it off. The metal radiated a pleasant warmth in the palm of my hand. I was touched both by the gesture and the beauty of the piece.

Despite how gorgeous it was, it was large and clunky. Any number of curses and blessings filed through my head to be catalogued. I had to assume Bruce wouldn't leave me a monkey's paw that caused my unspoken wishes to kill off a friend or raise a loved one from the grave. If I rubbed it, would a genie pop out? Would the genie have phenomenal cosmic powers?

I flipped it over and looked for markings. I couldn't

discern any directions to the Well of Souls—not even one-sided directions that would have me digging in the wrong place.

I watched too many movies.

Most likely, it was a pretty piece of jewelry Bruce thought I would like. I slipped it in my bag and forgot about it. It was going to be a long day. Mysterious amulets with hidden powers would have to wait.

# EIGHT

MOST DAYS I stopped off at a local coffee shop and grabbed a pastry and cappuccino. Since a delicious breakfast had been forced on me, I didn't need the pastry. Still, I needed the coffee. Coffee at home is one thing—I was grateful for the cup I'd been handed to wash down the sandwich. A venti for the office was non-negotiable, all the same.

The little coffee shop two blocks from my office was crowded, even for a Monday morning. I inhaled the heavy scent of roasted beans but the various perfumes and colognes of the customers jostled my nostrils in a hostile takeover. The woman in line in front of me was especially obnoxious. Her perfume was thick and flowery, assailing me like a child throwing a tantrum. "Look at me! Look at me!" it seemed to shriek.

I've always taken offense at people wearing heavy perfume. It's as if they have no respect for boundaries. If I wanted my personal space to reek of lavender and musk, I'd dump a vat of bath salts into the tub and go for a soak. It's rude to think everyone wants that stuffed up their noses. Whatever happened to subtlety?

I rubbed at my nose with the back of my hand, as if that might clear out some of the stench.

"It *is* a little much." The voice came from behind me in line, low and secretive, as if he didn't want anyone but me to hear him.

I was embarrassed. I had hoped no one else had caught me trying to wipe away the smell. I turned to answer and was caught off guard. In fact, I babbled like an idiot.

"You," I said, already kicking myself for my lack of suavity. "I saw you on TV the other night." He looked puzzled, probably afraid I'd confused him with an actor or talk show host. "You know," I said, trying to clarify, "on the news. Taking the grocery clerk to the ambulance. Or her body anyway." *Shut up, Zoey. Please shut up.* "It was a shock. I'd just been in there talking to her the day before. I bought cheese." *Oh for the love of the one-eyed god of wombats, will you stop now?* "I recognized you from earlier the same day when that man was hit by a bus. You do seem to be around when people die. What horrible luck. But then, you're a paramedic, right? So it probably happens to you a lot."

I stopped to take a breath and realized he was smiling at me. He nodded toward the counter and I thought I'd lost his attention. Not sure whether to be devastated or relieved about that, I realized he was urging me forward in line.

Excellent. I was an all-around doofus, not just the babbling kind. I turned to face front and closed the gap between myself and the stink bomb. Because I am a total glutton for punishment, I turned around and faced him again. One more try. I took a deep breath.

"I'm really sorry," I said. "Honestly, I didn't get much sleep last night. I'm not normally this way."

And then I tripped backward and bumped into the woman in front of me. Who was holding the coffee the barista had handed her seconds before.

"Dammit," the woman said. She didn't yell. It was a fairly low-key attitude for someone with hot coffee dripping from her sleeve.

"I am so sorry," I said. I grabbed napkins and blotted at her drips. "Please, let me get you another one."

"It's fine, it's fine. I hate this sweater. Only a little spilled anyway." She took the napkins from me and mopped up, then tossed the paper in the trash. "All better. No harm." She smiled and left.

I felt like a total shit for bashing her perfume.

There was no way I could make eye contact with Captain Dreamy behind me. Miserable, I placed my order for a venti cappuccino with a double shot of Irish cream. I needed the double shot. I only wished it were alcohol instead of flavored syrup.

I huddled in the corner waiting for my order to be called, hoping he wouldn't see me. If he were smart, he'd order a black coffee and clear out before I had to walk past him.

It turned out he wasn't smart.

He came over and leaned against the wall beside me. I pretended not to notice him, though I'm sure I wasn't in the least bit convincing. From the corner of my eye I could see he wasn't in uniform. His jeans were snug, but not '70s avert-your-eyes-you-can-totally-see-his-package tight. His green T-shirt hugged him affectionately without looking like he'd dressed from the kids department in an effort to look hot. No, hot came naturally. As much as I wanted a good, thorough look at him headlong, I refused to acknowledge his presence. A girl can only endure so much self-inflicted humiliation in one morning.

Regardless of how much attention I pretended not to be paying him, I was very much aware of it when he moved toward me. He lowered his head and brought his face next to mine. I could feel his breath on my cheek.

"Don't sweat it," he said. "The coffee probably improved her smell."

There is an excellent chance that I blushed at that point. I started to stammer a response, but having blurted out a stream of incoherence before, I swallowed it.

"If your name is Zoey," he said, "they've called your order three times."

I considered denying my name, but the damage was already so bad I couldn't see trying to repair it. Any chance in hell with paramedic guy was totaled. Call the insurance company and get a claim started; once the frame is bent, the shop can't do a thing.

I murmured a quick "thanks" under my breath, darted in to grab my coffee, and blew out the door before I could do something worse.

*Nice one, Zoey. You did everything short of fart-*

*ing in there. Maybe if you see him again, you can
tell him you have a yeast infection.*

I needed the brisk two-block walk to the office in
order to further my self-flagellation to the point of
depression. Never in my life had I behaved that way
in front of a guy—well, maybe in sixth grade. Since
then, I wasn't the smoothest talker, but I could hold
my own on witty banter. Today's display was wor-
thy of a night in bed with a tub of Ben & Jerry's. I
didn't own flannel pajamas, but I was considering
stopping at the mall to get some.

When I walked into the office, Sara glided from
her desk to meet me at the door.

"Good, you're here," she said. "The Dickson-
Strauss wedding is a week from Saturday and I have
a ton of errands to run. I'll be in and out all day. Can
you man the phones in case she's having a meltdown?
You're better at calming the storm."

She paced the office, picking up samples and
books, moving coffee cups, peeling Post-it notes
from one location and re-sticking them in another.
There was a frenetic energy I admired in secret—
Sara's mornings did not look like a zombie movie.
She never grunted before her first cup of coffee. Sara
was my idol.

"I have a two o'clock at the bakery, but other than
that, I've got it. If I have to leave, I'll forward to my
cell."

I plopped into my chair, trying to shake off the
utter dejection I'd built up for myself. I took a sip of
my coffee and managed to burn my mouth.

"Why do you insist on buying overpriced sugar disguised as coffee when we have a perfectly good coffeemaker here?"

"Why, indeed." I shuffled through a pile of papers and pulled what I was going to need for my meeting in an hour. "Probably because my ego is far too large and needs a good downsizing."

Sara's eyes narrowed. "Problem at Ye Old Coffee Shoppe?"

"Not a problem." I stretched my face into a bright, fake smile. "I'm going to die alone and childless. It's my fate."

"How much caffeine have you had today? You're not right."

I considered the question for a moment. "Hot chocolate has caffeine, right? So, a lot. I've been up since a little after three. This day is going to be fabulous."

"You sure I can leave you here alone?" I knew she didn't mean it. Sara was wearing her amused face, the one she used when she thought I was being silly and might start juggling bunnies and kittens any second.

Come to think of it, I might have seen that same expression on the paramedic's face. I groaned. *That's right. I'm freakin' adorable.*

Rather than outline my humiliation for her, I changed the subject.

"I have an appointment in an hour. What can I do to make your day easier, since mine's already trashed?"

Our office was small, but efficient. My desk was

along the wall on the right, facing the left wall. Hers was back in the left-hand corner facing the door. It was rare that we ever had simultaneous appointments, so this worked well enough without having individual offices. We had comfy seating facing both desks so clients felt pampered into parting with their money. The corner opposite Sara's desk had a coffee and tea area with a mini fridge containing milk, creamer and various juices. There was usually a pink bakery box sitting on the counter.

We liked cookies, and so did our clients.

The carpet was plush white, the walls a deep burgundy, and the whole thing came together with the air of a parlor rather than a cold, sterile office space. We used the work counter in the back room for crafty projects, assembling favors with birdseed, squares of tulle, ribbons, fabric, imitation flowers, candles, and endless jars of beads and sequins. We were prepared for anything.

Knowing this, I probably shouldn't have offered my open hour to Sara's needs. Without answering, she pulled me into the stuffy room and put me to work.

"Apparently," Sara said, "Gail Dickson's bridesmaids are not in the least interested in being helpful. I told her not to worry about it. We'd take care of the birdseed favors."

"Why do people do that? Why would you agree to be in a wedding unless you were going to help? Do people not read Miss Manners anymore?"

Sara shrugged. "My guess is they're already tired

of taking crap off of Mama Dickson—I'm sorry, Madam High Pubah City Councilwoman Dickson. She's even got me ready to slap her pompous little face, and I don't rattle easily."

That I could believe. Sara had taken point on this wedding, so I'd only been at the initial meeting. I was running backup. But I knew Councilwoman Dickson well. Everyone did. She managed to get her picture in the local paper on a regular basis, and anyone with a business in Sausalito knew pissing her off was a very bad idea.

This wedding would make or break us. Councilwoman Dickson's only daughter's wedding ranked a two-page spread in the local paper, and the politician had scored a promise of coverage in the *San Francisco Chronicle* as well. Being the head of the city council in a town as small as Sausalito shouldn't have been a big deal, but Alma Dickson had made herself into some sort of local celebrity. If everything went well, we could expect a long line of giggling debutantes clamoring for us to do their wedding.

But if Mama wasn't happy, we might as well pack up and move to another county.

An unhappy Alma was known to cause all sorts of trouble for business owners—parking tickets, building code violations, spontaneous sanitation inspections. I wouldn't put it past the old bitch to send someone over in the dead of night to dump cockroaches into the office.

No. This was one wedding we had to pull off without a flaw. Sara looked uncharacteristically frazzled.

Her eyes darted around the room like she wanted to pounce on the work table and get started.

"Go. I've got it. Well, some of it, anyway." I waved my arm in the air. "Run around town. Be efficient."

She looked relieved, but still edgy. "Are you sure you're all right?"

"I'm fine. Being an idiot isn't usually fatal. It's you I'm more worried about. Leave this. I'll help. It's what I do."

As soon as the words were out of my mouth, Maurice's voice reverberated in my skull. Was that all I was on Earth to do? Help people? *Might as well suck it up and accept it, Zoey. Helping is what you do. Just like Mom.*

After Sara was gone, I puttered around collecting seeds and ribbons and tulle and tiny fake flowers. It took a few minutes to find Sara's file on the wedding to double check the colors and number of guests. Sara is the put-together lady and I'm the spastic psycho, but underneath her pressed suit and my candy-striped socks, I'm more organized. The universe is an odd place.

The Dickson-Strauss wedding didn't look like any more fun than I'd predicted after the initial consultation. Two hundred guests, midnight-blue and silver color scheme, traditional, traditional, traditional. I made a face while I tied ribbons around the birdseed-filled bags of fabric. Both Sara and I would attend, as the bride had paid for on-site oversight of her big day, but I wasn't looking forward to it much.

My supreme organizational skills meant I could

assembly-line wedding favors faster than the Ford Motor Company. It didn't hurt that most of the materials were premade. Scoop the seed into the bags, tie the precut ribbons around the opening and add a tiny fake flower. Piece of wedding cake. I made it through a good seventy-five of them before I glanced at the clock and realized my Goth girl and her mother would be arriving any minute. Tying a bit of silver into an artful bow, I dropped it in the box and went out to settle at my desk to wait.

They were, of course, late.

While I waited, I pulled Bruce's amulet out of my bag and examined it. The gold was shiny and polished, as if it were brand new. Filigree edged a raised disk in the center inlaid with a black stone shaped like a dragon in profile stretching its wings. Diamonds and rubies ringed the outline of the beast, a single emerald chip at the dragon's eye. It was large. It was gaudy. And I loved it.

Maybe if I'd been wearing this antique chunk of crazy, I might have had more confidence and less idiocy at the coffee shop. I toyed with the links on the chain. Why had I fallen apart like that? It made no sense. Then again, much of the last few days had made no sense. I wondered what the hunky EMT must think of me.

And then it hit me. Normally, I wouldn't be asking myself what someone thought of me. I would know. That's why I was usually so much smoother when I met a good-looking guy. How could I be so stupid? My walls were up, blocking out everybody around me. Everything I'd been feeling that morning was coming from me. Nobody else was leaking in and giving me clues about how to behave. Apparently, this empath thing had been saving me from myself throughout my life and I never knew it. I needed to tweak the wall thing or I'd never survive without becoming a social pariah.

As I slipped the chain over my head, the door opened and a dark cloud—strike that—two dark clouds rolled into my office in the form of Spider and her mother.

# NINE

AMANDA "SPIDER" TALBOT was a Goth stereotype.
I doubted that she realized it or intended to come
off that way, but she'd hit overkill about three lay-
ers of eyeliner ago. Her hair was a bottled black that
had no shine and looked like an uneven, dried ink
splotch. Dark lace and satin engulfed her small frame
and dripped from her hands, allowing the tips of her
chipped black polish to peek out. Her expression, as
always, was dour. No doubt she was contemplating
her own death scene some years hence.

As if at war with her dark daughter, Mrs. Talbot
was dressed as a ray of sunshine—if sunshine came in
a medicine bottle and smelled like stale crackers. Her
yellow hair was frizzy and dried out, obviously a home
job. The two might benefit from a little cooperation in
the bathroom come dye-time. Neither was doing well
on her own. Mama Talbot wore a yellow sundress so
bright even I wouldn't have dared wear it. She had art-
fully applied the orange lipstick of my cosmetic nightmares. I felt vindicated; it looked like crap on her, too.

Despite her sunshiney outfit, Mrs. Talbot shared
her daughter's gloomy demeanor. Hers, however,
was the genuine article. It was neither for pretense,
nor a fashion accessory.

I braced myself and stood up to greet them.

"Ladies," I said, waving them in. I stepped out from behind my desk and met them near the door. "You both look lovely. Have a seat, please. Can I get you something to drink?"

Spider asked for tea and her mother said she'd like some, too. This, of course, prompted Spider to ask for coffee instead. Black.

This was their second visit to my office, so I was prepared for their mutual hostility. The initial consultation had also included Mr. Talbot, so there hadn't been any bloodshed. Daddy Talbot had a knack for keeping the two in line—or at least separated. After a brief interview, they all went home to discuss whether Happily Ever After was the right fit for the job. The fact that mother and daughter returned for a second consult was a positive note for the business, but I'd still have to earn their final approval. Difficult clients were my specialty. I would pull this off if it killed me.

I kept my smile steady and went to get drinks for them. It was already a rough start, and they'd only been there for thirty seconds.

The room wasn't large. From the coffee corner, I could hear everything the two women were saying to each other, and it didn't bode well for the rest of the appointment.

"Absolutely not," Mrs. Spider said. "A black wedding dress is inappropriate, in poor taste, and rude to your guests."

"Mother, it's appropriate for me. Our tastes are

vastly different, and my guests will applaud me for being true to myself."

"It's morbid and creepy."

"That's ridiculous. Black is elegant. Besides, it's perfectly appropriate for a graveyard ceremony."

I was focused on the drink prep, pointedly staying out of it until either the coffee and tea were ready or I was forced to spray them with a fire hose to separate them, but I'm fairly certain Spider's mother choked on a mint. It was probably the kind stuck to the bottom of her purse. With lint on it.

"There is no way in hell you're getting married in a graveyard. You'll get married in a church like a normal person. I won't have it. Getting married surrounded by dead people. What is *wrong* with you?"

Spider gave her mother a dramatic, condescending sigh. "Death is the ultimate expression of love, Mother."

And this is when I decided I'd better intervene before Mama throttled my bride to show her exactly how much she loved her.

"Here we are, ladies," I said. I carried the cups on a silver tray which I placed on my desk. "I highly recommend the shortbread cookies. My partner picked them up from the bakery this morning. She said she watched them come out of the oven. Shall we get started?"

"Your partner?" Mrs. Talbot looked uncomfortable.

*Oh, good Lord, she thinks I'm gay and she has a problem with it.* I blinked at her, my smile unwavering. "Yes, of course. My business partner, Sara. You spoke with her on the phone to make the appointment." *I need more sleep to deal with this.*

The bickering continued throughout the next half hour. Spider was doing her best to antagonize her mother at every turn. Her mother continued to speak in a condescending tone and tell her what was best for her.

Flowers, music, venue, décor—all of it was a tug-of-war between Mary Sunshine and Dracula's Bride. I had lost all control of the situation. This was not normal for me.

While they argued over the proper wedding shoes for bridesmaids, Mom making the case for dyed-to-match heels while daughter championed army boots, I took a moment to pull myself together. My hand strayed to my new amulet, fingers tracing the dragon. I thought this through.

I wasn't getting anywhere because I had them blocked. I pulled my attention inside myself and examined my bubble. I'd become pretty good at building and maintaining it over the last few days. It was time for a new exercise.

I inhaled deeply through my nose and let the breath out through my mouth. Had the two women across from me not been so engrossed in their own performance, mine would've caused them to wonder what sort of new-age hippie they were hiring. I ignored them as much as they were ignoring me.

In my mind, I examined my wall and traced my finger in a small circle, slicing through the material

like a laser. A gentle shove from my fingertips sent
the loose piece floating out to the ceiling, leaving
me a small window to pass information in and out.
It probably wasn't the best solution in the world, but
for the moment, it would have to do.

I opened my eyes and examined each of the snip-
ing harpies. I took in the older woman first, reaching out with my heart and mind, searching for what
she was feeling.

*Anger. Fear.*

*Helplessness. Loss.*

Loss. Ah. There it was. Buried beneath the anger
and fear, this woman was terrified of losing her
daughter. Once I'd located the underlying emotion
pushing at her, it was simple enough to put together
why she was acting this way.

Spider was a little more complicated.

First of all, she wasn't in the least bit pissed off,
contrary to her attitude. She was absolutely delighted
with the showdown. Tickled. Spider baited her mother
intentionally, with little or no conviction behind any of
her outrageous wedding demands. Where there should
have been some sort of passion, there was a void. The
only real emotion I was feeling from her was a twisted
kind of joy each time her mother's voice broke.

Interesting.

I cleared my throat, preparing to jump into the
fray. "Ladies, if I can direct us back to the worksheet,
we'll see if we can find a few things we agree on."

I took it slowly with them. "Let's start with the guest
list. Do we have an estimate?"

They answered simultaneously.

"Five hundred," Spider said.

"One fifty," her mother said.

There was a short pause before they started chittering at each other like angry monkeys fighting over the last banana. Any second, they might start the poo flinging, and I was pretty sure Sara wouldn't be amused by the carpet stains that would leave behind.

Mrs. Talbot's face turned an unhealthy pink. "That's a preposterous number you pulled out of thin air. You don't know that many people."

"I've already posted an open invitation to everyone who hangs at Coffins."

"You are not inviting a bunch of death-worshippers you just met in some club."

I could feel the tension in Mama Talbot building to a new level. She was winding so tight I expected an audible *sproing* as she shot out of her chair and hit the far wall. I hoped when she snapped she wouldn't take anyone's eye out. I knew I should stop it from happening, but my instincts are solid for this sort of thing. I let it run its course.

"It's my wedding, Mother." Spider had gone still, her voice low.

"Why can't you be normal, for once in your life?"

"Why can't you let me be myself?"

"You haven't been yourself for years. I hardly know who you are."

"Just because you were eight months pregnant and had a civil ceremony at City Hall, doesn't mean you get a do-over with my wedding. I don't have to pay for your mistakes."

And that did it. The camel's back collapsed in a heap of broken vertebrae. Mrs. Talbot was up and out of her chair, heading for the door before I could uncross my legs.

At the threshold, her head snapped around and she fixed her attention on me. "I'll be in the car. Do whatever the hell she wants. It's not my business."

The door slammed behind her. Her pain lingered for a moment, poking at the back of my neck like a sharp stick. Once that had dissipated, I was left with Spider's thinly veiled glee. She looked and felt like a marathon runner who'd just crossed the finish line to victory.

It was the ugliest thing I'd ever felt.

"She can be such a trial," Spider said. She stretched her legs in front of her and got more comfortable.

"Cut the crap, Amanda." I wasn't loud. I wasn't accusatory. My voice was calm and steady.

She blinked and sat up a little straighter. "Excuse me?"

"She's gone. You can put down the mask and let's talk."

"I don't think I like how you're speaking to me."

"I don't really care. If you don't fire me, and if I decide to stick with you, you're going to be honest with me and with yourself. Otherwise, I can't do my job. Are we clear?"

She nodded once, but looked wary.

"I have no idea what the problem is between you and your mother, but it has nothing to do with your wedding. You want this to be *your* wedding or hers?"

Her voice was small and quivery. "Mine."

"Then act like it. Every decision you've made so far has been based on what would piss her off the most. This is your wedding day—your first wedding day. We hope it's the only one, but even if you had ten more weddings, there's only one first. It is not a body piercing you can take out and heal over if you change your mind. It's more like a tattoo. Permanent. Do you want to be forty-five years old and look back at pictures of you looking somber in a graveyard? Do you want to think about your wedding as the day you got a major one over on your mom? Or do you want to remember a beautiful, perfect day in which you were joined together with the love of your life?"

I'm not a monster—maybe under my current circumstances I shouldn't throw that word around so lightly—but I will admit to the warm flash of pride that overcame me when I felt her deflate.

"I like the Goth style." Her voice was still weak and timid.

I relaxed. "I like it, too. We can work with it. Let's start with that. How long have you been part of the Goth community?"

"About a month."

Great. Excellent. I knew I'd spotted a wannabe the minute she walked in. *With* my shields up.

"And Eric is part of it, too?"

"He's okay with it. He wants whatever I want."

That was all I needed to hear. The entire catastrophe was instantly made moot. I do love my job.

Her appointment ran over by about a half hour—a

fact I noted in the books and would be sure to charge Daddy for—but progress was made. Against my own financial best interests, I talked her down to two hundred twenty-five guests. She agreed to tour a gothic mansion as a possible venue, and we discussed wedding dresses that had a gothic flair with splashes of black, red or purple.

In the end, it was a good first meeting. We had nine months to pull it together. I was pleased with myself.

We made an appointment for the following week, and I walked her to the door.

"Do you think my mom will be okay with what we're doing?"

"Does it matter?"

She looked at her shoes for a moment. "Yeah. I guess it does."

"She's been stuck in the car for forty-five minutes. Maybe you should take her for ice cream and talk about it."

"Maybe I will." And then Spider, the morbid, undead girl from Transylvania, smiled at me before she left.

Under all that black gook, I was betting she was beautiful.

It was a good day.

I went inside humming one of Maurice's nonsense songs and cleared up the cups of nearly untouched coffee and tea. An hour later, I was finishing the last of the birdseed bags when the phone rang.

"Happily Ever After, this is Zoey." I cringed.

I hated the name we'd agreed on, but none of my ideas had gone over well with Sara. I had caved, and now I was stuck with it. Even after five years, I still winced.

"Zoey, this is Gail Dickson. I need to talk to Sara."

Through the phone, the panic pattered at my cheek like hot drops of cooking oil.

"Sara's out of the office, Gail. I can help. What do you need?"

She must've pulled the phone away because the wail of frustration sounded like it came from a distance.

"The linens are wrong! My bridesmaids bailed on me, and I have to do the birdseed thingies all by myself, my mother-in-law hates the color scheme, and the caterers left the vegetarian choice off the menu!" She took a choking gulp of air. "The whole thing is ruined."

I glanced at Sara's notes. "Gail, deep breaths, honey. Sara's gone to take care of the caterers and the linens. I've already finished the seed bags. Your mother-in-law is not the one getting married, and no matter how much she hates the colors, it doesn't mean she hates you. It's also far too late in the game to do anything about it anyway."

"It's all falling apart." She sounded tired. Less than two weeks before the wedding, brides often hit panic mode and have a meltdown. This bride was especially prone. Growing up with an overbearing mother had undermined Gail's confidence and left her brittle and overly dramatic.

"Not at all. You have us to take care of things. That's what you pay us for. The only thing you need to concentrate on right now is looking good. Stress is counterproductive. We stress for you."

"I want it to be perfect."

"It will be. We'll be there to make sure of it. Just breathe, let us know if anything comes up that needs handling. And go get a massage."

"But what if it's too late to fix the menu?"

"Can you imagine anyone telling Sara 'no'?"

Her giggle came out as more of a wet hiccup. It was a vast improvement over hysteria and tears. "No, you're right. I'm a little scared of her myself."

"Oh, you have no idea. I thought she was going to make me go home and change the other day."

"Were you wearing that pink skirt with the orange dots?"

"No, but I think she may have broken into my house and stolen that one. It's been missing for two weeks."

"She wouldn't!" That had her laughing.

"She might. Fashion is very important to her." The oily spatters of panic were gone. Now all I felt from her was weariness. "Gail, if you need anything, you call, okay? One of us will always answer. We forward the phones at night, just in case. Go get a massage. I want to see you looking radiant."

"Thank you, Zoey. Thank you so much."

After I hung up, I felt drained. Between Spider and Gail, I wasn't sure if I could take another bridal outburst. I considered patching the hole I'd lasered through my wall, but I depended on the emotional feedback from my brides. A small hole was easier to deal with than my previous wide-open state. The lowered level made a difference.

Before I'd learned to shield myself, I'd have had a debilitating migraine by now. I may have been taking in less of other people's garbage, but I was still giving more of my own energy than non-empathic people probably did. I didn't know how not to do that, or if it was possible to cut back. A nap would have been an enormous help. Alas, I still had one more appointment to go. All I could do was hope Helen Cranston and fiancé Steve Welsh were having an especially good day. Besides—there would be cake. Cake can fix any number of problems.

With almost two hours to kill, I made a run to Best Buy in Marin City. Maurice had cooked for me, cleaned up after me, implemented home security, worried over me and sat up with me when I was scared. I could certainly help him with a little noise during the day.

I looked at clock radios, but they seemed cheap. I was surprised to find that the store stocked boom boxes, but those weren't quite right, either.

After lingering in the aisles for twenty minutes and brushing off four different instances of "Can I help you find anything, ma'am?" I knew what I wanted. I supposed I'd known what I was after all along, but I'd been putting off the inevitable. This was going to be expensive.

To avoid wincing in public, I asked the girl at the

checkout not to say the total out loud. I signed without looking and took my bags. iPods don't come cheap, and neither do clock radios with docking stations. Money wasn't the issue. I made enough. I'd inherited my house, and my own needs were few. Still, I couldn't help the feeling that this sealed an enormous relationship commitment. I had no idea how long he would stay, but in the meantime I could at least make him feel comfortable and welcome.

I grabbed a burger on my way to the office, abiding by one of the steadfast rules of wedding planning: Never go to a cake tasting on an empty stomach. I felt guilty about the fast food and hoped no one would see me. Maurice would be upset that I hadn't let him pack me a lunch, and Sara would lecture me on taking care of my body. Both were far more concerned with my well-being than I ever had been.

I parked the car up the street from the bakery and clattered down the sidewalk in my buckled heels. The day was warm and I was beginning to regret the sensible suit jacket. I made it to the appointment with two minutes to spare. Unfortunately, Helen was already outside waiting for me.

And she was crying.

# TEN

I'D HAD SUCH high hopes for a calm end to my day. Helen had, so far, not had a bridal meltdown in front of me. Her wedding was still four months away, so she wasn't scheduled to break down for at least another two.

She wasn't hysterical, so that was something. She also wasn't with her fiancé, which was probably the problem.

I rummaged in my bag and pulled out a travel pack of Kleenex before I approached her. Best to be prepared.

Handing her the tissues with one hand, I put the other on her shoulder. "Hey, you okay? Where's Steve?"

She gave an embarrassed sniffle and rubbed a tissue across her cheeks. "I'm fine. I was having a little pity party. I didn't mean to get caught. Steve had to take a client to the golf course for an emergency meeting." She wiped her nose and gave me a wry smile. "It's very important to keep the clients happy."

I reached through the little hole I'd made in my mental wall. I felt embarrassment and frustration from her, but nothing catastrophic. Not a meltdown after all. I squeezed her shoulder and opened the glass door to the bakery.

"Chocolate," I said. "Let's go taste some creamy, fluffy goodness."

Helen was a refreshing change from my average client. A little older, a little wiser—I felt more like I was helping out a friend, less like I was holding her hand through a crisis. I liked her. She was blond, blue-eyed, and had a way of making casual clothes look formal—well prepared for the role of corporate spouse. But she maintained a wicked sense of humor that didn't mesh with the look. I appreciated that about her.

We were greeted at the door by the owner, Moira Eccles. She buzzed around us in short bursts of energy like a tiny hummingbird fluttering from flower to flower. I had no idea how a woman who worked with pastry all day could be so damn thin, but I suspected it was from flying back and forth around the customers.

Splendid Creations was my go-to for cakes. It wasn't often that a client had me attend the tasting with her, but I tried to steer them there whenever possible, even if I wasn't going to be present. Moira knew what she was doing. She was an artist, but she was also a superb businesswoman. An order from her never went astray and was always on time.

She brought us a platter loaded with thin slices of cake, globs of icing and puddles of filling.

"Try everything," she said. "Any combination you can dream up, we can create."

She sat with us to ask all the pertinent questions about the construction of the cake. Size, shape, colors, theme. Round or square? Fondant or buttercream?

"Chocolate," Helen said. "Chocolate, chocolate, chocolate."

Moira smiled. "For the cake, the filling, or the icing?"

"Yes."

I laughed. "She's having a bad day." I handed Helen her fork. "Taste first. Flavor decisions after."

She set her attention to dragging her fork through different combinations. One slice was getting more attention than the rest. "What is this one?" she asked.

Moira leaned in to look. "That's red velvet."

"Can we do chocolate with it?"

"Honey, you can do anything you want. You're the bride."

"What about red velvet cake with the chocolate ganache filling and a cocoa buttercream frosting. Is that too much?"

"It's never too much. You can have more than one filling if you like. It's your cake."

I could see the wicked sense of humor ticking behind Helen's eyes. I wondered what she was up to.

She picked up her fork and took a small piece of red velvet. Then she dragged it through the chocolate ganache, added a second layer of the same cake, pushed on a little raspberry filling, then finished it all off with a dab of cocoa buttercream icing. She smiled and winked at me, then shoved it into her mouth. Her head tilted back and she fluttered her eyelids for comic effect.

"Well?" I said, trying not to laugh.

"Perfect. Moira, have you seen this combination before?"

"I can't say that I have, though I think it's a good choice."

"Can I name it?"

"Name it? Sure. Let's have it. I'll put it on a menu in your honor."

"Red Velvet Death by Chocolate. Make sure the raspberry filling is extra thick. I want it to bleed when we cut into it." She leaned toward me and gave me a conspiratorial wink. "That'll teach Steve to bail on me."

I knew there was a reason I liked her.

To be sure of the choice, Moira jogged to the kitchen and whipped up a full slice to the new specifications. It did indeed "bleed" when we stuck our forks into it. And it was delicious. Moira did a sketch of a three-tiered square cake draped with fondant and dripping with flowers. It was going to be lovely. Helen was thrilled, we were filled with cake, and nothing but positive emotions were bouncing across the room.

I had forwarded calls to my cell, so I didn't have any reason to go back to the office. Neither of us had anything pressing left to do for the day, so we walked down to the coffee shop and grabbed a table.

With all that sugar coursing through our veins, the only logical thing to do was to pour caffeine into the mix.

While we chatted over our cappuccinos, my eyes kept darting to the door. It did not go unnoticed.

"So spill it," Helen said. "Who are we waiting for?"

"I'm not waiting for anybody." I shrugged and smiled in a way that felt as unconvincing as it probably looked. Against my will, I glanced at the door again. Sometimes my body doesn't listen to orders.

"Okay. Let me rephrase, then. Who are we afraid of?"

I groaned. "If I'm afraid of anybody, it's myself. And I'd be glad to tell you who he is, but I don't even know his name."

"Ha! I knew it was a guy." She sat forward in her chair, both hands clutching her cup. "Dish. I'm not letting it go."

I knew she wouldn't. I was cornered. I considered dropping my coffee to cause a distraction, but I'd already spilled somebody else's that morning. I didn't want to get myself banned from my favorite caffeine dealer. That would be tragic.

"He's a paramedic," I said. "And he's gorgeous. I keep running into him. Today he talked to me and I made a complete ass out of myself. I dumped some woman's coffee on her. I babbled. I told him I bought cheese, Helen. Who says that?"

Helen's face contorted. She seemed torn between commiseration and raucous laughter.

"So?" she said. "You got it out of the way. Next time you'll stun him with your poise and charm. Clever girl, putting him off guard like that."

"From your lips to God's ears," I said.

"If you keep running into him, maybe he's already fallen madly in love with you and you don't know it. Or fate is conspiring to put the two of you together."

I snorted. "If that's true, fate has an evil way of running things. Two out of the three times I've seen him, there was a dead body involved."

She shrugged and picked at the paper heat guard around her cup. "Take what you can get."

"At least he's got a job. That's more than I can usually say for my ex."

"Having a job isn't necessarily a selling point for me at the moment." She peeled the paper apart at the seam and unwound it. "Money's nice, but I'd like to see my fiancé from time to time."

"Have you talked to him about it?"

"He says he's building our future. Providing for the children we'll someday have. I know he loves me. Is it so bad to wish for a little bit more of him?"

"I don't think it's ever bad to wish for more, especially when it comes to love."

I could feel it now. Her disappointment leaked through the little porthole in my wall. It trickled over me like soft feathers brushing my arms. I wanted to take it away from her, make it better, but honestly, it wasn't an overwhelming emotion. Not strong, like so many of the others I'd been hammered with lately. I had a feeling this was an emotion she kept inside and rarely let out for air. It was a constant companion, but not one that absorbed her full attention except on days like this. Days when she could let her guard down.

The voice of wisdom inside me was silent. I had nothing I could say to her that could fix this or make her feel better. But that was okay; she didn't expect me to help her. Sometimes all a person needs is for someone to listen.

I reached across the table and squeezed her hand.

"If nothing else, you'll have him all to yourself on the honeymoon."

"There is that," she said. "I've never been to Fiji. Two weeks alone with Steve and maybe I'll be glad for him to go back to work. You think?" She grinned.

"And then you can spend all your time eating left-over wedding cake."

"Red Velvet Death by Chocolate wedding cake." She held her cup in the air and we banged them together in a toast.

"Do you think he'll mind?"

"Eh. He should have come for the cake tasting if he cared that much."

I never hung out with clients outside of appointments. Helen was the first exception. Socializing wasn't really my thing, and I had a tendency to hide out at home most of the time. Sara had to cajole me into going out, and we'd been close ever since we were roommates in college. Now that Andrew had pointed out my dreadful affliction—excuse me, *gift*—my solitary lifestyle made a lot more sense. I didn't bond well with individuals because they handed me too much emotional baggage. Getting too close to people overloaded me. Sometimes grocery shopping drained me to the point that I had to take a nap when I got home.

It seemed my hermit phase was coming to an end. Between my house guests, Andrew and this spontaneous coffee date with Helen, I wondered if learning to control the influx of stray emotions might be changing the way I interacted with the world. With the exception of the paramedic, it was turning into a pretty good thing. I was as sociable as the next person, given half a chance. Who knew?

We sat there for over an hour, chatting like old friends.

When our cups were empty, I went to the counter and got us refills. I'd probably regret the caffeine and sugar overload later, but I was enjoying myself. When I came back, the conversation made a natural turn from making fun of the college kid in the corner who was lip-syncing and making faces to the music on his MP3 player, to wedding plans.

"We need to make some sort of decision on the table linens and draping for the reception," I said.

"How do we do that? Do we go to a showroom and pick it out?"

"We could. Or I could bring a sample book by and we could go through it."

She clapped her hands. "I like flipping through samples. I had loads of fun picking out drapes for the house."

"Is that sarcasm?"

"Sadly, no. I really do like it. It's a dirty little secret."

I thumbed through my appointment book. It was something I didn't do very often in public, conscious of how much of a relic it was. It may have looked behind the times, but I liked my ratty appointment book. It was substantial. Sturdy. I knew where everything was and how to get to it without clicking buttons or keeping it charged.

"Tomorrow..." I ran my finger down the page. "Nothing. God, really? I have nothing tomorrow? How's tomorrow look for you?"

"Tomorrow's good. I have Pilates at eight, but I'll be home by nine-thirty. That okay?"

I penciled the time into my schedule. "Nine-thirty. That works. I'll bring the book and we'll make some decisions so I can place the order."

We stood up and gathered our things. As I slung my bag-o-crap over my shoulder, I glanced at her tiny designer bag. How could she hold anything in it? My big clumsy satchel suddenly felt awkward. Maybe Andrew was right. I should find a replacement. Something a little less bulky and a little more dignified. At the very least, this one wasn't very professional.

I knew Helen had crossed the line from client to friend when she made a face at my monster purse.

"How about we go shopping sometime for something more suitable?" she asked. "Something lighter and easier to search through."

I sighed and agreed. It was time to give in to the masses and replace my old standby.

We tossed our empty cups in the trash and stepped out onto the sidewalk.

"My car's that way," she said, pointing up the street.

"I'm the other way. I'll see you in the morning. Have a safe trip home."

There was an awkward moment where a hug sometimes goes. She was my client, and despite having had a good time hanging out with her, we weren't exactly BFFs. We were in that weird gray area. If we were men, we'd say something gruff like "See ya, buddy" or "Take her easy." We would then slap each other on the back or shake hands. Guys had it so much easier. Frankly, I was grateful for the awkwardness. Had she given me one of those bizarre air-kisses near my cheek, the whole afternoon would have been spoiled.

I settled for a short wave of my hand. She waved back, then turned and walked down the sidewalk to her waiting car.

In that moment, my amulet did something odd. The fact that it did anything at all was enough to be alarming. I was beginning to get used to monsters and myths popping up, but if inanimate objects started doing things on their own, I was turning in my resignation.

The chain went icy cold against the back of my neck. Not just chilly, but so cold it burned. It stung as I wrapped my fingers around the disc and pulled it over my head, frowning. Feeling silly, I looked up to see if anyone was watching me.

A pair of emerald-green eyes stared at me from a cluster of people across the street. The amulet bit into my fingers and ice crystals flaked from the links.

The light changed and the pedestrians at the corner crossed toward me, a quarter of a block away. I couldn't get my feet to move. *Deep breaths, Zoey. Deep breaths.*

I could see Sebastian's dark head bobbing up and down in the middle of the crowd, his eyes focused on mine across the distance. Frantic, I reached inside myself and jammed a mental chunk of crystal into the hole I'd made earlier. I sealed it up as well as I could, but the circumstances were not ideal. I needed a quiet place to do it right. I needed to concentrate. I needed to breathe.

The crowd dissipated around him, and he stood still on the corner by himself, facing me. I hammered and nailed and sanded my mental wall, trying to seal the cracks before he got to me. I was sure he could read the hysteria on my face. *Faster, Zoey, faster. He'll be here any second and Andrew won't be here to save you.*

Sebastian nodded his head at me, acknowledging me acknowledging him. The oiled curl in his beard jutted out at me in greeting. If I could get my feet unstuck, I might've been able to dart into the coffee shop until he was gone.

I wasn't going anywhere.

He lifted his hand in a half wave, the frilly white sleeve of his pirate shirt fluttering over the crimson smoking jacket.

Like an idiot, I nearly lifted my arm to wave back.

He spun on his heel, and with a casual swagger, walked away from me down the street.

# ELEVEN

MAURICE WAS NOT happy. He paced across my living room, his high-top sneakers galumphing over the Egyptian rug. I worried for the integrity of the weave.

"You're not going to work tomorrow, that's the first thing."

I didn't know what to say. He was right, of course. In the face of an incubus, I'd frozen, and I couldn't be let out alone.

"This is ridiculous. I don't have to go into the office tomorrow, but I do have to go out. And I can't hide the rest of my life."

"I can't protect you when you're out there." His pacing became more frenetic. "Did the amulet work, at least?"

"It got cold. Really cold. Is that supposed to mean something?"

"It's a warning. Next time, don't wait, just run."

"How did you know about the amulet? I only found it this morning. Did you tell Bruce to leave it for me?"

"I did." Molly hopped onto the coffee table and stared up at me, her face solemn. "I told him about the incubus, and he said he had just the thing. It will warn you if you are in danger."

"Thank you, Molly. I appreciate it. If Bruce comes back, please thank him for me." I caught Maurice by the elbow as he made a circuit past me. "Hey. Don't worry so much. I let my guard down. It won't happen again. After my appointment tomorrow, I'll spend the day working on my defenses. I'll be all right."

He looked doubtful, but the pacing had stopped for the moment. That was a good thing. Time for a tactic I'd mastered: changing the subject.

"I got you a present," I said. I grabbed my +2 Bag of Holding and rummaged around for the Best Buy bag. With my arms almost elbow deep, I managed to pry the price tags off, then I freed the plastic sack. "For you." I handed it over.

He looked surprised. Not as though he was surprised that I would think of him—more like surprise because he'd never received a present in his life. He stared at me wide-eyed, clutching the bag without looking inside.

"Open it," I said. Seeing his shock, I almost wished I'd taken the time to gift wrap it. If presents were so rare, I should have made it more special. Well, lesson learned. I decided I'd make up for it at Christmas.

Christmas? That was three months away. Apparently, I had settled on the idea he was staying.

He peeked inside the bag. I couldn't tell if he was excited or worried something would jump out and bite him.

His breath sucked into his chest in one enormous gulp before he ripped open the bag like a little kid at Christmas. "An iPod! Oh, Zoey, that's crazy!

Molly, I got an iPod!" He pulled out the other box
and erupted a second time. "A clock radio, too?" He
danced around with the boxes, doing what looked
like an impromptu merengue.

Thank goodness I hadn't cheaped out. This was
the most fun I'd had in ages.

When the initial excitement wore off, Maurice
stopped dancing with his boxes and tore into them.
He spent the next hour pouring over directions,
charging the devices and perusing iTunes on my
laptop for music to transfer.

Crisis averted. Just call me queen of the subject
change.

I was pleased my laptop was getting some use. I'd
only purchased the damn thing because Sara kept
harassing me about living in the dark ages with my
flip-phone and my battered appointment book. We
had a website built for the business, and when re-
minded, I checked e-mail in case prospective clients were looking for information. I knew it wasn't
a priority though; Sara checked it religiously. I was
more of phone girl. On the rare occasion I found an
e-mail in there, I called with the requested information. It drove Sara nuts. Twitter and Facebook were
beyond my patience.

While Maurice was absorbed, Molly and I moved
into the kitchen.

Having successfully bashed a hole through my
carefully constructed barriers, I was unsurprised
by the headache clamping my brain in a strangle-
hold. Thanks to Andrew, I was prepared. I offered

to make Molly something else, but she insisted on trying the tea I'd brought home from Andrew's shop. I warned her about the sweat-sock aftertaste, but she said she was game and had a small headache herself. I shrugged and set it to brew.

Over one giant cup for me and a tiny Barbie cup for her, we sat in the warm, cozy kitchen, chatting like old friends.

"How's your eye?" I asked. "It looks a lot better."

In reflex, her hand went to the side of her face. "It is much better, thanks to your friend. My people know a great deal about herb lore. It is not so common for one of your kind, especially one who is not of the Hidden."

I sipped at my tea, feeling the headache unclench inside my skull. "He knows a lot of things. I think I owe him my life."

She nodded, her face solemn. "That you do."

I pulled the necklace from inside my blouse and examined it. Both the chain and the amulet were warm to the touch. I must not have noticed it earlier, since I'd worn it outside of my shirt.

"How does this work, exactly? It was freezing when Sebastian showed up. Would it do that for anything that threatened me?"

"The amulet cannot warn you of impending disaster, say a car accident or a lightning strike. There must be a conscious mind in the vicinity, someone who wishes you ill."

"I see." I traced my fingers across the filigreed

edges. "How did you know Bruce had this? Where did it come from?"

"Dragons hoard. One cannot know what they have in their treasury, or how they came by it. I explained the danger. He brought you this."

"I'm grateful to you both. After a lifetime of taking care of others, lately I need constant help just to stay alive."

"There is no shame in needing others, Zoey. We all need help sometimes."

I nodded, thoughtful. "I suppose you're right."

Maurice stuck his head in the kitchen. "Zoey? Can I borrow your credit card?"

"For what?"

He rolled his yellow eyes. "I have to pay for the downloads, Zoey. Piracy is illegal, you know."

I stifled a smile. "No, of course. I wouldn't want you going to jail." I rummaged in my purse for my wallet. "Dammit. I'm going to have to admit defeat and give up this purse. Everybody's right. It's too big. I can't find a damn thing." At the bottom, wedged between a pack of cheese-and-peanut-butter crackers and a mini toolkit, I finally found my wallet. I handed over a credit card.

Maurice reached for it, and I pulled it away. "Don't go overboard."

He nodded, smiling, and I gave it to him. He disappeared around the corner, humming Abba. I shuddered to think what he was downloading.

"Your kindness is what draws the Hidden to you," Molly said. "You have a kind heart."

I shifted in my seat and stared down at my hands folded on the table. "I don't feel particularly kind, Molly. I just don't like people to be unhappy."

She shook her head and placed her pink cup on its pink saucer. "Most people are not so concerned with the feelings of others. Your gift makes you vulnerable, but it also makes you special."

"I'm just getting used to this whole empath thing. Up until a few days ago, I thought everyone's brain worked this way. I honestly don't know how people communicate without it."

She smiled. "We get along the best we can. And if we misread one another, we try again. It is how regular folk do it, human and Hidden alike."

We sat in silence for a few minutes, each deep in our own thoughts. I was concerned about Molly. I'd helped people in abusive relationships a time or two in the past. Based on my experiences, the chances were high that she would end up going back to him for another round. I had to broach the subject with some delicacy so I didn't drive her in his direction. But I couldn't remain silent on the subject.

"Molly, you know, I love having you and the kids here." I took a sip of my now tepid tea. "You're welcome to stay as long as you like."

She nodded her thanks and dabbed at her mouth with a torn square of paper towel. "We like it here very much, Zoey. Thank you. We will not stay forever, but it is good to know we have a safe place to be for now."

I wanted to blurt out the question foremost on my mind, whether she was planning to go back to the asshole, but I toned it down. "Do you have any plans?"

"I have to think about my children first," she said. "Even drunk, Walter would never touch the little ones. But Fred is older. He broke my boy's arm. That is inexcusable."

She sat up straight and tall, and I was struck again by how much dignity was packaged into such a tiny, delicate person. "Molly, hitting you is inexcusable as well."

She nodded. "I know this. If he did not drink…" Her voice trailed off.

"But he does."

"He could change."

"Yes, he could. Or he could kill you."

"There is that possibility." She lifted her hand and ran her fingers over her darkened eye.

"You don't have to make any life-changing decisions right now, Molly. You're here to heal, and it's only been a few days. You have all the time in the world."

"Until he figures out how to get past the fairies."

"That won't happen. I promise."

That was an easy promise to make. After everything I'd gone through so far, I knew Maurice had spared no favors on security.

Molly excused herself to check on the kids and

get some sleep. As tired as I was, I still had some work to do. I'd used what amounted to an imaginary jackhammer to tunnel through my walls earlier in the day, and stray emotions blew in through the gaping hole I'd left. What was supposed to be a small, controllable leak was more like a burst pipe.

What I needed was some beach time on my rock to sort it out. After changing out of my work clothes and into sweats and sneakers, I headed out for a walk.

As I crossed the fairy line on my way out of the yard, I was accosted.

"Woman, where's my damn family?"

I looked down at my feet, puzzled. It was fairly dark, and the small, brown figure was difficult to make out. I bent lower. An irate, male brownie shook his fist at me.

*Ah, this must be Walter.*

"Sleeping," I said. "If you don't mind, I have things to do." I took a step forward and fell flat on my face.

From the ground, I could see him much better. He had a handsome face, though the unwashed hair, grizzled beard and hateful expression erased any good impression it might have made. I sat up and examined my shoes. Nice. The laces were tied together. "Real mature," I said, picking at the knots.

The little bastard took advantage of my diverted attention and launched himself onto my knee. This placed him within inches of my face. Despite his diminutive size, his whiskey breath packed a hell of a wallop from such close range.

"You have no right keeping them from me," he said.

"Whoa," I said, pulling my face away. "One, breath mint, and two, personal space."

I lowered my knee and nudged him off with the palm of my hand.

"Pushy bitch," he said in a low voice. "Somebody needs to teach you a lesson." I didn't think he intended for me to hear him.

I had a strong urge to pick him up by the back of the shirt and dangle him several feet over the grass. I wanted him to feel helpless in the hands of someone bigger and stronger. I wanted him to suffer for what he'd done to his family.

But I was never that kind of person. Even if I wished I could be.

I ignored him and retied my shoes in silence. Then I rose, brushed off my pants and made my way toward the beach.

Of course, he followed me.

All the way through the forest and out across the sand, he yammered.

"You can't get away with this," he said.

I said nothing.

"I'll get through eventually. You can't keep them from me."

I plopped on my rock and began to meditate.

"Look at me, woman!"

He was beginning to go past irate and into ballistic. If he spontaneously combusted, that would certainly solve a number of problems.

I was surprised by how easily I was able to tune him out. It was becoming simple for me to flush out the day's collection of unwanted emotional debris. From there, I had to decide whether to take down my walls and rebuild, or try to patch up the hole I'd hacked out earlier.

This posed a problem. Better to take the whole thing down and rebuild from scratch. A patch job, imaginary or not, wouldn't feel very secure—and since the whole thing was in my mind, the illusion of security was important. However, taking it down in front of Molly's husband was an invitation for all sorts of emotional crap I did not want to own.

I opened my eyes and returned my attention to the small man next to me.

"...tell her that I love her, and then I'll go."

I sighed. "Are you drunk right now?"

"I've had a few, but that's not your business."

"No, it's really not. Neither is anything else you've been saying. Molly is currently healing from the beating you gave her. Fred's arm might be broken. Go sober up. You have no business with them or me right now."

"They belong to me. I'm not going anywhere until I talk to her."

"We're done. I have nothing to add, and you have nothing I want to hear. Go home."

He plopped his tiny ass in the sand, folded his arms across his chest and glared at me.

An idea formed, and it occurred to me I'd need someone around to try it out.

"Suit yourself," I said.

With my eyes closed, I pictured a tiny crystal dome, heavy and solid like a mad scientist's equipment. It dropped over the top of him into the sand. I followed the bottom edges and imagined them tunneling beneath him, expanding and lengthening until they met and locked, forming a seamless glass bubble. I could hear the echoes of his anger, depression, insecurity and guilt banging around inside. But he was sealed up tight, and his emotions along with him.

I'd learned a new skill.

Satisfied, I dropped my own walls and rebuilt from scratch. This time, in the wall at eye level, I built myself a window. Rather than tunnel through the thick crystal completely, I rubbed at it with my palm. I thinned it enough to let in a little emotion, but not a lot. Like a screen door—it let in the breeze but kept out the bugs.

This was a learning process. I was determined to keep learning this until I could figure out the best way to control the incoming and outgoing signals. I was sure someday I'd get it right.

When I was done, I opened my eyes again. Walter was gone. I was relieved, but wary. I didn't trust him to give up and go home so easily. I scanned the area, making out the shadows in the dim moonlight.

Halfway to the tree line, I saw him. He dangled by his shirt several feet off the ground, being escorted from the area. Apparently, the skunk-ape had no moral issues with treating him that way. The joy I felt at the sight seemed hypocritical. I now had "people" to do for me what I refused to do for myself.

This was a moral dilemma I wasn't prepared to tackle. I'd been up since three-thirty and was on my last legs. I hauled myself to my feet and made my way to the house, almost wishing the skunk-ape would come back and carry me, too.

I wondered if he really smelled as bad as his name suggested.

I OVERSLEPT, OF course. Not having an appointment until nine-thirty meant I could sleep in a little later than usual. Because of this, I ignored my alarm clock when it went off and woke up much later than I had planned.

I had enough time to throw on some clothes, brush my teeth, grab my sample book and fly out the door. Maurice trailed after me waving a toaster waffle with peanut butter.

"You have to eat something." He followed me to the car and shoved it through the open window. "Eat."

I grabbed it with one hand and backed out of the driveway with the other. "I'll eat it, I promise. I'm only going to be gone for a few hours."

He shouted after me as I pulled out. "I'll have a nice lunch ready!"

I hate being late. I was running about fifteen minutes behind schedule. Rush hour was over, so I could probably make it up on the drive out to Helen's house on the north side of Sausalito.

I needn't have rushed. When I got to her house, it was surrounded by a large collection of emergency vehicles and personnel.

A chill ran up my back. I could only think of one reason why paramedics would be milling about. Helen was dead. And it was probably my fault.

# TWELVE

I PARKED MY Bug on the curb behind two cop cars.
An ambulance sat in the driveway, pointed toward
the street.

I sat for a moment in the quiet car, contemplating
what to do. I shrugged off the feeling of certainty
that Helen was dead. If I acted like it wasn't true,
maybe it wouldn't be. Should I call her from my cell?
Should I just walk in?

Denial is one of my best skills.

I practiced it on my way up the walkway. *She'll
want to reschedule, of course. I won't intrude. I'll
only stay a moment, long enough for her to know I
came for the appointment.*

A police officer met me at the door.

"Ma'am, you can't come in here."

His considerable girth blocked the doorframe. I
couldn't see in, and I wasn't getting past him.

"I have an appointment with Ms. Cranston," I said.
My mouth was dry and my stomach was clenched. I
could go through the motions of denial all I wanted.
My body knew exactly what was coming.

"I'm sorry," he said.

He didn't say anything else. He fixed me with

his eyes and refused to budge, with no further explanation.

"Would you please tell her I'm here? I don't mind rescheduling. I can see she has other things going on. But I'd appreciate a word with her, or at least if you could pass on a message."

The big man swallowed. He looked uncomfortable. His mouth moved as if he were trying to form words when a low voice prodded him from inside the house.

"Excuse me, Nick. We're coming through."

Officer Nick wiped a bead of sweat from his brow and stepped aside. I could feel my eyes widen as I moved out of the way on autopilot.

Two men rolled a stretcher toward me, a sheet pulled up to cover the still form laying on it.

A small part of my otherwise-occupied brain registered the familiar paramedic at the far end of the operation.

The men lifted the stretcher over the steps and wheeled it to the waiting ambulance. I watched, horrified. My denial skills were thinning by the second.

I tore my eyes from the sight of the body being closed up in the back of the ambulance and focused on Officer Nick.

"Please tell me that wasn't Helen." My heart sank. If I wished and begged hard enough, maybe I could change reality.

He shook his head. "I'm sorry, ma'am. May I ask the nature of your business with Ms. Cranston?"

My throat tightened up and I had trouble forming words. "I'm…I'm her wedding planner. She's getting married."

"I'm going to need a number where I can reach you, in case the detectives have any questions."

"Of course." I fumbled in my bag and pulled out a business card. As I handed it over, I noticed how much my hand shook. "Can you tell me what happened?"

"I'm not really at liberty to say, but at the moment, it looks like natural causes. We'll know better after the autopsy."

The whole thing had a surreal quality, like a dream sequence. My thoughts were scattered and disconnected. How could she die of natural causes when she was so young and healthy? Where was Steve through all this? One of the cops trampled through Helen's flowers. It was a shame. She'd told me how much trouble she had getting those roses to bloom. Sara was going to have a fit over all this. The loss of income on this wedding was going to hurt the business. I looked down at my leg. I had a run in my hose. That would teach me to get dressed in a hurry. The taste of my morning coffee lingered on my tongue. I'd never have coffee with Helen again.

I wandered to my car, unsure what to do next.

"Hey, you all right?"

I looked up from the pavement and six feet of dreamy paramedic was leaning against my car.

Because that's exactly what I needed right then. The universe had a sick sense of humor.

My eyes focused on the top button of his shirt. I

couldn't pull them any higher. His undershirt peeked out, and the button was only half in the hole, looking undecided as to whether it wanted to remain closed.

"I'm okay," I said. "I just need a minute to process. I saw her yesterday and she was fine. We had coffee. We were going to go over fabric samples today." *That was good. Coherent, almost.* My attention wandered to the front seat of my car where the sample book lay forgotten. "I left my waffle in the car." *And now you've moved into babbling again. Come on, Zoey. Pull your head out.*

"You brought her a waffle?"

Okay, this was getting worse.

"No, I was supposed to eat it."

"Breakfast is important. You should always eat breakfast."

I nodded. "That's what Maurice says." *Oh, great. Why'd you have to mention Maurice?*

"Maurice is your boyfriend?"

"No! Oh, God, no. He's my, well, he's a houseguest? Roommate? I don't know what to call him. He cooks for me."

"He's your housekeeper." He cocked his head, clearly puzzled by my poor explanation.

"Well, no. Though he did get the stain out of the rug. It's been there for years. I don't even like red wine. It looked like Phyllis Diller." *Oh, much better, Zoey. You've now gone into full-on idiot mode. Go on. Tell him about the yeast infection.*

I tried again. For some reason it was important to

me that this man knew I wasn't a complete bubble-head. And that I didn't have a boyfriend.

"His wife threw him out," I said. "He needed a place to stay. She was sleeping with a bridge troll." The words dropped out of my mouth so fast I had no time to recall them. In panic, I finally looked up at the man's face. He really had such beautiful eyes. He was grinning at me.

"A bridge troll? Well, that hardly ever happens. He's lucky to have you as a friend."

He was obviously humoring me. Waffles and bridge trolls—I was quite the conversationalist.

My brain flailed around, grasping at something to change the subject. I stuck my hand out. "I'm Zoey, and I'm an idiot."

He grabbed my hand with a firm grip and shook it. His face was solemn. "I'm Riley, and I like idiots."

After we shook, he held my hand for a moment longer, releasing it a few beats short of being uncomfortable.

"Fate does seem to be moving us around in each other's way," he said. "Normally I have Tuesdays off."

"Lucky me."

"It could be luck." He drew his face closer in a conspiratorial wink. "Or a nudge from the universe."

I felt my cheeks get hot. He smelled incredible.

"The universe is pretty twisted then. So far the only thing drawing us together is coffee and dead bodies."

"Not entirely true. I've seen you around. You're... well, you're special. People notice you. That day on the street was the first time I'd managed to get you to make eye contact with me, and I'd been trying for months. I'm especially fond of the black fedora with the peacock feather, by the way."

I wasn't sure what to do with this information. I had a stalker. A stalker besides Sebastian. A *gorgeous* stalker. I should have been a little unnerved, but instead I felt a wicked thrill.

A commotion on the front stoop pulled me out of the exchange before I had to respond. Steve Welsh came tearing down the steps, sobbing.

*Grief.*

*Guilt.*

*Loss.*

As if someone had hurled a stick of dynamite at me, my walls shattered, and I stood emotionally naked and vulnerable on the sidewalk.

"I just want to check on her before she goes to the hospital," he said. "Maybe she woke up. She needs me."

His anguish was overwhelming and I had to lean against the car for support. Emotion burst from him like a charging bull and rammed me in the center of my chest. I inhaled with shock, but the air was trapped. I couldn't exhale.

Two officers had followed him out of the house to the back of the ambulance. They each put a gentle hand on his elbows and pulled him toward the house.

"Sir," one said, "she's in good hands, I promise you. There isn't anything more you can do. Let's get you back inside where you can be more comfortable."

"What about Helen's comfort?" A sob hitched in his throat.

I couldn't catch my breath.

"She's as comfortable as possible, sir. Really, you should come inside."

They led him like a lamb gone astray. He was docile, but mumbling to himself. His sadness carried down the pristine lawn to the sidewalk and puddled around my ankles, sucking at me.

"I should have checked on her before I left. She looked so peaceful and happy. I didn't want to disturb her."

I struggled to draw air into my lungs, my palms flat against the car door, grasping at bricks of solid light to rebuild my mental walls. It wasn't working. Steve's devastation squeezed at my chest and made it impossible to concentrate.

"Sir, is there someone we can call for you? You should have someone with you."

"I should have spent more time with her. I didn't know there wouldn't be any more time. I didn't know..."

They ushered him through the door and out of sight. The pressure released me and I bent double, coughing and gasping.

"Hey, hey, easy," Riley said. He knelt beside me, his warm palm rubbing my back. "Deep, slow breaths. That's it. In through the nose, out through the mouth."

It took a few minutes, but my breathing was my own again. I stood on shaky legs.

"Thanks," I said. I was embarrassed, but what else

was new with this guy? How could I explain to him what the hell was wrong with me? I'd already proven my lack of communication skills. I didn't need him knowing I was a freak, as well.

But he didn't ask any questions. "I suppose I'd better get back to work," he said.

"Sure, of course. It was nice finally meeting you."

"I'm sure I'll see you soon, Zoey." He waved and walked up the driveway to the waiting ambulance.

I didn't stay to watch him go. I threw myself into the front seat and tore away from the house. I had to get home. I had to put my walls up. I had to eat my waffle.

OF COURSE, EATING the waffle was out of the question. The way my stomach churned and flopped on the drive home would have made it an unwise choice.

There was also the crying. You should never eat when you're crying. That's a good way to choke yourself.

I was halfway home when the dam broke.

Helen was gone. She had a garden and wedding plans and a wonderful sense of humor. She was my friend. We'd made plans to go shopping for purses. There was so much more I wanted to learn about her. And now she was gone.

*He got her. It's my fault. He got her because of me.*

I had no idea what to do next. Staying home forever and never coming in contact with anyone again seemed the best option. But I had a business to run. And groceries to buy.

Every time I stepped out my front door, I was putting people in danger.

"Bastard," I said. The tears were beginning to dry on my face. Sadness and frustration were turning into a good strong case of pissed off. I hadn't wanted to admit it, but deep down, I knew the dream I'd had about Selma, the grocery clerk, had been real.

This was the second death I had caused, not the first.

By the time I pulled into my driveway, I was past pissed off and well into irate. I wanted the asshole dead.

When I walked into my kitchen, Maurice was playing Monopoly at the table with Molly's kids. He was busy moving play money and property cards around the table for them.

I could feel four sets of eyes on me as I stormed in, slammed my purse and unused sample book on the counter, tossed the uneaten waffle in the trash, and banged the teakettle onto the burner I set on high.

"No waffle?" Maurice said. His voice was quiet, as if afraid he'd be the focus of my anger.

I felt guilty. "I forgot about it. I'm sorry."

"What happened?" His face was still, but his eyes flicked around the table at the children.

I wasn't about to unload this in front of them. I took a deep breath and filled a clean cup with Andrew's tea leaves. Whether from devastation overload or crying-related sinus irritation, my head was ready to explode.

Maurice was perceptive. "Fred, why don't you

take your brother and sister outside to play? We'll finish up the game later."

Fred gave me a long look, then turned to the others. "Who wants to look for mushrooms?" He took Abby's hand and waved Aaron over to the edge of the table. Together, the three tiny figures took a leap into the air and landed on the tile floor as if they'd had parachutes.

"Where's Molly?" I asked. "What if her husband shows up while they're out there?"

"She had some things to do. Errands, I guess. I told her I'd keep an eye on them. And Iris won't let that drunken assclown anywhere near them." The kids were already in the living room. "Stay inside the fairy ring!" he said before they could make it out the door.

The kettle took forever to boil.

"Sit-sit-sit," he said. "I'll take care of the tea. You look like hell."

"I feel like hell. But I can't sit down. Not yet." I walked around the kitchen nudging canisters and opening cupboards. I picked up the sponge to wipe the counters, but since Maurice had moved in, everything was pristine.

He was patient, I'll give him that. He followed me around the kitchen with his big yellow eyes, refraining from questions or comments. I knew it was making him crazy, but I didn't have words yet to convey the feelings I had jumbled up on top of each other.

The kettle finally whistled at me. For someone with a headache-curing tea prescription, the sound of a kettle whistle was ironically piercing. I poured hot water over the collection of leaves and bark in the cup and brought it to the table. I sat.

"So," Maurice said. "You're home early."

That was a good opener. I stared into my cup and wondered if I should buy a tea steeper instead of letting all the muck stay in the bottom of my cup.

"Appointment was cancelled," I said.

I was still holding it in. I felt lost. I'd liked Helen. I'd liked her very much.

"You'll reschedule," he said. He watched me poke at the floating bits of twig in my cup. He took out a clean cup and a small strainer. "Give me that. You'd think you never made tea in your life." He poured my now well-steeped tea through the strainer and into the fresh mug. I took it from him and sipped.

"Can't reschedule. She's dead." I could hear my voice hitch a little, but it also sounded strangely cold. I wrapped my hands around the cup and tried to absorb the warmth.

Maurice widened his already enormous eyes. "She's dead?"

I was fighting a battle with my tea. I wanted it to go down, but it wanted to come up.

"He got her." There. It was out. I'd said it and now Maurice could tell me I was crazy and this whole thing would be tragic rather than terrifying.

"Oh, Zoey, no. How could he know her? That's insane."

But it wasn't insane. I had known from the moment I'd pulled up behind the cop cars what had happened.

Tremors attacked my body full force, and I had to put my tea down in case I dropped it. The tears I was holding in spilled over, making fresh tracks on my sticky face.

"Don't you see? He had no intention of coming after me yesterday. He was trying to scare me." My voice was becoming more shrill and panicked. "He wasn't walking away from me. He was following Helen."

I buried my face in my hands and sobbed. Maurice was up in seconds with his skinny arms wrapped around my heaving shoulders. I snuffled into his shoulder and made a wet spot on his blue and yellow paisley shirt. My words were hardly more than a whisper. "I got her killed."

I cried it out and he let me. Nothing he could say right then could stop the flood of guilt and sorrow, and he knew it. After a few minutes, I started to regain my composure enough to think how ridiculous it was to be sobbing on the shoulder of my greatest childhood nightmare.

My life was nothing if not interesting.

I pulled away and wiped my face. I don't know where he got it, but Maurice handed me a handful of tissues. The guy moved fast sometimes.

I took a gulp of tea and forced it down my constricted throat.

"This can't go on," I said. "I can't hide from him forever, and I won't let him kill any more women."

"Women?" Maurice's nonexistent eyebrows lifted.

With such big eyes, I wondered why nature had failed to provide him with eyebrows to protect them from dust and stray cat hair. "Zoey, have there been other deaths?"

"The clerk from the grocery store a few days ago. I don't have any proof, but I know it. He showed me in my dream. I thought it was part of the crap dream, all some meaningless nightmare, but now I'm sure he was showing me how he killed her."

"Zoey, you can't blame yourself."

"Maybe not for Selma, but I should have seen what was coming for Helen." I stood up and walked around the kitchen, pacing with my cup held between my palms. Grief and self-pity time were over. I was pissed again.

"What were you going to do to stop it? You can't do anything, Zoey."

"Well, I'm not going to hide from the son of a bitch, and I'm not letting anyone else get killed."

"I can't protect you out there. You can't exactly walk into work with a skunk-ape trailing behind you."

"I have to protect myself, Maurice. And I'm tired of being on the defensive."

"He's so dangerous, Zoey. Have I mentioned he's a demon?"

"I don't give a shit if he's Satan himself. I'm going to learn everything I can about his kind. And then I'm going to hunt the bastard down and kick his ass."

# THIRTEEN

I NEEDED INFORMATION, and I needed better control of my power. But the need for rest was more immediate. After I calmed down in the kitchen, Maurice went to check on our brownie family, and I went back to bed.

The tea had helped, but it couldn't fix everything.

As exhausted as I was, it took time for me to settle in. The curtains in my room let in too much light, the humming of bugs and the clanging of my wind chime collection were too loud. I flipped my pillow over twice. The sheet was too heavy. I was cold without it. I got up and shut the window. The room became stuffy.

I gave up and decided to watch some television.

My body wouldn't move to reach for the remote. Somewhere in the tossing and turning, I'd fallen asleep, and my brain hadn't caught up yet.

After a moment or two, bright lights flashed around my bed. I tried to blink my eyes, but I was paralyzed. I wasn't afraid. There was a logical part of me that understood I was dreaming and that fighting to move would wake me up. That awareness began to fade, and I smiled at the dancing lights. They were pretty.

My paralysis faded with my lucidity and I sat up.

The lights circled around me and zipped out the door. I followed them through the hallway, into the living room and out into the yard.

Sebastian waited for me against the oak tree at the end of my driveway.

For a moment, fear shot through me. I felt for the amulet around my neck and found it hanging under my shirt, warm and soothing. At first, I thought it wasn't working. I scrutinized the dark, velvet-clad man. No. It was working fine. He couldn't hurt me here.

*Okay, so I'm asleep.* He was here to taunt me, harass me and make me feel like my heart was being ripped from my body. But he could only bring illusions to my dreams, not realities.

I remembered something else: I was seriously pissed off.

With the sureness that only comes in dreams when the dreamer knows she's in control, I marched myself across the grass, stepped over the invisible fairy ring and looked him squarely in his disturbing emerald eyes.

"Fuck you," I said. That felt pretty good.

He looked startled. His gaze became more intense and I could feel it licking at the edges of me, trying to find a way in.

"No," I said, as if he were a dog trying to hump my leg. If I'd had a newspaper, I'd have rolled it up and whacked him on the nose.

Beyond all logic, he tilted his head back and laughed at me. The sound was hideous, deep and throaty like a wounded buffalo. "Well done, Dream Girl," he said. "Now we can really start having fun."

From the trees that separated my house from the beach, I heard a long, anguished scream.

I ran.

I was at the tree line in seconds and broke through into the brush and branches. The twigs and brush prodded and pulled at my clothing, slowing my progress. I shoved them aside and kept going. The deeper I went, the more difficulty I had. The train of my flowing black dress snagged and I yanked it free.

I stopped.

No, no, no. I was not wearing this thing again. What kind of twisted psycho was he to keep throwing this monstrous black wedding gown on me?

*It's a dream, Zoey. Take it back.*

I closed my eyes and made the dress go away, replacing it with the sweats and T-shirt I'd pulled on for my nap. The idea that I didn't have to play out the dream—that I could wake myself up—didn't cross my mind.

I reached the clearing in time to see Sebastian bending over Helen's body.

She was naked, writhing and floating three feet above the ground. He turned to me, smiled and gave a wave of his velvet-and-lace-clad wrist. He turned to Helen and stroked his hand down the length of her body. She threw her head back and moaned in fear that had a disturbing dose of ecstasy mixed in.

He walked around her prone figure, trailing his fingers across her skin, and settled on the other side of her where he could watch me while he worked.

"Helen was a feisty one, my dear. No clandestine

meeting in the dirty back room of a store for her. She had so much more to give me." He bent low and kissed her lips. Her legs spasmed. "It took hours to drain her. She thanked me for it."

I had never been so angry in my life. I threw myself across the clearing to get him off of her.

And fell through him onto my face.

He waved his finger at me, grinning like a badly carved jack-o-lantern. "Ah, ah, my darling Dream Girl. If I can't touch you, you can't touch me." He made a sick parody of a child's pouty face. "It's only fair, you know."

"Get away from her," I said. The words felt stupid in my mouth. The damage was done. He was replaying the highlights of a game he'd already played and won. I couldn't save her.

"She was an insatiable little slut, my Helen. Took it right there next to her man while he slept like an infant. It made her that much tastier, to be honest."

"That's twisted and sick." My throat was dry.

He looked smug. "She invited me in, Zoey. They always do."

At the sound of my name, I felt gut-punched.

"That's right. She gave you up right along with herself. She wanted to please me in every way she could." He bent forward and darted his tongue across her exposed nipple. She bucked and buried her hands in his tacky coat. "It's a simple thing, a name. It's a part of you that you give out every day to strangers without a thought. Yet it holds so much power."

He nuzzled her neck, nipping at it. She sighed,

shivering, her knuckles white from clutching the cheap velvet so tightly.

"You have nothing of me," I said. I walked straight through him, knowing now he wasn't solid. I stalked across the clearing toward home.

"How long will you hold out, my love?" he called after me. "When I'm hungry enough, I'll call for you. And you will come."

The double entendre gave me a case of the screaming willies.

I turned to face him and fixed him with my best bad-ass-chick look. "No. I most certainly will not. But I will find you, and I will carve my name in your chest so you can see how much power it has."

He bit down on the earlobe he was teasing with his tongue, and Helen arched violently, then went limp and still. He snickered. "Dream Girl has her brave-panties on today. I bet they're way too tight. I'll get them off. Don't worry."

I turned my back on him, walked out of the woods and woke up.

I lay in bed for some time, staring at the bumpy things on my ceiling. As a child, I used to connect the dots in my mind to form faces and animal shapes. I was not looking for foxes and koalas this time. I was making a list.

Number one: gather information. You can't fight something you don't understand.

I padded through the house and found it empty. Laughter poured in through the front door. I poked my head out.

Maurice ran in a serpentine pattern in the grass, three pieces of string held aloft in his hand. All three brownie kids were tied to the other ends, a swatch of fabric fisted over each of their heads.

Maurice had made them into kites. Or tiny para-sailors. Or something. It looked dangerous.

"Maurice, are you insane?" I strode down the front steps, my hands on my hips. "You're going to get them killed!"

Abby squealed with laughter.

"No I'm not, Zoey. They're safe, honest." He made a motorboat sound with his lips and tore back the other way.

The kids squealed as they changed direction, whipped around and followed in the air behind him. Maurice jerked his wrist and the kids dropped a few feet, their high-pitched screams sounding like they were flying down a steep hill on a roller coaster.

I glared.

Maurice slowed and the kids fell to the earth in a gentle motion like dandelion seeds caught in the wind. It didn't look like they'd been in danger at all.

"See?" he said, walking up the steps. "They can't fall. It's part of their nature."

I should have known he'd never risk their safety. "I guess I'm a little on edge," I said. "Sorry."

"It's okay. You need some lunch anyway."

I followed him into the house. "I can make my own lunch, you know."

"I know. But I do it better."

I couldn't argue with that.

He stuffed me full of sandwiches and homemade potato chips while I explained what I wanted.

"Can you make more of those muffins?" I asked.

"If I can go get the ingredients."

I thought about the risks and the moral repercussions of stealing a few strawberries and oranges from my neighbors. "I don't have time to argue about it. Go ahead."

I was about to add something else, but he was gone. I still hadn't figured out if he could turn invisible, translocate, or was just so damn fast my eyes couldn't follow him.

I was betting on speed. Within ten minutes he was back and already putting the muffins in the oven.

After a quick shower, I pulled on a fresh pair of jeans and the plainest sweater in my closet. I went out the door with precise directions and a basket of warm heaven and trudged through the woods behind my house.

My skunk-ape bodyguard crackled through the brush nearby, keeping pace. I caught a glimpse every so often, but he kept out of my way.

I had my ideas of what to expect of Aggie's house. Small, dark, probably an overgrown garden. Aggie herself would be hunched over and would cackle a lot. I shifted the basket to my other hand and kept walking.

What I found on the other side of the trees was a yellow two-story with black shutters and a white picket fence. The garden was alive with flowers and butterflies. Hummingbirds zipped between three feeders. Aggie stood at the gate, as if waiting for me.

She was neither hunched nor cackling. Her hair

was that peculiar blue older women sometimes get when their hair turns white and they use a rinse. Her smile was so bright, it outshone the garden, and when she laughed, it sounded like a tiny bird chirping. I didn't know what to make of her.

I stopped short of her gate and stood there, confused. How could I never have seen this house or this woman? I'd lived here all my life, with the exception of college. Still, if Maurice hadn't told me where to go, I never would have found it.

While I stood confused, she flew out of the gate and threw her arms around me.

"Oh, my! You turned out so beautiful! I knew you would. You were such a beautiful child."

I returned the hug, though I felt awkward about it.

"I was?" When had she ever seen me before? Why did I not remember?

She ignored the question and pulled me through the garden and into a side door that led into her kitchen. It was as yellow inside as it was outside. I wanted to be polite, but I couldn't think of any words. Every surface was covered in ticking clocks.

"Do you have something for me, sweetheart?" she asked.

Fairy tales flitted through my head and I started to panic. A gift. You don't walk into the heart of a witch's home to ask a boon without some sort of gift. I was frantic. I could give her my earrings. All I had on me besides earrings was my dragon amulet, and she couldn't have that. Oh God, she was going to take my first born.

She smiled kindly at me. "What's in the basket, dear?"

I felt like an idiot. This was not a new feeling for me, especially lately. I relaxed.

"Maurice made some muffins for you," I said, handing her the basket.

She clapped her hands in delight. "Oh, I do love that boy's cooking. How thoughtful."

She pulled out a muffin and took an enormous bite. After a long, thoughtful chew, she swallowed and smiled. "Wonderful. I was wondering where my strawberries went."

I was mortified.

"I am so sorry. I only found out recently he was doing that. I've asked him to stop." This was not entirely true, of course, since I'd told him to go ahead for the emergency muffins. Had I known the strawberries were from her garden, I'd have asked him to make something else.

"Nonsense, dear. They'll only go to waste anyway. Sit down."

I sat.

"You tell that boy he can help himself to whatever I have in my garden."

"You're very kind," I said. "And thank you for the protection-bag-thingy for my car."

She waved a dismissive hand in the air. "Of course, of course. When that sweet boy came over and told me Clara's girl was in trouble, well, I couldn't just sit here enjoying the garden, now could I?"

Hearing my mother's name gave me a start. "You really knew her?"

She blinked at me. "She was here all the time. And

so were you. You don't remember? You used to play here while she and I visited."

I shook my head. "I barely remember her at all."

Aggie frowned. "You were eight when she left, isn't that right?"

"Yes."

"Don't you think it's odd that you don't remember the first eight years of your life?"

"I hadn't thought about it. I guess that is odd."

"Odd indeed. And perhaps even odder that you never thought to question it."

"I don't remember anything about her leaving. I remember missing her, months after the fact, but every time I try to think about the time surrounding her leaving, the memory feels cold and slippery, like a block of wet ice. I can't focus on it. I figured it was too painful to think about. But now, I'm beginning to wonder. Were you there when she left? Did she say anything to you?"

Aggie smiled. "Of course I remember. We had tea every morning together, sometimes here, sometimes in her kitchen. That day, I was..." Aggie's pleasant smile drooped into a frown. "Well, I was...you know, I can't remember it either." Her voice faded out at the end of the sentence, and she looked out the window at the garden, a little dazed.

I touched her sleeve, and she pulled back from wherever she'd gone. "Do you remember what happened after? Were the police looking for her? Surely, they would have come to question you."

She shook her head. "I don't recall there being

any police. There must have been an investigation, but I don't recall it. How odd. It's as if I remember spending every morning with her, then I remember missing her, as if she'd been gone for months."

That felt far too close to what I recalled, though having been eight, I didn't have much to remember before that day. It was as if someone had robbed us not only of my mother, but of most of our memories associated with her. For me, that apparently meant memories of my time with Aggie, as well.

"So, before that day, we knew each other? Why didn't I see you after that?"

"You were over here all the time, dear. I wondered why you stopped coming to see me after she was gone. I didn't want to intrude, so I let it go. I thought you were hiding from the memories, but it looks as though maybe the memories were hiding from you."

Every clock in the house went off at that moment. Cuckoos, digital clocks, the oven timer, brass alarm clocks. Never in my life had I heard so much noise in such a confined space.

A minute later, they all went back to their quiet ticking. I wondered if she ever slept.

She patted my hand. "It seems our past has a mystery. But that's for another time. A time, perhaps, when your life isn't hanging in the balance?"

"Yes. I do have a more immediate problem."

"I thought you might. Maurice wouldn't say exactly what had frightened him so badly. Only that you needed some protection when you were away."

"I have a demon problem."

"Oh, demons are quite bad. That *is* a problem. How can I help, dear?"

"I need to know how to kill one."

She shook her head, her blue-white curls bouncing around her face. "You can't kill a demon. They aren't alive."

I dropped my head on the table and covered myself with my arms. "I don't know what I'm going to do, then."

She made soothing noises and patted my arm. "You can send him back. That's always an option."

My head popped up. "Send him back?"

"Of course. What kind of demon is it?"

"Incubus."

Aggie blushed. "Oh, my. Well, we can't have one of those nasties strutting around town, now can we?"

"He's already killed two people because of me."

Her face dropped. "No, we can't have that at all." She scuttled out of the room and was gone for several minutes. I was left in the bright yellow kitchen, listening to the ticking of hundreds of clocks.

When she returned, she had an armful of dusty books. She dropped them on the table and rubbed her arms.

"These are yours," she said.

"Mine?"

"Your mother kept them here. There's more, but these are most likely to help us."

I didn't know what to say. What *was* my mother?

We pored over the books through two more silence-shattering clock announcements of the hour.

We hadn't learned much that was specific to incubi, but I had enough demon lore to work up some kind of solution.

I'd pictured a ritual involving candles and a big circle drawn on the ground. In truth, it was simpler than that—but it meant getting a better handle on my empathicness. My empathitude? The empath thing.

"Anything worth doing takes practice," she said, walking me to the door.

"I have no idea where to start."

"You'll figure it out. It took Clara some time to adjust to her gifts, too."

"Was she a very powerful empath?"

Aggie laughed. "Oh, my heavens, no. She wasn't an empath at all. She was more of a healer. It made her quite unpopular with the local reapers of the time. Bad for their business."

At the gate I turned and looked back. A white rosebush grew in the corner near the house.

"Salamanders," I said.

Her face lit up. "Yes!"

"I played with them by that rosebush. They were on fire."

"They're elementals. But they were very careful not to burn your fingers."

The memory was clear and sharp, as if it had happened the day before. "I remember. I made piles of dried leaves and they would race in and set them on fire. Mommy hated that game."

Where had my memories gone? And why did this one sneak in?

Aggie nudged me out the gate. "Time enough for that later, dear. Right now, you have a sex demon to vanquish."

"If I can find him."

"If you don't, he'll find you, no doubt."

That thought chilled me.

"Thank you for your help, Aggie."

"Anytime, dear. Come back whenever you need me. But don't forget to come back when you don't, too."

She hugged me and stood back to look at me. "Beautiful. Just like I knew you would be." She turned away, still smiling, but not before I saw the moisture in her eyes.

# FOURTEEN

WHEN I GATHERED up my things to leave for work the next morning, nothing was where I had left it.

I was sure I'd left the sample book on the kitchen counter with my purse. Neither was there. I looked everywhere. Circling through the house, I came back to the kitchen counter. Sometimes when you lose something, it's not really lost at all, and it ends up right where you knew it was in the first place.

Not this time. But what I hadn't noticed before was a small, multicolored bag with a gold clasp. I picked it up and opened it. It weighed hardly anything and the inside was also a patchwork of colored fabric. It was beautiful. I stuck my hand in and pulled out my cell phone.

That was weird. I hadn't seen it in there. I stuck my hand in again. Out came my wallet. I repeated the trick until I had a large pile of crap on the counter—tissues, mints, my appointment book, a banana, two handfuls of stray receipts.

There was no way a fraction of that should have fit in the tiny purse.

I examined the bag more closely, running my fingers over the small squares of fabric held together by the tiniest, most even stitches I'd ever seen.

I couldn't help myself. I giggled.

I'd complained about my purse in front of Molly a few nights ago. Last night, I left my sample book next to my purse.

I read *The Shoemaker and the Elves* when I was a kid. I'd been elved. Or brownied.

I put everything in the bag, still marveling at how well it fit. I was going to have to order a new sample book. Those didn't come cheap. A bag like this, however, was worth a warehouse of sample books.

It was priceless.

I wanted to thank her, but the house was oddly silent. I considered the story of the shoemaker and the elves. When the shoemaker's wife thanked the elves by making them clothes, they left. Was there a brownie etiquette book that warned against thanking them? Getting advice from old fairy tales was probably not the best way to handle things. I would have to ask Maurice what to do.

Strange that he wasn't around either.

I turned to leave when another thought occurred to me. How much would the bag hold? I picked up one of the dusty tomes I'd lugged home from Aggie's place. Brushing it off smeared the cover and made clumps of dirt, so I blew on it too. A cloud rose up and choked me. I hated the idea of putting the dirty thing in my pristine new bag. Whapping at it with dishtowel did a better job. Satisfied it was the best I could do, I compared it to the size of the purse. *You are seriously demented if you think this will go in there, Zoey.*

I shrugged. Stranger things had happened over the last week. I opened the clasp on the bag and shoved. The book disappeared.

What's more, the weight of the purse didn't change an ounce.

Best. Present. Ever.

Feeling less encumbered than I had in years, I headed out the front door.

"Have a good day," I said over my shoulder. I had a strong feeling I'd been watched the whole time.

I WAS THE first one into the office. That hardly ever happened. I glanced up at the clock and saw it was five after nine.

I flipped on the lights, took the calls off forward, started a pot of coffee for thrifty Sara, and settled into my desk with my overpriced cup of sugar and caffeine. I had a long list of vendors to call. I'd never had a client die before, but I had some experience in undoing a wedding. Sometimes weddings were cancelled. It happened.

I could have waited for somebody to call me from Helen's family, but there seemed no point. The sooner I made the calls, the better chance I had of getting some or all of the deposits back. Not that Steve needed the money. Still. It was my job. If I didn't cancel everything, that would be a reflection on my business. I didn't want to risk my reputation simply because it was an awkward situation. The likelihood of Steve or another member of the party having the wherewithal to cancel anytime soon was slim. Better to have it done before it occurred to him to call and ask me to do it.

It was a truly awful morning. I poured every ounce of concentration I had into thinking of "my client" rather than "Helen." I had to depersonalize or I'd never get through it.

The first call would be the worst, so I thought it best to get it over with. Moira had spent a lot of time with Helen and me, planning the cake. I liked Moira, and I knew she liked Helen. This wouldn't be easy. I dialed her number, feeling queasy.

"Zoey, wonderful to hear from you!" She was always so cheerful. I hated to be the one to kill that cheer.

"Not so wonderful, today, Moira. I'm afraid I have to make a cancellation."

"Oh, that's too bad. Did someone get cold feet?"

I swallowed hard. *Come on, Zoey. It's just business.* You can do this. "Helen…" I choked. Nope. Not easy at all. "Helen Cranston passed away yesterday."

Moira was quiet on the other end.

"Moira?"

"I'm here. Sorry. That's so awful. I'm having trouble understanding it. Was she sick?"

"Not that anyone knew." I thought about poor Steve blaming himself and having to be dragged from the ambulance. No. She wasn't sick. But I knew a bastard incubus who *was* sick. "Anyway, I'm really sorry, Moira. I guess Red Velvet Death by Chocolate will never make it to the menu." I stopped. What a morbid name for a cake, now that Helen was gone.

"Don't be silly," Moira said. "I'm putting it on the menu with her name on it. It's the least I can do. I really liked her. Don't you worry, Zoey. I'll cancel it and send you the deposit back to give to her fiancé."

When I hung up, it took me a few minutes to pull myself together. If every call I had to make was even a fraction of the difficulty of the first, I wasn't going to make it. At twenty after ten, Sara finally showed up.

"Good morning!" she said as she sashayed through the door.

"Morning, sleepyhead. Decided to take it slow today?"

She glanced at her watch, surprised. "Huh. I guess I'm running behind." She poured herself a cup of coffee and set it on her desk without further explanation.

I came in late all the time. Unless I had an appointment, I didn't see the point to opening the door promptly at nine a.m. It wasn't like our business encouraged spontaneous walk-ins. But Sara always came in early anyway.

She took off her coat and hung it on the coat rack.

"Your shirt is untucked in the back," I said.

She patted herself down and shoved the blouse into the waistband of her skirt, satisfied. Her hair, though not messy by any stretch of the imagination, wasn't as neat as usual either.

"Anything you want to tell me?" I leaned back in my chair, bemused.

"About what?"

She seemed bewildered—as if her appearance and behavior were nothing out of the ordinary.

"Nothing. What have you got going today?"

"Not a lot. Still have to finish the birdseed favors for Gail. I was thinking of cutting out early today. I didn't get much sleep last night."

"They're done. I finished two days ago. I told you." I was torn between amusement and worry over her distracted state.

"Oh." She sat in her chair and rummaged through her purse. "I guess I forgot."

"I guess." Maybe all she needed was a good night's sleep.

She pulled out a tube of lipstick and mirror and hummed while she touched up her lips. "What are you up to today?"

"Canceling vendors." I flipped through my Rolodex—another dinosaur Sara often harassed me about—and looked for the number of the caterers Helen had chosen.

Sara looked up from her compact. "Cancellation? Who's canceling? We can't have a cancellation."

I felt better. This was more like the Sara I was used to, not the distracted, humming Sara. "Helen Cranston died yesterday." There. I blurted it right out without wincing too much. Maybe this would get easier.

Sara was silent. I glanced up from my phone number search to see her frozen with her lipstick hand hanging halfway to her mouth.

"I just talked to her last week," she said. Her hands

fluttered into activity, capping the lipstick and tucking it with the compact into her purse. She was up and next to my desk in seconds, her hand held out.

"Give me the file. I'll help you make the calls. Crap, crap, crap."

There's an old saying that goes "Tragedy breeds efficiency." Okay, so maybe there is no saying that goes like that. But there should be. It snapped Sara out of whatever fog she'd been in, and my day's work was cut in half.

Misery loves company—now *that* one is real. It made a shitty morning a little less shitty having her there to help. In a matter of hours, we managed to cancel all the carefully laid plans it had taken me months to put together. We also were fortunate in getting back most of the deposits. There seemed to be some sort of unwritten "bridal-death clause" I hadn't been aware of. It wasn't as if I'd had cause to know about it before.

The only holdout was the catering company. In their case, I couldn't really blame them. Helen had requested some very expensive caviar that had to be pre-ordered. The caterers weren't getting their deposit back on the goods, so they weren't willing to give it to us.

Around one, we decided to call it a day. We'd done everything we could for Steve Welsh, checked in with Gail and tied up a few other loose ends. It was an awful day, but it made me remember why Sara was my best friend. I'd been so busy lately, I hadn't realized how much I'd missed spending time with her—even under such lousy circumstances.

Sara's arms were full when the phone rang, so I picked it up.

"Happily Ever After, this is Zo—"

"What sort of business are you running over there?"

Alma Dickson was the absolute last person I wanted to deal with that day. "Mrs. Dickson, how are you? What seems to be the trouble?"

Her voice grated in my ear like girders scraped together on a construction site. "I understand the menu has errors, the linens are wrong and something has to be done about these lazy bridesmaids. I won't have my daughter's wedding ruined because of your incompetence."

It was too much. The day was one horrible moment after another, and this harpy was going to be the reason I snapped. I opened my mouth to speak, then slammed it shut again. I felt like a guppy, but I had no appropriate words to give her. I had plenty of other words, but none that were appropriate.

Sara saw my distress from across the room and jogged over. "Dickson?" she asked in a whisper. I nodded and she took the phone from me.

"Mrs. Dickson, how lovely to hear from you. This is Sara. I'm sure you'll be happy to know that we caught the problems with the caterer before any harm was done, and I changed the linens as you requested." She paused, listening. "Yes, of course. I was over there yesterday." She rolled her eyes. "No, as we discussed, that silver pattern was unavailable.

If you'll take a look in the notebook I gave you, you'll see the pattern you actually chose."

Sara wandered back to her desk and sat down. "Absolutely. Roses are lovely, but I'm sure I can get the florist to add some gardenias to the bouquets."

Sara went quiet again, a sure sign that Mama Dickson was off on a new tirade. Sara threw an eraser at me and made a strangling motion with her hands. "I understand, completely. Bridesmaids can be difficult. But controlling them isn't something I can do for you, Mrs. Dickson. However, you'll be happy to know we've taken the birdseed favors into our own hands. They're nearly finished." She winked at me.

I tried not to think about the crazy bitch dressed all in black and sneaking into our office after hours with a box of cockroaches or dead rats.

The conversation went on for some time. Usually I was responsible for calming a difficult client, but this woman, especially on this day, was far beyond my capabilities. I worked out people's emotions. Sara knew how to schmooze. I was infinitely grateful to have Sara taking care of Grand High Pubah Councilwoman Dickson.

Sara hung up the phone and groaned. "Good Lord, that woman is a nasty piece of work. I'll be so glad to have this wedding behind us."

"She's all sorted out?"

"There wasn't anything to sort. I think she makes stuff up as an excuse to throw her weight around."

"Well, she's lost my vote next election day."

Sara ran her fingers through her hair. "God help us if the business she brings in gives us any more mothers like her."

I shook my head "She's one of a kind. I doubt there's anyone in Marin County as difficult as she is."

"Don't say that. You'll jinx us."

"Lunch?" I asked as we cleared up our desks.

"I think I'm going to head home. I feel like I'm coming down with something." She did look a little gray.

I tried to keep my disappointment to myself. Obviously, she needed some down time, and she'd been a huge help. "Go. I'll forward the phones to myself and lock up. Get some rest. You kind of look like ass."

She gave me a weak smile. "You're such a flatterer."

"If I say you look pretty, will you go home to bed?"

"Yes."

"You look pretty. Go home to bed."

"I'm going." She grabbed her coat and walked toward the door.

"Sara?"

She stopped. "Yeah?"

"Thanks."

"I'll always have your back, Zo, you know that. As long as we stick together, we can get through anything."

My stomach knotted as I watched her walk out the door. There was so much I couldn't tell her. For the first time in ten years, I didn't have Sara at my back.

# FIFTEEN

THIS TIME THERE was no lead-up, no nonsense in a tattered black wedding gown, and no trip through the woods. I fell asleep, and there he was.

"Good evening, Dream Girl. You're looking lovely."

My throat tightened in fear, but I refused to back down. He couldn't hurt me here. I shouldn't be afraid. Except, of course, I was.

"You're looking tasteless and flamboyant, as usual," I said. "I admit, I like pirates over ninjas, but I think you're doing it wrong."

He raised an eyebrow in surprise. I wasn't sure whether it was because I wasn't showing fear, or because I was making fun of him.

"You seem different," he said, after looking me up and down in a way that felt like I was being prodded by a curious monkey.

"I am different. I'm not taking any more shit from you."

He smiled. "Language, my dear. Naughty words tend to reveal a need to cover something up. Are you certain you're all right?"

"I'm better than I have been in quite a long time, thank you."

"Then why are you shaking?" He took a step forward and grasped my quaking hand. I hadn't realized it was doing that. That was no good. Hard to show bravery when you look like you're having a seizure.

"I'm asleep. Probably, I kicked the covers off and I'm in my bed freezing."

"No doubt you're right. I can't imagine why you would be afraid of me."

"I'm not." I stuck my chin out in defiance. I figured if I continued to stand by the lie long enough, it would become true.

"I have a gift for you." He tugged at my hand. I was surprised the contact didn't affect me. It was a dream, of course, but still. I would have expected something to happen.

He turned me around to face the way I had come.

There hadn't been time for my sleeping mind to develop any sort of landscape when I first came into the dream. Now he was creating it for me.

A circus tent was pitched in the middle of a baseball field. Sebastian led me to the entrance, and I let him. Why I allowed it, I don't know. His lacy sleeve tickled my wrist and brought to mind centipedes crawling on my skin.

Lest the thought create the bugs themselves, I turned my attention to the tent. It was several stories high and covered in thick black and purple stripes. I stepped through the entrance, and he let go of my hand. I rubbed at my wrist to erase the itchy feeling of skittering insects.

There was a single ring in the center, a red spotlight shining on it.

Nothing was in the center for the light to show. I let him guide me to a front-row seat, and I sat on the bench to watch. I knew whatever was going to happen was something I didn't want to see. I had no control over it. I couldn't look away.

A calliope rolled into the arena, a tall, sallow man running his fingers over the keys. The music sounded like a sick merry-go-round. Somehow, the musician made the most cheerful of instruments sound like a dying rhino. A bright orange spotlight followed his progress until he rolled to a stop at the far side of the ring. He continued to play the grating music as six black poodles danced on stage.

They hauled a sled with a large box covered in black silk. The parade of yapping dogs made a full circuit around the ring before pulling their vehicle to a stop in the center.

Sebastian stepped out into the light, his tacky red velour jacket a poor substitute for a ringmaster's coat. The top hat he'd added to his ensemble looked badly fitted, as if it were made for someone with a much smaller head. I snorted. His head was quite large, both literally and figuratively.

With a flourish, he removed the fabric from the hidden box and stepped aside.

The box was casket-shaped and made of glass, much like Snow White's fabled coffin. A woman lay still within the confines of the small space, her hands folded peacefully over her bare breasts.

Black roses were scattered around her. I didn't want to look at her face. Honestly, I didn't want to look anywhere else either, since she was completely naked. My eyes tried to look everywhere, anywhere else, but they were drawn to her face.

Her black hair puddled around her head. Dark lashes rested against her cheeks, and her black lips formed a peaceful smile.

I moaned.

"No, no, no," I said. Spider opened her eyes from inside the box. She turned her head toward me and licked her lips in a way that made me feel unclean.

"Leave her alone!" I jumped to my feet and tore across the arena.

Spider's eyes rolled back, revealing only the whites. She convulsed, her back arching in agonized pleasure. Her hands slammed against the glass in an effort to find something to grip. The fingers splayed against the sides, sweaty prints marring the surface and leaving behind streaks of residue.

I reached the center and clawed at the seams of the casket, trying to find a way in. She squirmed and writhed inside, her body wracked in powerful orgasm. The terror in her eyes gave truth to the lie of pleasure. I banged my fists against the cool walls.

"Open it, you bastard." I spun and faced the demonic ringmaster. "Leave her alone. Let her out."

He smiled, his finger stroking the oiled curl of his beard. "Why? She seems happy enough. Why would you want to interfere?"

Dream Zoey decided she'd had enough. All the

helplessness I'd been feeling, all the times someone had to look after me or pull me out of the situation I'd put myself in piled on top of each other at once. I was tired. And I was pissed.

I hauled off and kicked him in the nuts.

Now, I was fully aware that I couldn't touch him, it was just a dream, and I was not a kick-ass chick with judo skills and a gun. But there's only so much a girl can put up with before resorting to violence, no matter how impossible or untrained that violence might be.

When the kick connected, I think he was as surprised as I was.

He doubled over, clutching his groin. My confidence grew three sizes, and I followed up my kick with another to his head. I've never been terribly coordinated, and when the maneuver went straight through as if I were punting a cloud, I fell sideways with the momentum and into the casket.

The glass shattered, and water spilled out like from a smashed aquarium. A considerably shrunken Spider gave a weak flip of her tail and went still. Her single, visible fisheye, outlined darkly in eyeliner, clouded over in a milky haze.

"Now you've done it, Dream Girl. I wasn't done eating that." Sebastian squatted on the ground, regarding me with a critical eye. "I'm still a little hungry, truth be told. What else are you serving up tonight?"

"Get out."

He shrugged. "I go where I like. You give me so

many delicious choices. Since I met you, I've developed a gourmet appetite. I don't think I want to give that up."

I was so angry, I wanted another go at his testicles. Unfortunately, I knew I'd landed a lucky shot because he hadn't been expecting it. No way was I going to get away with it a second time.

My eyes narrowed. "Are you putting on weight, Sebastian? I think maybe you need to go on a diet."

His brows rose in surprise. "My dear, that was hurtful. Why do you say such things? You know it's not true." He patted his belly anyway, as if checking for excess pounds. He was a vain one.

It was my dream, I knew that now. I was in control. I closed my eyes for a moment and imagined.

When I opened my eyes, the circus was gone. In its place was a vast stretch of nothing all around us. In my mind, I created a casket of my own, black and empty.

Sebastian stared at me with cold, pale eyes. The deep green I'd grown to fear had leeched out to a weak imitation—or maybe this was their real color without the artifice.

"Sweetheart," he said, reaching manicured fingers toward me. "Don't do anything you'll regret."

"I already regret not thinking of it sooner." I placed my hand on his chest, and without thought of the impossibility of the contact, shoved him backward into the box. I waved my hand, and the lid slammed shut. Sebastian didn't make a sound, but the last glimpse of his face showed resignation tinged with fear. A satisfying click locked him inside.

I turned my back and walked away.

Getting rid of Sebastian had been easier than expected. Waking up was hard. The landscape of the dream filled itself in with every step, as if it were a canvas in mid-paint. I needed help before I lost myself again.

"Maurice!" I yelled his name repeatedly as I ran through a meadow lined with seashells. If I could make enough noise, he might hear me and wake me up. I leaped over a turtle and kept yelling. "Maurice!"

And then I was awake, with Maurice by my bed looking down at me.

"You okay?" he asked. "You kept shouting for me, but you didn't sound scared like before. I wasn't sure if I should wake you up."

"I'm awesome, actually. I think I got rid of him, at least in my dreams. I doubt he'll be coming in through that route anymore."

Maurice scratched the tip of a pointy ear. "What'd you do? Liquify him with a bucket of water?"

"Funny. No. I locked him in a casket." I paused, grinning. "Also, I booted him in the balls. Wish I could do that again, actually. Really satisfying."

It was four-thirty in the morning. I was wide awake, so there wasn't much point in tossing and turning for an hour or two. I'd likely fall asleep in time for the alarm to go off, which would make for a crappy morning. I was better off staying up.

I had three hours to kill before heading out to work. I showered. Maurice made me a huge breakfast. I went for a walk. I was too agitated to sit still.

Spider was most likely dead, another victim I could blame myself for. If Sebastian kept to his pattern, it was too late for her. My priority had to be figuring out a way to keep him from killing anyone else. But I had no clue where he would strike next.

I used up all the time I could pacing around the house, fiddling with my hair, staring out the window at the swimming pool in the backyard. I kept thinking I saw something out of the corner of my eye, but nothing was there when I looked directly at it. After feeding me breakfast, Maurice had disappeared into his closet with the laptop and my credit card. I thought about knocking on his door to ask him to check the pool, but decided against it.

I had way too much on my plate for something to have taken up residence in my swimming pool. I didn't want to know if something was there.

After puttering around for two and a half hours, I gave up and made the drive to work. The line at the coffee shop was much shorter than usual. *Maybe I should go to work early every day.*

I snickered. That would be crazy.

It was no surprise that I beat Sara into the office that morning. I was early even by her standards. She might even come in late again since she was fighting a bug.

With my brides dropping like flies, there wasn't a lot to do. The Dickson-Strauss wedding, with a little over a week left till show time, was ready to go, provided Mama Dickson didn't throw us any more curveballs. I had an appointment booked with Spider and her mother for the next day, but I had a strong hunch I didn't need to prepare for that one. Eventually, I'd have to suck it up and find out for sure. I wasn't ready for that. I'd rather live for a little longer with hope than find out for sure that hope was for chumps. Avoidance never pays off in the end, but like a trooper, I continued to try.

I went into the back room and examined the birdseed favors for Gail. They hadn't been moved since I'd finished them. Sifting through the boxes and jars lining the shelves, I pulled out seed beads and pearls, feathers and lace.

I spent the morning embellishing the bags, making each one a work of art. If I didn't keep busy, I would lose my mind.

Sara dragged through the door two hours later, yawning. She dropped her bag on her desk and slumped in her chair.

"Hey," I said, sliding a cup of coffee to her. "Still not sleeping?"

"Bad dreams."

I raised an eyebrow at her and sipped my own coffee. "Must've been a whopper."

"I've been having a lot of those lately."

"You and me both."

She looked exhausted, and her cheeks were a little flushed. I put my palm on her forehead and made a thoughtful face.

"Am I dying?" she asked, rolling her eyes.

"Maybe a little warm. Should you be here? I can handle the office. You should've stayed home."

"Eh. I'm okay. A little run-down. I'll take some aspirin. Will that make you happy?"

Sara and I had nursed each other through a number of ailments over the years. Flu, colds, the self-induced results of alcohol over-exuberance. About eight years ago we found out that Sara, who was generally good at everything, was not particularly good at skiing. I spent half a semester in our dorm room fetching things for her while her broken leg healed. She did the same for me when I broke my wrist in a skateboard accident. For the record, I was watching the skaters, not participating. I have a knack for standing in the wrong place.

"What would make me happy is if you were at home in bed. But since it doesn't look like I'll get that right now, I'll get you some aspirin."

As tired as she was, Sara was on top of things when Mrs. Dickson called with a new, self-manufactured problem. The councilwoman's voice over the phone was loud enough for me to hear across the room.

I couldn't make out every word, but it was clear that someone in the string quartet we'd hired had pissed her off.

"Mrs. Dickson, I'm so sorry to hear you're unhappy with the cellist. I'm certain she had no intention of cutting in front of you at the grocery store. If you could…" Sara palmed her face in exasperation. "Yes, of course. I understand. I'll see what I can do to find you a replacement."

The rant would likely go on for another ten minutes if allowed, but Sara reined her in, repeated her assurance that we'd straighten it out, and disengaged. She tossed the phone on her desk and moaned.

"A week and a half from the wedding and the bitch fired the entire quartet. We'll need a miracle to find a replacement in time."

I'd heard enough of the conversation that I already had a list ready. It took less time than I expected for Sara to call the musicians we'd hired and apologize, while I ran down the list until I found someone with an opening to replace them. The Bay Area was full of talented musicians, and September wasn't prime wedding season. I felt a little guilty that it was so easy.

"It's like we're rewarding her bad behavior," I said. "If it weren't for Gail, I'd be inclined to tell her there wasn't anyone else."

"Oh, she'll suffer," Sara said. "I'll see to it she pays for both quartets. Not that she's likely to notice when she gets the invoice. She's a politician. Invoices are beneath her."

Sara gave in and went home around lunchtime. I startled her when I grabbed her and gave her a hug.

"Take care of yourself, okay?" I said.

She smiled, amused. "It's just the flu. I'm fine."

"Yeah, but, you know." I brushed a stray hair out of her eyes. "I need you."

"Of course you need me. You're a wreck." She eyed me up and down. "When I'm feeling better, I'm coming over and throwing away that skirt. And a few other pieces of your wardrobe."

I brushed at the bright green sequins striped down my hip. "What? It's cheery."

She shook her head and put on her sweater. "I know the thing with Helen shook you up. But I'm not going anywhere, Zo. Well, except home to bed. Hold down the fort. I'll see you in the morning."

She made a show of giving me elaborate, noisy air kisses to make me laugh, then slipped out the door. Nope. Sara never missed anything, even when she was coming down with a bug. I was letting Helen's death freak me out.

Which brought me back to Spider. I had to face up to the task I'd been dreading all morning.

I dialed Spider's mother, my stomach doing gymnastic flips and leaps. It took several rings before she answered, and when she did, she was so quiet I wasn't sure I'd heard her.

"Mrs. Talbot?"

"Yes."

"This is Zoey Donovan from Happily Ever After. I'm just calling to confirm we have an appointment with you and Amanda at nine-thirty tomorrow morning."

"Oh."

Oh? What did that mean? I wanted to throw up. I knew what it meant. "Mrs. Talbot?"

"Yes. No. We…we won't be able to make it tomorrow." She didn't offer me anything more. It was like yanking out my own appendix with salad tongs.

"I'll be happy to reschedule. When is a more convenient time?" It was a good thing I'd been doing this

job for a while. I took comfort in having something
near to a script. I didn't have to think about what I
was saying until I had more information—which I
knew would come pouring out any second. There
was a long silence on the other end. "Mrs. Talbot?"

I could hear her breathing in big gulps of air as
if she were trying to calm herself. "She's…Mandy's
gone." Her breath hitched and she was quiet again
for a moment, gathering herself together. When she
spoke again, it was a whisper. "We found her two
days ago. My girl is gone."

Two days ago? The bastard waited two days to
taunt me with it. For a second, I imagined spiking
him through the heart with a wooden stake. But of
course, that was vampires. I hadn't figured out yet
what to do about an incubus. "I'm so sorry, Mrs. Talbot. She was a wonderful girl. If there's anything I
can do…" I didn't know how to end that sentence.
There was nothing anyone could ever do. This poor
woman's daughter was dead. I couldn't cancel ar-
rangements for her because we hadn't made it that
far into the planning stages. And let's not forget, it
was my fault.

"You've already done more than you know," she
said. "She was different after we saw you. I don't
know what you said, but I had my little girl back
for a few days. At least," she paused as her voice
cracked, "at least I knew before she left me that she
didn't hate me."

She cried for a while. I cried with her. I was never
so grateful to have my walls up and strong as I was

during that conversation. I shared my tears with her. I wasn't mirroring her emotions back at her. I was beginning to understand how regular people interacted with each other. It was possible to share emotions between people by expressing them instead of psychically exchanging them.

I was exhausted when I hung up the phone. Apparently, dealing with my own emotions was as much work as dealing with the ones that used to leak in from other people. I had so much to learn about my gifts, as well as how others functioned without them. It was all so new, and time was so short.

# SIXTEEN

THE DAY HAD begun sunny, but like any other Bay Area day, had gone from cheery to overcast when I wasn't looking—much like my mood.

I made my way down the sidewalk, anxious and toying with my amulet. Every dark-haired man who passed, every splotch of red, made me catch my breath and clutch my necklace tighter. It remained warm in my palm. If I didn't walk out in front of a bus or get struck by lightning, I was safe. Considering my luck lately, that was a pretty big if.

The only weapon I had against Sebastian was knowledge. The few hours I'd spent with Aggie had given me a few insights, but I needed more. I had a load of books in my magic bag that I hadn't yet plumbed. If anyone could help me dig out the wisdom they might offer, it was Andrew.

I pulled the door open and stepped inside Andrew's shop. He was in a corner talking in a low voice with a customer. He glanced over and smiled at me before returning his attention to the woman next to him. I took a step forward and was nearly sent sprawling by a ball of fluff flinging itself against my legs.

"Hey, Milo. Come on up here, sweetheart." I

scooped up the little fox and took him to settle with me on the couch at the back of the room. He was excited and raced up and down from the floor to my lap and back again, his tongue flapping in a foxy grin. I pulled him up and pinned him so he'd hold still for affection. When I rubbed his ears, he flopped on his belly and gazed up at me with adoring eyes.

I heard the door swing open and shut, then Andrew stood over me, grinning.

"I was going to tell you we missed you," he said, "but I guess Milo beat me to it."

"It's appreciated from both of you," I said.

Andrew plopped into the overstuffed chair near me. "I have had the weirdest day. Three different people came in here today asking for marijuana. Seriously. Two of them actually argued with me that I was holding out on them."

"Well, it *is* an herb shop."

"Funny girl. 'Cause I've never heard that before."

"Did you look them right in the eye and ask them if they were police officers?"

"I did not. Cop or no, I'm not selling weed out of my store to anybody. I'd very much like to keep my business and not go to jail."

I wondered if he sold it outside his store and decided I didn't want to know.

"Bruce is gone," I said to change the subject.

He leaned forward. "Gone gone or dead gone?"

"Sorry. He went home, I guess. He left me this." I slipped the chain over my head and handed Andrew the amulet.

He examined it and gave a low whistle. "That is some serious blingage."

I nodded. "It freezes when I'm in trouble, too. Sort of an early warning system."

He handed it over and I put it on, tucking it under my shirt. "Doesn't exactly match every outfit, but when did that ever stop me from wearing something?"

He looked me up and down with a critical eye. "Nice skirt. Thinking of switching jobs to magician's assistant?"

I grimaced. "Don't you start on me, too."

He spotted the purse sitting on the floor. "Do my eyes lie? This is not the handbag of a homeless person. Somebody went shopping."

"Nope. Somebody lives with a houseful of brownies and left her sample book on the kitchen counter."

"No!" He picked it up to examine it closer.

I smiled. "Oh, yes. Go ahead. Get something out."

He reached in and pulled out my phone. "You have a text," he said.

I took the phone. "Keep digging."

He pulled out my wallet. "It's roomier than it looks."

"Don't stop."

He reached in again and pulled out a banana, then my small toolkit. "This is freaky."

I motioned for him to hand me the purse and he passed it over. "Watch this."

I stuck my hand in, felt around, then pulled a big book out of the tiny opening. It landed on the table in a cloud of dust.

"All right, show-off. I'm impressed. Please, no elephants. I'm not zoned for large animals."

I snorted. "One more thing." I made fancy motions with my hands, like a magician over a top hat. I reached in and pulled out a plastic container. "Ta da!" I said with a flourish. "Muffins!"

"Much better than an elephant."

"I like elephants."

We ate while I told him everything that happened since seeing him on Saturday, and what I planned to do about it.

"You know you're insane," he said, taking a bite. "You should be huddling underground in a bunker, and you want to go looking for him."

I bobbed my head and grinned. "Uh huh. Insane. Will you help me?"

"Of course I'll help you. Although I should tie you up and take you back to Maurice."

"Kinky."

"You wish."

I pulled out two more books from Aggie and propped the first one open. "Help me figure out how to find a demon that's running around downtown. He has to go somewhere when he's not stalking me or killing people I know."

We flipped through the book, grimacing at some of the gruesome pictures.

He tapped his finger on a page. "How about this? 'Demons of the third tier are bidden to return each fortnight to the location of their causing.' What's that—'causing'?"

I shrugged. "What's a third-tier demon?" I turned the page. "'Demons of sensuous nature are restricted to one prime victim or sub-victims of the original.' I'd say that's a big yes on being a demon of a sensuous nature. He's the biggest pervert I've ever met." I shuddered.

Andrew frowned. "What the hell is this book?"

I closed it and looked at the cover. The letters swam around in curlicues and didn't form any words I could recognize. "Aggie handed me the pile of books and said they might help. I have no idea where they came from. This one reads like a Demon Handbook."

"'Restricted to one prime victim or sub-victims.'" He looked thoughtful. "I think that's you, Zoey. You're the prime. Sub-victims are people you've been in contact with, people who contain some of your energy."

"That's cheery. At least we know he can't go after just anybody."

Andrew fanned through the pages and stopped at a page with a faded color picture of a good-looking man and a beautiful woman. They both looked arrogant and cruel. "Ha! Found you, you bastard."

I leaned forward. The heading at the top of the page said Incubi and Succubi.

The print was faded and difficult to read, but I could still make it out.

"'The incubus and succubus are second-tier demons. As such, they have no clearance to move outside of a three-kilometer radius of their point of arrival in the human world.'" I flipped to the cover and frowned. Kilometers? Clearance? When was this book written? There was no copyright mark, so it was impossible to tell. The cover was ancient, but the writing was more modern. There was no fathoming the ways of the demon world. I returned my attention to the article and continued reading.

"'Any distinguishing marks left on victims that put the demon community in jeopardy will not be tolerated.

"'Feeding outside the prime victim's circle is prohibited.

"'Violation of any and all rules will be punished immediately, and license to travel in the human world will be revoked.'"

I turned the page. A full-page picture of a demonic bunny stared up at me. I slammed the book shut. "Looks like that's it."

"Not much to go on."

"Nope. So, he can't leave the city, he can't leave any suspicious marks, and he can't have anyone but me and those I've come in contact with."

"It's good to know he's got some rules, at least."

"It didn't tell me how to find him, though. I can't exactly stand out on the street all day as bait, hoping he'll come along."

"No, and I can think of several of us who wouldn't allow it." He went still and quiet, staring at me. He'd done it once before, so I knew what he was up to. He was reading my aura.

I stayed quiet so he could concentrate. It made

me self-conscious and a little twitchy. After a few minutes, he relaxed.

"Honey, I think there might be another way to get to him."

"You read his cell phone number from my aura?"

"No, but almost as good. The dreams you've been having—he's been sending them to you, right?"

"As far as I can tell."

"If he can get to you that way, maybe it goes both ways."

"You want me to hunt him down in my dreams."

"Sort of, yeah. Your aura looks so much better than when I met you. But you have this dark spot, and it trails behind you like a dirty piece of twine."

"He tagged me."

"I guess. It doesn't look healthy, and I've never seen anything like it. So to my mind, you have three choices. One, ignore it, two, try to hack through it, or three, follow it and see where it goes."

"You're hoping I'll go for option two, aren't you."

"Hoping, yes. Expecting? Not on your life."

"Good call. I have no intention of ignoring it or letting the son of a bitch go before I'm done with him."

"What can you do in your dreams? You already said you locked him in a coffin. Can't you just leave him there to rot? Cut the cord and be done with him."

I shook my head and ran my fingers through Milo's soft fur. "I suppose I could. But that doesn't lock him up in real life. As long as he's still connected to me, he's out there in reality, stealing lives. If he doesn't know I'm coming for him, maybe I can find out where he spends his waking hours. And once I do, I'm pulling the plug. If I can't keep him locked up, and I can't kill him, maybe I can at least take away his food supply. And then, maybe we can figure out how the hell to send him back home."

Andrew picked at a loose thread on the arm of his chair. "What if you can't find him?"

"I can still cut him off. One problem at a time."

"God, Zoey. Be careful."

I shrugged, but my nonchalance was fake. "I'm being as careful as I can. And if that doesn't work, I'll wear steel-toed boots in case I get another whack at his family jewels."

"Remind me never to piss you off."

MAURICE WAS ADAMANTLY set against my plan.

"Why would you intentionally engage with him, Zoey? No good can come of it."

He puttered around the kitchen, compulsively cleaning counters that were already spotless. Molly sat on the table, folding a pile of tiny shirts and socks. I was relieved that some unknown rule of brownie etiquette hadn't forced her to leave after gifting me with my new purse.

"I can't sit here and wait until he's ready for the main course," I said. "And I can't let anybody else die in my place."

Maurice wasn't happy. For that matter, I could tell by her silence that Molly wasn't very happy either.

"He can't hurt me in my dreams. I have to do this.

Hell, there's an excellent chance I won't be able to do it. But I have to try."

The two of them exchanged a look I didn't like. Maurice opened his mouth to object.

I was saved by "The Wedding March" chiming on my phone.

Thanks to my new purse, I reached right in and pulled it out. No searching, digging or swearing necessary.

I didn't recognize the number, but it didn't show that it was a forwarded call. I hoped like hell it wasn't more bad news. I'd pretty much reached my limit. I flipped it open.

"This is Zoey."

"Zoey. Hi. This is Riley."

I swallowed. It was the last voice I'd expected to hear.

"EMT guy?"

He laughed. The sound was warm and made my toes curl. "Yeah, the EMT guy. Though 'paramedic guy' is preferable. Nick gave me your number."

"Nick?" I sounded like an idiot. Again.

"The officer you spoke to the other day."

I nodded my head, knowing full well as I did it that he couldn't see me.

"Listen," he said. "The universe keeps throwing us together. I was thinking maybe we could get a jump on it and do it ourselves next time."

"Uh huh." *Sheer intellectual genius. Keep it up.*

"Do you like sushi?"

"Sushi?"

"There's this place I really like. I'd love to take you there. How about Saturday night?"

"Sure. Saturday."

"I can come pick you up or we can meet there."

My brain snapped out of its fog. There was no way he was coming out here to get me. If he got past the fairies and the skunk-ape, Maurice was sure to give him the big brother treatment. "I'll meet you. It's kind of a drive to my place."

He gave me directions to the restaurant and we agreed to meet at seven-thirty. By the time I hung up, I was grinning like an idiot, and Maurice and Molly were staring at me.

"What?" I felt guilty for some reason.

"Nothing," Maurice said. "You're just acting goofy is all."

"I have a date. On Saturday. With the hot EMT. No. The hot paramedic!" I did a little dance around the kitchen table. I stopped in mid-step, stricken. "Oh my God."

"What?"

"I hate sushi."

# SEVENTEEN

DESPITE MY INSISTENCE that I knew what I was doing and that I wouldn't be able to get hurt, I was sure of neither of these things. Being occasionally aware that you're asleep by no stretch grants the ability to chase after a bad guy in your dreams. This posed another question: Did demons dream? Did it matter?

I took a long, hot bath and settled into bed. I knew once I was asleep Maurice would be hovering around me, watching. Rather than make me nervous, this gave me a measure of calm. In theory, even if I could get hurt in my dreams, the danger would be gone the minute I woke up. Maurice wouldn't let Sebastian pull a Freddy Krueger on me.

I shuddered. Thinking about Freddy Krueger right before going to sleep is never a good idea. It's especially bad when you're going into dreamland to hunt down your enemy.

I lay in the dark trying to stay focused enough to retain control of my thoughts, yet relaxed enough to drift off to sleep. Not an easy trick.

I thought about Riley's eyes and the way his laugh gave me goose bumps. I could eat sushi for him. What's a little raw fish and seaweed? *No, focus. Think about the rope that connects you to Sebastian so you can follow it. Come on, Zoey. Build a mouse-trap now, romance and googly eyes later.*

I knew I was getting drowsy. My thoughts were wandering loose. I tried to follow them and rein them in, but it was like herding cats.

I remembered the game Mousetrap from my childhood. Daddy and I used to play it together. All those pieces were so complicated. We didn't always get the mouse. Maybe if we'd used Gruyère. Maybe the mouse was snooty. I tried to pluck the mouse out of a tiny jail cell, but the tweezers I was using brushed the bars and set off an alarm. I jumped and woke up.

*Way to concentrate, Zoey. Pull your head out and try again.*

I concentrated on the line Andrew had said that, in theory, tethered me to the incubus. In the dark behind my eyelids, I imagined a thread tied around my ankle and winding out the window. I followed it, pulling the length through my hands. I climbed out the window into my garden. Grass brushed against my legs. When did my lawn get so long?

The moon was overhead, spinning like a wind-mill and singing a wordless tune. The thread in my hands bit my fingers and I dropped it.

I bent to pick it up and found a wet, flopping fish at my feet. It went still and stared up at me with one glassy eye.

"The problem is," the fish said, "you have to have movie-time attitude."

I pondered this bit of sage advice.

"Should I make popcorn?" I asked.

"No, you must wear a tiara. And maybe you should be awake."

I looked over my shoulder at my open window.

"Dammit," I said. "I lost the thread." This dream-journey thing was harder than I'd thought.

I picked up the thread and followed it again. When I reached the tree Sebastian had been leaning against the last time, Bob Saget stepped out from behind it.

"I'm very disappointed in you, Zoey," he said. "Getting your friends killed is not very responsible. I think you should go back to your room and think about it."

My stomach knotted up with shame. I was about to apologize and turn around when I realized Bob Saget was not, in fact, my father.

I began to wonder how much was the work of my wandering mind, and how much was meant to intentionally distract me. If Sebastian knew I was coming and was placing barriers in my way, it meant he was afraid. I marched past Bob Saget without engaging.

Of course, if this was my own mind throwing up roadblocks, it meant I was afraid. But I already knew that.

I followed the thread down the road and onto Highway 1. It looked nothing like the real road I traveled every day, but I knew where it led. I was going to Sausalito. I could see the city lights in the distance and knew the journey wasn't real. I was making good time on foot, whereas it was a good forty-five minutes by car. Dream math.

My feet made a crunching sound on the gravel. I knew I was being watched. I squared my shoulders and followed the thread, which had thickened in my hands. The deeper I went into the dream, the more it grew. At this rate, it might get so big I'd have to climb my way over it before I was done.

At the crossroad, I halted. There's always a crossroad in dreams.

Riley stood waiting for me, wearing a red and green striped sweater and Freddy Krueger's hat.

"Hurry up," he said. "The coffee's getting cold. Everybody's waiting."

He motioned me to follow him down the left fork. I could hear people celebrating, glasses clinking. I took a step forward and dropped the rope.

"Come on," Sara said.

"What happened to Riley?"

"Who's Riley?" She tugged at my hand.

I looked at the road that forked to the right. Clouds had drifted in. They looked angry.

"This is a horrible idea," one said. Its face was puffy and soot-stained.

"Which one?" I asked. "Your way or theirs?"

He shrugged his billowy shoulders. "Doesn't much matter, does it?"

I turned to follow the left branch. The clouds had folded over and enveloped both roads. Which way?

"Zoey, baby. You have to concentrate."

My mother stood in the road. She smiled and reached out her hand. I took it. "Concentrate," she said again.

The confusion cleared from my muddled head.

"Thank you," I said. I reached down and picked up the rope. It felt oily and frayed. I must've been getting close.

The path through Sausalito was convoluted and wound in and out of shops and offices. Demonic rabbits, a rain of soap bubbles, and my ex-husband hanging upside down from a tree didn't distract me as I made my way.

I stepped out of an empty warehouse and blinked in the sunlight. I stood in the street, and the blackened rope hung limp in my hand. The end stretched out and hovered in the air, culminating in a dense, oily cloud that reached into the distance. It went everywhere and nowhere. I was both relieved and disappointed. Tracking down the incubus was impossible.

But I could still destroy the connection.

I closed my eyes and formed a sturdy, sharp pair of scissors in my hand. Light glinted off their surface. My grip on the rope was firm.

Unfortunately, scissors are never sharp enough in real life, and this is equally true in the dream world. It was a bit of a moment-killer. I'd been hoping for a single, dramatic snip to do the job.

I worked it down to a few last threads. I was torn between confident elation and the fear that Sebastian would pop up and stop me before I could finish.

I focused. I cut. And before I was all the way through, my vision shifted.

The rope didn't change. It lay dead and frayed across my palm. The city didn't change. It was still empty, a distorted version of the real Sausalito. The change came from me.

I was glowing. All over my body were thin, wispy threads of silvery blue. They shot out in all directions, breathtaking and ethereal. I picked one out and followed it with my eyes. In the distance, I saw the other end connected to a tiny woman. I squinted to see better. Molly waved at me.

I followed a second line, and it led to Moira from the bakery, and a third and fourth were for Gail and Alma Dickson. The threads were infinite in number and spread out across the town. Mrs. Talbot. The barista at my favorite coffee shop. The lady who delivered my mail.

Sara.

Every woman I'd come in contact with was connected to me.

The rope in my hand throbbed and squirmed like a tentacle. Its inky blackness leached into every single line that was bound to me, infecting it. Every one of those women was in danger.

I hacked at the final few threads of Sebastian's rope until the last bit snapped loose, and I was free.

It was too late. Incubus rot pulsed down the lines toward the women. I tried to cut those lines from myself, to amputate them before the sickness flowed all the way out, but these were connections of emotion, not so easily severed. Wherever my blades touched, the lines puffed into mist, then reformed.

I slumped to the ground, devastated. He didn't need me to track them anymore. I was too late. Every woman in Sausalito was a potential feast.

I had accomplished nothing.

The dark cloud at the other end of the rope condensed and took form.

I imagined what Sebastian might look like as his true self. He could be some monstrous Cthulhu-like creature with tentacles and red, bleeding eyes. He might be ten feet tall, covered in open sores and have filthy, twelve-inch claws. He might be a two-foot-long slug with lightning reflexes and speed so fast I wouldn't see him until he was oozing up my legs and gnashing at my flesh.

I backed up faster.

In dreams, that which we fear is the exact thing which will come for us in the dark. If we don't think about it, it isn't there. But I had thought about it.

I did the worst thing a person can do in a dream. I panicked, turned my back and ran.

I was no longer captain of my fate. I had nothing under control. I wasn't aware anymore that I was dreaming. I only knew the squelching sounds behind me were getting closer and my feet were moving too slowly. Something brushed the back of my calf.

I tried to scream. Nothing came out but a low, garbled sound like I was choking on a mouthful of hard-boiled eggs.

I dove into my office and tried to climb under my desk to hide. I was too slow. It grabbed me by the shoulder and sunk its claws into my skin.

I thrashed, refusing to turn and face it, terrified of what I would see.

I tried again to scream. My throat closed up and the sound refused to travel up my windpipe.

The unseen thing squeezed and shook.

"Zoey," it said.

It knew my name.

"No!" I thrashed harder.

It shook me like a rag doll. "Zoey, stop it."

I batted at it with fists. "You can't have me!"

"Zoey, wake up!"

I opened my eyes to find Maurice holding me down as I flailed my arms. Molly was standing on my nightstand with a worried expression, and beyond all reason in my sleep-fogged state, I saw a large furry face pressed against the window, fist braced to break the glass.

"I'm awake! I'm awake!" I said, tearing loose. "Don't let him break the window!"

The skunk-ape opened his fingers and let his hand drop to his side. He grinned at me.

"We were worried," Molly said. "You would not wake up. We thought he had you."

"I'm fine. I didn't see him. Just a regular bad dream. Maurice, would you open the window, please?"

He squeezed my shoulder before releasing me, then patted my arm, as if to reassure himself I was whole. "You keep scaring the hell out of me, Zoey. How am I supposed to get anything done around here?" He crossed to the window and slid it open. "You take daredevil risks that make my hair fall out. Look at my hair!" He pointed to the top of his head. There didn't seem to be any less than he'd had when he first got there, which hadn't been much to begin with. It seemed prudent not to mention it—though the single bobbing tuft still winked at me. I never had offered him that hair gel.

I dragged myself from under the comforter and moved to the window. The skunk-ape looked stricken, as if he might bolt.

"Thank you for looking after me," I said. "I don't even know your name."

The hairy creature clicked his tongue and grunted.

"He does not speak your language," Molly said, having appeared on the windowsill when my attention was focused elsewhere. I really needed to find out how these people moved so fast. "His name is Iris."

I glanced at Molly, questioning whether I'd heard right. She nodded once and went still, giving me a warning look. I returned my attention to the skunk-ape.

"Well, thank you, Iris." I leaned out the window and offered my hand. He looked at it a moment before wrapping it in an enormous, gentle paw.

His palm was rough, but bare, the rest of him covered in bristly gray and white fur. Parts of his face were naked as well—a long straight nose, saggy lips, the apples of his ruddy cheeks, and two very human blue eyes. I had expected a skunk-ape to smell to high heaven. To my surprise, he had a flowery scent, as if he'd soaked in aromatherapy bath salts. It was nice, not overwhelming.

I placed my other hand over the back of his, giving him a warm, two-handed squeeze. "You don't need to stay so far out of sight," I said. "You're welcome here."

He grunted twice.

"He thanks you for your kindness," Molly said, translating. "He prefers the cover of the woods, but will always be near if you need him." Iris clicked his tongue and made a few guttural noises, then disappeared.

"Iris?" I said after he was out of earshot.

"He likes flowers. Skunk-apes usually live in the Southeast, but his aversion to the natural musk of his people caused them to shun him."

"Let me guess. He moved west until my mother took him in."

Maurice smiled. "You're getting good at this."

"It seems to be the answer to most of my questions these days." I dropped into the padded chair near the window. "Unfortunately, it's not the answer to all of them."

"What happened in the dream, Zo?" Maurice asked. He took a seat on the edge of the bed.

"I cut the cord, but I didn't actually find him."

"But you were so frightened," Molly said. "You did not see him?"

"That was my own brain throwing up. I wasn't exactly the picture of mental self-control in there." I grabbed a black and green throw-pillow and buried my face in it. I groaned. Molly and Maurice were silent, letting me pull myself together. When I was done, I pushed the pillow away and looked at them both. My chest was tight with hopeless, unshed tears.

"I was too late," I said. "I cut him off, but he tagged every woman I'm connected to. He doesn't need me anymore. He's got a nearly endless supply without me."

"Oh, Zoey." Maurice shook his head. "You can't blame yourself. How could you know he would do that?"

"There's very little I do know, Maurice. I don't know a damn thing that's useful. He's going to keep killing people I care about, and I can't stop him."

There was one thing I could do, but I could barely think it to myself, let alone say anything to Maurice and Molly.

If I were dead, he'd have to go back. It said so in the Demon Handbook.

# EIGHTEEN

I WASN'T SUICIDAL. I sure as hell didn't want to die. But I didn't know what to do, either. I was distracted most of the day, twitching every time the phone rang, certain each call would be news of another death.

Sara still looked run-down, but she tried not to show it. It was a battle between us to see who got to take care of the other one. She knew something was wrong with me, but there wasn't a damn thing I could tell her.

I considered talking to her about all of it. Aside from the unbelievable supernatural shenanigans, I had a relative stranger living in my house. Sara would not have approved. A predator on the loose? Sara would call the police. Small, uninvited creatures living in my linen closet? She'd have the number of a good exterminator.

Add the supernatural to the mix, and my no-nonsense best friend would be rolling her eyes at me and offering to lighten my workload so I could "take a rest." Sara did not approve of what she called woo-woo business. She wouldn't even get her palm read on the boardwalk when we were on spring break back in college. Sara liked things neat and tidy, and that included her view of reality. I didn't relish the idea of shaking that up. She put her palm on my forehead, the same as I'd done to her the day before. "Feels warm," she said, lips pursed in disapproval. "You should go home."

"You can't tell if someone has a fever if you have one yourself. I'm fine."

She dropped her hand. "Whatever this bug is, we both have to dump it before next week. Bad enough if one of us is sick for the Dickson Family Circus."

"I'm not sick, Mom. I'll be fine. Maybe just need a little fresh air."

I walked out to the street and inhaled the smells of salt and fish and engine exhaust. My walls were solid and tight. I wanted no chance of making any more connections, possibly ever. So much damage had been done with this curse of mine. Since I'd cut the connection to Sebastian, any new contacts I made would probably be safe from him, but I wasn't going to chance it.

I walked with no destination in mind. I needed to think. I needed to breathe. I stopped at a light and looked around. I was sealed up so tight there was a surreal quality in being surrounded by cars and sidewalks full of people. I'd never experienced life the way other people apparently did. It was cold, empty and frankly, pretty lonely. The faces around me were a mystery, as if I were viewing them on a movie screen. I could guess at their stories, their feelings, but I couldn't know.

A woman stopped at the light had her phone to her ear. The other hand gripped her steering wheel with white knuckles. She appeared agitated, possibly yelling at whoever was on the other end of the call. A kid walked down the sidewalk, his hoodie pulled over his head, the obligatory wires dangling from his ears. His stride was slow and deliberate, his look thoughtful. Was he depressed? Thinking about some plan to take over the world? Simply keeping time to the music?

How did people function this way?

I continued up the street, watching the crowds. Two women strolled past, laughing and holding hands. They looked to be in love, but how could I know without feeling it for myself? A cop car flashed its lights at a green Toyota. The man being pulled over looked resigned, glancing several times at his watch.

I supposed I could take all the physical cues and put them together to form the stories of the people around me. But they'd be guesses. I was accustomed to *knowing*. Maybe all these years I'd been an emotional Peeping Tom. That was an icky thought. I hadn't considered the moral implications of emotional voyeurism. It was one thing to do it unconsciously, but now that I knew what I was doing— well, it didn't make me feel so good about myself.

It was a little cool in the Bay breeze and I pulled my sweater close. I walked past restaurants, the obligatory Sausalito houseboats, trendy shops and scores of strange, empty faces that carried no emotion to distract me, connect me or lighten my load.

I grew tired of feeling alone in a sea of faces. I needed to think without distractions. Around a curve in the street, the buildings gave way to an incline of rocky, empty coast.

I stepped off the sidewalk into the sand and trudged down toward the pylons beneath an abandoned dock. The spot looked perfect for some quiet meditation. My brain felt too heavy with dark thoughts. Listening to water lap against the shore would help me sort things out.

As I neared the underside of the dock, the cool air dropped at least another ten degrees. Then my amulet kicked in. It was as if it had been in a deep sleep and was startled awake. The cold bit into my skin, and the chain vibrated with the chill.

Fear made me nauseous, and a meteorite in my belly flipped over with a solid clunk. I'd walked right into Sebastian's lair.

My first instinct was to run, but my thoughts sped up before my feet could move.

*Maybe it's a sign. Maybe the only way to fix this is to give up.* I lifted my chin and tried not to show fear. *Bring it.*

The area beneath the dock was not spacious. Sausalito wasn't exactly a beach-boardwalk type of place. It was cramped under there. And dark. And cold.

The sand crunched beneath my boots, and the sound of my own shaky breathing filled my ears. The tide lapped at the pillars several yards away, and I couldn't remember if it was on its way in or out at this time of day. If I went in there, and the tide came in, I could be trapped.

I stood at the edge, one foot under the dock, the

other still out in the sun, deliberating. The amulet was like an ice cube beneath my shirt. I pulled it out and let it rest above the fabric. Warning duly noted.

I gripped the wooden support with my right hand, took a deep breath and moved into the darkness.

It took a moment for my eyes to adjust in the dark, cramped space. I was hunched over, unable to stand up straight. Shadows formed around me, some more substantial than others.

When I was able to pick through them, the shadow closest to me, three feet away, moved.

"Ah, room service," it said. "How thoughtful."

A spark flashed, then a candle flared to life. Sebastian sat in the sand, his green eyes staring up at me.

I checked my walls and felt them for cracks. Airtight.

I wanted to say something witty about the AAA rating on his accommodations and how room service wasn't included, but my tongue was stuck to the roof of my mouth.

His gaze tried to penetrate my defenses. I could feel it prodding and caressing at the walls, but my work was sound. He could try all he wanted. There was no way in, not until I had no other choice.

"You've been busy, Dream Girl," he said. He did not look happy.

My tongue unstuck. "Buffet's closed." My voice came out stronger than I'd expected, but not nearly as iron-willed as I'd hoped.

He chuckled. "I can live on your leftover scraps

for some time to come. Still, I'll miss our night times together, Dream Girl. Cutting me off like that was cruel." He pouted and picked up a seashell, examined it, chucked it aside. "Did you find a magic word you want to hurl at me to send me home? Shall I hold still for you while you draw a circle around me to do a hex?"

I frowned, suspicious. "How did I find you? I wasn't looking for you, and I know this isn't a co-incidence."

He shrugged, the cheap velvet of his coat scraping against the pillar behind him. "I knew I couldn't see you anymore in the dream world, so I put out a call. I hoped you'd answer, and here you are." His smile was broad and self-congratulatory.

I could feel the blood leaving my face. It made me queasy to think he could call me to him like a pet, despite my efforts to disconnect us. Some connections go deeper than we think. I shuddered.

And then I knew. I saw him sitting there, smug and bloated like a tick, and I knew what I had to do. If I filled him so full of emotions, maybe he would burst like an overfed leach. Disgusting, yes, but it had to work. It was the first time I had hope since he'd arrived.

Of course that plan had a killer problem: I'd emptied myself that morning of every emotion but my own. I'd been wandering the streets walled up against the tiniest bit of feelings from the wealth of people around me. I was isolated from the crowds now, unable to reach out to them. All I had was me, and me wasn't anywhere near enough.

I was a small woman standing in a dark, concealed area, with a hostile man twice her size.

For the second time in less than two weeks I wished I were a kick-ass chick with multiple weapons strapped against my body and black belts in several forms of martial arts. And I was in trouble.

Hunched over like I was, I couldn't move very quickly, but he was seated, so I had a head start. I backed up a step, trying not to provoke him. If I could get back to where there were people, I could regroup. Maybe I'd have a chance at beating him.

"Where are you going, little one? We were having such a nice visit."

"Go home, Sebastian. You won't get anything more from me, and you're done killing my friends." Brave words meant for distraction. I slid my foot behind me another step.

"Oh, but there's still plenty out there for me. I'm nowhere near finished."

"No. You touch no one from here on out. I'm giving you fair warning." Fair warning of what? I still hadn't quite figured it out. All I had was the beginnings of a plan. I was bluffing, and we both knew it.

Sebastian was up and on me so fast he was a blur. His hands gripped my arms and his face was inches from mine. "I don't think you understand," he said. "You're mine now. If I can't get in one way, I'll find another."

He crushed his lips against mine and kissed me. The physical contact sent cracks through my carefully constructed walls. My mind struggled against

him, but my body betrayed me. I kissed him back.
God help me, I wanted to give everything I had to
him. His lips parted and I was grateful to feel his
tongue probe mine. I breathed in the scent of him
in all its over-soaked cologne. I melted against him,
my body craving contact with his skin and fretting
over the fabric that separated us.

His caress sent shattered pieces of my wall spinning out from my body, leaving me as bare and un-
protected as the rest of his victims. His arms slid
around my waist and something in me snapped. The
last of my defenses lay broken in the rocky sand. I
was relieved to have it gone. Now I was his. I didn't
have to fight anymore.

He broke the kiss and moved his hands up to my
face, cradling it. I looked into those green eyes and
felt despair. I slid my hand between us, wanting to
touch his chest where the skin peeked at me from
the top of his shirt. On the way up, I brushed against
my amulet. The cold shock ran up my arm and broke
the connection between us.

I did the only thing left within my power to do—I
screamed.

# NINETEEN

IN THE MOVIES, a scream is usually a harbinger of death. It means someone isn't going to make it. In the real world, screaming is a last resort, when all one can hope for is a passerby who will intercede.

In my case, the passerby was the last person I'd expected to see.

Riley came whipping around the corner and knocked Sebastian flat on his ass. I'm not against having a handsome prince ride in on his white horse and save me. I'm all for women's lib and for taking care of myself, but sometimes a girl, especially a stupid one like me, can get in over her head. I knew in the end I'd have to defeat my boogeyman myself, but today was not that day.

I don't know which of us was more surprised to see Riley. Sebastian, despite being sprawled in the cold sand, recovered first.

"Death takes a holiday, I see," he said. He wagged his finger at Riley. "That's naughty."

That made no sense to me, but I couldn't begin to fathom what he meant by it.

"Not your business," Riley said. He took my arm and pulled me toward him. Part of me wanted to bury my face against his chest and burst into tears of relief and gratitude. The other part never wanted to be touched by a man again. That part wanted a long, scalding shower. Perhaps with lye soap. And a peroxide rinse.

He led me out into the sun and up to the sidewalk.

Sebastian's voice carried out to us from the dark. "Take good care of her for me, grave digger. I might be hungry again later."

I stopped. Grave digger? I looked at Riley and back at Sebastian. The incubus smiled, his grin splitting his face and showing a double row of spiky teeth.

"I love weddings. See you soon, Dream Girl." His image wavered and disappeared. I shivered.

"Where's your car?" Riley asked, tugging me down the street.

"A few blocks that way," I said, pointing. My knees were shaking and my head kept swiveling around of its own accord, checking to see if we were being followed. "He knew you. How did he know you?"

Riley didn't answer right away. He kept a hand on my elbow as we crossed the street. "We don't know each other," he said. "I know his kind. I see a lot of predators and victims in my line of work."

"As a paramedic?"

"Sure. Yeah. As a paramedic. Zoey, what the hell were you doing under there?"

"It's a long story. A stupid one. I should go back to the office."

"No. You have to go home. You'll be safe there.

He might not give up today, and I can't stay with you. I have another appointment soon."

"Appointment?" Paramedics didn't have appointments. They had emergencies.

"Promise me you'll go home?" Once again, I had the distinct feeling I was being handled. I wanted to object, take back the power over my own life. But if I was honest with myself, I had to admit all I wanted was to go home. And I wasn't getting any concrete answers out of Riley at the moment.

He shuttled me into my car and waited while I buckled up. I felt like my dad was hovering over me. I rolled down the window.

"Thanks for rescuing me," I said.

He reached into the car and locked my door. "Tomorrow at seven-thirty?"

I was surprised he still wanted to go out with me. There was no stopping this guy, apparently. "Sure. Yeah. Tomorrow." I forced a smile and hoped it looked sincere.

I pulled away without looking back. The farther away I drove, the warmer my amulet became. I tucked it under my shirt. I was still freezing, and the extra warmth was welcome.

For someone who had escaped certain death only minutes before, I drove as if death were not a concern. I was going far too fast on the winding roads. After a few close calls squealing around curves, I took note and let up on the accelerator.

I had the heater on full blast and the chill deep inside me finally eased a little. I usually talked to myself, but not out loud. This was a good sign that I was losing it.

I had no idea what to do next. There was a flaw in my new plan. If I opened up to throw emotions at him, that left me vulnerable. I couldn't fight him with my shields up, and I couldn't resist him with my shields down. And now, to make matters worse, I found out physical contact rendered my shields useless. I was a sitting duck, and so was every woman he'd tagged through me.

At home, Maurice took one look at me and ushered me in, took my sweater and purse, pushed me down on the couch, and went to run me a bath.

"He found you. We were afraid he would. Was it very bad?"

I jumped. Sometimes I forgot how many people were living in my house. Molly had climbed up on the armrest. She regarded me with a critical eye.

"It could have gone worse," I said. I pulled off my boots.

"You are alive. Some days we must be satisfied with that."

I leaned my head against the cushions and closed my eyes. "I suppose that's pretty good, for today." I still heard the echo of Sebastian's voice rattling inside my skull. *I love weddings. See you soon.*

"Abuse is worse when they make you thank them for it."

I opened my eyes and looked at her dainty face, the bruises across it now a sickly yellow. "That does make it so much worse. It makes it my fault because I allowed it."

"No. What someone does to you is never your fault. It was you who taught me that."

My lips formed a weak smile. It made me happy to know I'd made a difference in this woman's life. Maybe I sucked at vanquishing demons, but at least I could still help my friends.

Maurice came down the hallway, saw Molly and frowned. "Let her rest, Molly." He grabbed my hand and pulled me up from the couch. "Let's go. In the tub. Your skin is icy, and you need to warm up."

He led me down the hall into my bathroom. "I can do this on my own," I said. He winked at me and shut the door. A second later I opened it and poked my head out to see him walking away. "Maurice?"

He stopped and looked over his shoulder. "Hmm?"

"I'm glad you're here. Thanks."

His smile was weary. "Somebody has to look after you, Zo. You're too busy taking care of everybody else to look after yourself."

FOR THE REST of the day and all day Saturday, I was on lockdown again. I felt like a naughty child who had been grounded. I accepted my punishment with grace, for the most part. I had screwed up. I made a few phone calls for work, but mostly moped around the house getting in Maurice's way.

"Zoey, go read a book or something," he said. He had been trying to clean the windows, and I'd knocked the bottle of cleaner on the floor. It busted open and leaked everywhere.

"Let me clean it up. My fault." I bent to mop it with the rag he'd been using to dust.

He snatched it out of my hands. "Go find something to do. You're making me crazy."

I felt horrible. I almost got myself killed by my own stupidity, and now I was behaving like a six-year-old. My voice was soft. "I'm sorry." I turned to go to my room so I'd be out from under foot.

"Don't you have a date to get ready for?"

I stopped. "Is everybody going to let me out? I thought I was stuck here."

He appeared to consider it. "Riley saved you. I trust him to keep you safe. Promise you'll go straight there and straight back? No stopping off for milk. You stay with him, and always in public. You can't be alone in town. Not for a minute."

"Of course." The thought of running into Sebastian made my stomach clench.

"I'll tell Iris and the fairies to let you go. They were only trying to protect you."

"I know. I'm sorry I worried everybody."

"Go get ready. I have to clean this up." He was a little brusque, but I knew it was because he was worried. I was lucky to have friends who cared so much.

IT ALWAYS SEEMS the more time I have to get ready, the worse my hair looks. On this momentous occasion, I had a first date with a gorgeous, mysterious guy who, for whatever reason, thought I was worth pursuing, despite my constant social disasters in his presence. I had a good three hours to screw up my hair, and I did a spectacular job. After two hours of blowing it dry, straightening it, re-curling it, then straightening it again, I had about forty-five minutes left to jump in the shower, rewash it and start all over. The Medusa look hadn't suited me at all.

The second time around I let it air dry. The curls were natural and fell where they wanted. The less I did, the better it looked.

I debated for a while over what I should wear. Using the Sara-rule about wearing only one quirky item per outfit, I chose my favorite little black dress, black hose and Iron Fist heels with red and green zombies all over them. I wore green, dangly earrings to go with the shoes, and of course, my outrageous dragon amulet.

Okay, so maybe that's two quirky items, but since I had to wear the amulet everywhere, it would be unfair to count it. Besides, this was a date, not a business meeting. Sara didn't get a say in it.

I felt like I turned out pretty hot. I walked out into the living room and found the entire brownie family lined up on the back of the couch, with Maurice standing next to them. Apparently, I was required to model before I could leave.

"Pretty!" Abby said, and clapped her chubby hands.

"Spin around. Let's see," Maurice said. I spun. He frowned. "It's a little short, don't you think?"

Molly laughed. "Leave her alone. She looks very nice."

A shadow moved in the window and I glanced

over. Iris had his face pressed to the glass in a big, toothy grin. He gave me a double thumbs-up.

*I have the weirdest family on Earth.*

They followed me out to the car and waved as I pulled out. In my rearview mirror, I could see them all, very small to very large, standing in the driveway. What an amazing life mine was turning out to be. At that moment, I felt the bad stuff was almost worth all the good that had come with it.

I was also grateful I hadn't let Riley come pick me up. No matter how much I loved these people, there were some things too impossible to explain on a first date.

MAURICE WOULD HAVE been pleased. When I pulled into the parking lot, Riley was already standing outside waiting for me.

"You look…" He paused and gave me a once-over that wasn't uncomfortable so much as tingly. "You look amazing."

I think I blushed. I never did that, except recently around him. "Thank you. So do you." And he did. His dress pants fit like they'd been tailored, and I was anticipating the first chance I could get to examine them from the back. His dark blue shirt made his gray eyes look duskier. He smelled so good I had to stop myself from burying my face in his neck.

He held out his hand and I took it. It was warm and fit around mine like it was made to go there. If it had been several hundred years earlier and I'd been wearing a corset, I likely would have swooned.

He led me inside, and the hostess seated us at a small table in the corner by a window. It was a breathtaking view of the San Francisco Bay, lights beginning to twinkle on as the sun set. I couldn't imagine a more beautiful start to the evening.

The server started us off with a bottle of wine. And then we opened our menus and panic set it.

*Raw fish, raw fish, raw fish.*

I had no idea what to order. In all honesty, I'd only tried sushi once and I'd been by myself. Feeling adventurous on my lunch break, I'd found a small, out of the way place where I could try it without an audience. I have no idea what the hell I ate, but it was gross. And slimy. I suspect it might have been squiddish.

"What are you thinking of having?" he asked.

I waffled. I "um"ed a lot. I bit my lip. I turned pages back and forth. I read and reread the entries.

And then I gave up. I didn't have the ability to find a graceful way out.

"I don't know," I said. I folded up my menu and looked him in the eye. "I have no idea what I'm look-ing at."

He smiled. "Do you want me to order for you? Have you had sushi before?"

"Once, sort of."

"I'll be gentle." He winked at me. "Don't be scared."

He ordered a number of things that had the word *roll* in them, which sounded hopeful. And bless him, he started us out with vegetable tempura. Vegetables. Fried. Now *that* I knew I liked. I had no idea going to a place that served raw fish meant you could also have deep-fried vegetables. I was tempted to ask for my fish rolls to be tempura-ed as well, but I didn't think that would go over very well.

I had a little trouble with the chopsticks, but I was determined not to continue looking like I'd been living in the back hills of nowhere all my life. I knew how to use them. I was out of practice was all.

I was feeling pretty good about the night. The food was much better than I'd expected, the conversation suffered few awkward pauses and, so far, I hadn't slopped any food down the front of my dress. Aces.

Riley didn't look like he had any of the first-date nerves I'd started the evening with. Everything he did—whether it was unfolding his napkin, flipping through the menu or sipping from his wine glass— had a lazy ease about it. His movements were so self-assured and casual. I doubted he'd ever spilled so much as a toast crumb. I was betting if Riley ever did drop a piece of toast, it would land butter side up.

My belly was nicely filled with crunchy, deep-fried tastiness, mysterious fishy stuff rolled up with rice and seaweed, and a good three glasses of wine. I gave a contented sigh and placed my chopsticks across my plate.

"What's the verdict?" Riley asked, wiping his napkin across his mouth.

I pretended to think about it. "Hm."

He tossed his napkin at me. "You loved it. Admit it."

I balled up the fabric and threw it back at him. "I was hungry. I'd have eaten anything."

He grinned and sang at me like a little kid. "Zoey loves sushi, Zoey loves sushi."

I tried to take a swallow from my wine glass to cover my silly smile, but it didn't work. He was making me laugh. If I took a sip now it would likely spew out my nose. Aside from the extreme embarrassment involved, it would probably hurt like crazy. Not to mention, a waste of good wine.

The sun had gone down, leaving the Bay to sparkle with fairy lights from the boats scattered across the water. Foot traffic was thinning on the sidewalk outside the window. The type of traffic had shifted, too. There were less business suits and more casual or club-wear. It was a gorgeous, clear night, and I was with the most amazing guy I'd ever met.

The night had turned out pretty spectacular.

I was content to sit and share the view with him, my head spinning a little from the wine. He reached across the table and took my hand. It might have been awkward, but I suppose he'd been planning his move for some time. He'd managed to slide his arm between dishes without anything getting in the way. Smooth.

His fingers laced through mine, and his gray eyes lit up in the candlelight. "Thanks for coming tonight," he said.

"Well, you know, I didn't have anything life-threatening to do. I thought I'd take the night off from throwing myself into mortal danger."

He squeezed my fingers. "Funny girl. Any chance

you'll tell me now what you were doing under the dock?"

I squeezed back and smiled. "You just saw me eat. Don't you think that's enough shocking information for one evening?"

"You barely got any on you. It wasn't as interesting as you think."

"Maybe you should've taken me for pasta then. I can make a hell of a mess with that."

"I'll keep that in mind for next time."

My breath caught. Next time? The Zoey inside my head clapped her hands and jumped up and down. On the outside, I used my free hand to reach for my water glass and take a slow sip of water. Unfortunately, as I did this, I also glanced out the window.

Not six feet away, Brad stood outside on the sidewalk, staring into the restaurant at me. I sputtered water down the front of my dress in the least graceful move I had in my considerable, clumsy repertoire.

"Oh, God," I said. I grabbed my discarded napkin and dabbed at the front of myself. I released Riley's hand so I could pull the fabric taut and mop it all up. "I'm so sorry. You didn't see that." Out of the corner of my eye I peeked out the window. Brad was heading right for me. I was sure the panic on my face was easy for Riley to read.

He looked out the window.

"Don't look out there," I said. "Just a homeless guy. Nothing to see."

He looked anyway. Can't say I blame him. The

minute somebody tells me not to look at something, looking is the first thing I do.

"Why is that homeless guy staring at us?" he said.

That's when Brad shouted my name and banged on the window, inches from my face.

# TWENTY

I WANTED TO crawl beneath the table and die. Up to that moment, the date had been going so well.

"So," Riley said. "Friend of yours?" He looked as uncomfortable as I felt.

Brad banged on the window again, the flat of his hand leaving a smeary print on the glass. His lips moved and I could hear my name as if from far away.

I rubbed my forehead with the pads of my fingers. "Worse. A stray that followed me home a very long time ago and won't take divorce for an answer."

"Ah."

Through the restaurant window, Brad crooked his finger at me. His lips formed enthusiastic words. "Come here, Zoey!" He held up a finger and mouthed the words *one minute.*

Completely humiliated, I returned my attention to Riley. His eyebrows had risen in surprise.

"If I don't do something, he'll never go away," I said. "I'll be right back, I swear. I am so sorry."

Riley looked from me to Brad and back again. "Want me to go with you?"

"I appreciate that. But no, he's harmless. A pain in the ass, but harmless. Except maybe to my pride and my bank account." I grabbed my purse and headed out the door, mumbling threats of decapitation and disembowelment.

Brad must have watched me get up, because he was by the door when I came out.

"Zoey, baby! I can't believe how lucky I was to run into you like this."

"You didn't 'run into me,' Brad. You accosted me through a window. Get away from here. You're ruining everything."

He looked genuinely surprised. "You're on a date?"

I rolled my eyes. "I'm in a nice restaurant with a guy. What else did you think was going on?"

His face fell. "I had no idea you were seeing anybody. You could have given me a heads-up."

"Brad, we've been divorced for eight years. I don't owe you any explanations."

"That's cool. I understand."

He was pouting. Brad's blond hair, blue eyes and dimpled cheeks could give any girl wobbly knees. It had worked on me once upon a time. For a brief second, I felt bad. I snapped out of it pretty quick. I was growing less and less susceptible to his manipulations.

"What do you want?"

"I was going to call you. I didn't mean to interrupt. I'll go." He turned to leave, his head hanging like a kicked dog.

I knew he was manipulating me. We'd played out similar scenarios countless times in the past. I always caved, and I could feel it happening again.

I sighed. "Brad."

He stopped and lifted his head. "Yeah?"

"What do you need?"

"It's nothing, Zoey. I'll find somebody else. I know people."

That was a laugh. The people Brad knew couldn't help themselves out of a bathtub, let alone help anyone else.

"I don't have time for this, Brad. Say it or don't. This is your only shot."

He stood still for a moment, staring at the sidewalk. I could tell he was trying to put the words together for one hellacious sales pitch. I glanced through the window and saw Riley watching. "Hurry it up, Brad. My date is getting cold."

"I want to go back to school," he said, the words streaming out in a rush of air. "I can't live like this. I want to be better than I am. I want to be better for you."

"For me?"

He nodded.

"Why would I have anything to do with it?"

"You make me want to be a better person. You make me want more." His eyes slid over me, making me feel uncomfortable and half dressed.

"After everything you've put me through over the years, why would I lift a finger for you now?"

"You always help people, Zo."

That startled me. "Not this time, Brad. I'm done. I'm going in." I swiveled on my fancy zombie heels and headed to the door.

"I'll call you," he said. "When you're not so busy, I'll tell you my plan."

Of course Brad had a plan. It made me tired thinking about all the plans he'd had over the years. "If I see you through that window again, I swear, I will change my number and hire a bodyguard to keep you away."

"I'm going, I'm going. You're not in a receptive mood anyway. We'll talk."

I ignored him. I knew he'd call. And I knew I'd find some way to help him without completely ruining my self-esteem. No matter how irritating he was, no matter how pathetic, I still felt he was somehow my responsibility, at least in some measure. I hadn't been able to fix him, and that was guilt I carried with me.

There was no one at the front of the restaurant. The hostess station was empty. That saved me the embarrassment of looking her in the eye as I slunk in.

As I stepped into the dining area, I could see why no one had been up front. People were clustered around a table by the far wall. A middle-aged man stood by his vacated seat, flapping his arms.

"Someone do something, please!" he said. "Help her!"

I had noticed the man and his wife when they came in. He was short and stocky with thinning blond hair. She was tall and sharp angled, her brown and gray-streaked hair so bushy it devoured her thin face. She was currently flopping on the floor, her mouth gaping like a frog and her lips turning blue.

Servers and patrons alike stood watching, unsure what to do. *Shouldn't someone be giving her the Heimlich or something?*

Even if I were experienced at giving the Heimlich and/or CPR, I couldn't have crossed the room and waded through all those people in time to do a damn thing. As I stood frozen, one of the servers broke free of the herd, reached down and yanked the poor choking woman upright by the armpits.

While his wife was being squeezed repeatedly from behind, the pudgy husband continued waving his arms and marching back and forth, pleading for help which had already come.

It was a shame there wasn't a paramedic present.

I scanned the room for the one person I knew was qualified to handle the situation. Riley sat at our table. He glanced up at the circus across the restaurant, then bent his head over his phone, apparently reading a text message.

*Seriously?*

There was a disgusting gagging sound, and the bird woman coughed up the wad obstructing her airway. The crowd murmured approval, followed by scattered applause. Apparently, the good news didn't reach her husband. He continued to parade between the tables, hollering for help.

I still hadn't budged from my spot, so engrossed was I in both the performance of the players and the lack of performance from my date. I had a perfect view of the entire floor when short-pudgy guy stopped yelling for help on behalf of his perfectly safe wife, and instead turned purple, clutching his chest. He went down so fast it was a few seconds before anyone noticed.

In the same way time had both slowed and sped up when I witnessed the businessman being mowed down by the bus, I saw the choker's husband go down with perfect, helpless clarity. My body was caught in a slow-motion movie reel, my arm coming up to point at the speed of dark.

Someone shouted, and the crowd shifted its obsession with the wife to the husband. He lay sprawled on the floor, unmoving. I heard someone yelling for a 911 call. A patron bent down and hit the man's chest with a fist.

From our table by the window, Riley slid his phone into his pocket, took a sip of his drink and watched.

Time converged and my movements returned to real-time mode. The patron giving CPR was having no success. He kept pumping, though the pudgy man showed no signs of reviving.

Riley checked his watch and took another slow sip. He rose and walked across to the busy mob.

He squatted down and felt for the man's pulse.

"Has anyone called emergency services?" he asked.

"Robert!" The bird-lady was screeching at her husband's prone body. "Get up, Robert! What do you think you're doing? Why is everything always about you?"

Everyone but Riley turned their heads to view the crazy harpy berating her dead husband. I still stood across the room, viewing it in full screen. I saw Riley take that moment, with everyone's attention away from him, to place his ring over poor Robert's mouth.

The previous time I'd seen this, I hadn't been sure. I'd been over-saturated with incoming emotional charges. I'd been clear across the street with crowds of people separating us. This time was different. I had a clear view of the gray, oily substance oozing out between the dead man's lips and into Riley's ring. Riley pulled at first, as if the stuff resisted, but then it flowed out of the man's mouth and into the ring as if it were seeking shelter. It took a few seconds to complete, but it was over before anyone else turned around.

By then, Riley had his hands overlapping each other and pressed against the dead man's breastbone, pushing rhythmically in what I knew was a pantomime of resuscitation.

I was appalled. Riley hadn't tried to save him. For that matter, he hadn't tried to save the wife while she was choking, either. What kind of a monster was I dating?

Sirens were faint in the distance and snapped me into movement. I returned to the table and sat gulping my ice water. I wasn't sure what to do. I wanted to clear out before Riley got back. I wanted to confront him, ask him what the hell he was. I wanted to hide in the bathroom until they closed the restaurant and I could sneak out.

I wanted to call my dad and have him come pick me up.

Indecision often forces the issue. Minutes later,

the ambulance arrived. Scurrying became more fren-
zied as people moved out of the way for the paramedics. They took over for Riley, giving up shortly
thereafter to load Robert onto a stretcher. Robert's
wife was checked and put into a second ambulance.
They were still working when Riley came back to
the table and sat down across from me.

He didn't say anything. He fixed me with his
lovely gray eyes and waited for me to speak.

"You could have saved him." My voice was shaky.
"You didn't try."

"Zoey, it was his time."

"How can you say that? How can you be a paramedic and say something like that? Isn't it your job
to save people?"

He looked a little sad, but his eyes never wavered
from mine. "Sometimes."

"Sometimes? Were you there in time to save Helen?
Was it her time? Who are you to decide? You don't get
to decide whose time it is. You're supposed to save
them." I stood up and banged my empty water glass
on the table. I gritted my teeth and spoke through tight
lips. "Thank you for a lovely evening, but I must be
going now."

"Wait, Zoey. It's a cliché, but really, I can explain."

I bent close to him so he could hear me whisper.
"I saw what you did to him. I've seen it twice. I don't
know what you are, but I have experience with monsters—even ones that appear to be human. Whatever
you stole from that man, I don't want to know. But
know this—I saw you do it." I turned and walked out.

I could hear him protesting behind me, but I was so angry and worked up, I wanted nothing more to do with him. Ever. I didn't care how dreamy he was or how tingly he made me feel. After being tasted by an incubus, I wasn't about to get suckered in by whatever the hell Riley was.

I was so angry I don't remember the drive home. Considering that and the glasses of wine I'd had with dinner, it was a miracle I didn't hurt anyone.

I came through the door to immediate sympathy.

"I am sure it was not as bad as you think," Molly said.

I was curled up on the corner of the couch, eating cookie dough from the mixing bowl. I don't know how Maurice had known to make it for me, but it was in the fridge when I got home.

"Oh, it was as bad, trust me." I shoved a spoonful in my mouth, crushed a macadamia nut between my teeth. "No way can this night be recovered."

Maurice sat across from me and passed a napkin across the coffee table. "Your dress isn't tucked into the back of your hose, and there's no sign of toilet paper on your shoe. Spinach in your teeth? Let's see."

I groaned. "If only it were that easy."

They sat in silence, waiting for me. I let them wait. I had no idea where to begin. Half the bowl of dough was gone before I shoved it away and took a deep breath.

I might as well tell them. From our post-night-mare talks in the kitchen, Molly and Maurice were both well aware of the endless problems with my ex-husband. This one was extra special, though. Even I couldn't believe it, and I'd been there.

"Let's start with Brad."

"Oh, no," Molly said. She leaned down from her perch on the back of the couch and patted my shoulder. "Why did you answer the phone?"

"He didn't call," I said. "He accosted me through the window at the restaurant."

Maurice gasped. "How the hell did he find you?"

"Bad luck, I suppose. I had to go outside and deal with him."

"We have got to do something about that guy."

"Nope. Doesn't matter. I'm going to die alone anyway. Brad wasn't remotely the worst part of the night, as ridiculous as that sounds."

"How could it get worse?" Molly asked.

I told them. I regurgitated the conversation with Brad, which seemed so far in the past it was like another life. I described the scene I found when I went back into the restaurant, from choking wife to heart failure husband.

And I told them about Riley. I told them everything he did, but more importantly, I told them what he didn't do.

When I was finished with my pathetic tale of heartbreak and woe, they weren't looking at me. They were looking at each other.

"What?"

Maurice cleared his throat and ran off into the kitchen with the cookie dough bowl. I could hear him

clanking around in there preparing to bake my left-
overs. I turned to question Molly, and she was gone.

"All right, guys. Not cool. What do you know
that I don't?" There was no reply from anywhere
in the house. Whatever they knew, they wouldn't
share it with me. I unfolded myself from the couch,
prepared to head into the kitchen and grill Maurice
for information.

The doorbell rang.

I reacted the way any normal person would. I went
to answer it. My hand was on the doorknob before
I realized there shouldn't be anyone at my door. No
one should have been able to make it through the security posted outside. Getting as far as the front step
should have been impossible.

I glanced at the doorway to the kitchen and saw
Maurice look out, then duck his head. I shrugged.
If Maurice wasn't worried, I shouldn't be. I turned
the knob and opened the door.

Riley was standing on my doorstep, holding a
bouquet of flowers.

I was stunned for a moment and stood there like
an idiot, my jaw slack.

"Can I come in?" he asked.

I looked out over his shoulder at the darkness behind him. Iris was out in the yard, leaning against
a tree. He shrugged at me and held his furry palms
up, as if to show his inability to stop this particular intruder.

"How the hell did you get in?" I said.

Riley smiled and shoved the flowers in my hands. "Doesn't matter how good your security is. Nobody can stop Death."

# TWENTY-ONE

I COULD FEEL connections in my brain banging against each other, misfiring and refusing to coalesce. Without being conscious of having moved, I stepped aside and let him in.

I needed a moment to pull myself together. Stalling, I dipped my nose into the flowers and inhaled. They were pretty, white and yellow roses with purple sprigs of something dried mixed through. They smelled lovely, but I wasn't paying close attention. They could have smelled like floor wax, and I probably wouldn't have noticed.

I was, however, acutely aware of Riley's fingers on my elbow, guiding me to the couch. Angry as I was, afraid of whatever he might be, the heat and electricity of his touch shot up my arm and warmed my cookie-dough-filled belly.

I felt a little queasy.

He settled me onto the sofa. Maurice appeared out of nowhere with two glasses of lemonade, gave Riley a polite nod, took the flowers and disappeared. He was no help whatsoever—wouldn't even meet my eyes on his way through. Traitor.

"I have to explain, Zoey," Riley said. He took

hold of my arms and pulled me around to face him.
"I know it looked bad."

I focused on a spot on his jaw, a spot he'd missed
while he was shaving. It was probably easy to do. I
did it all the time when I was shaving my legs. Not
tonight, of course. I'd inspected every part of my legs
to make sure, you know, just in case. The bristles on
that tiny spot on his face looked soft and touchable.
*Focus, Zoey.* He was staring at me.

"You're supposed to save people," I said. "It's
what you do."

"No, it's really not. At least not in the way you
think."

Something in my head clicked. I grasped at it.
"Maurice isn't afraid of showing himself to you."

"No."

"You came through the fairy ring."

"Yes."

"Iris didn't stop you."

"No."

It came together in a short, three-word sentence.
"You're not human."

"Not exactly, no."

"What the hell does that mean, 'not exactly'? Either
you are, or you aren't."

"I was. And I will be again. Right now—I'm not."

I dropped my eyes from scrutinizing his jaw to
analyzing the lines on my hands in my lap. I was
afraid to ask. I had to ask, but the potential answer
scared the hell out of me. I took a deep breath, held
it, let it out slowly. "What are you?"

He lifted my chin with his fingertips, forcing me to look him in the eye. "I'm a reaper, Zoey."

I swallowed. "Like the Grim Reaper? Scythe and skull, collecting the souls of the damned?"

He smiled and pulled his fingers away. I missed the feel of them on my skin. That was a bad sign. *Pull it together, Zoey. You are not falling in love with Death. That is not cool.*

"It's not like that."

"No? Then tell me."

"First of all, I wouldn't know which end to hold if somebody handed me a scythe. I get a text message with when and where if I'm the closest reaper to the scene. I can't interfere. I wait, then take the soul if somebody dies and gets stuck."

"Stuck." This was weird, even for my bizarre life.

"Sure. Sometimes when death comes suddenly, a soul is too surprised to leave."

"Like a car accident or a heart attack."

"Or an incubus murder."

I nodded my head, beginning to understand. "Let me see your ring."

He held his hand out for me to examine the clunky metal wrapped around his right-hand ring finger. It was a smooth, silver band with a large, multifaceted garnet. It didn't look like anything special, except for the size of the stone being near the edge of ostentatious. I peered into the gem, hoping to catch a glimpse of something ethereal. It was flawless and dark. I was a little disappointed.

"Why the EMT disguise if you're not there to help? It seems more than a little dishonest."

"I don't spend all day collecting souls, Zoey. Sometimes I do get to help the living. Besides, a guy's gotta eat."

"So being a Grim Reaper's a side job."

"No, it's what I am. And 'reaper' will do. I don't feel very grim, most of the time. I'm a pretty cheerful guy, on the whole."

I thought about the setup for soul collecting. There were a lot of missing parts to the process I didn't understand. I had questions. They tumbled over each other and spilled out in a barrage.

"Who texts you with the assignments? Where do the souls go after you do the sucky thing with your ring? How long have you been doing this? If you were human once, what are you now and how did that happen?"

He laughed. "I can't answer all of that. I have bosses, and the souls I collect are collected from me, that's all I can say. I'm not supposed to be telling you any of this, but I've already broken one major rule when I pulled you away from the demon. What's one more infraction?"

"I was supposed to die that day, wasn't I." I sat up straighter and sucked in my breath. On some level, I knew I was lucky to be alive, but the idea that it had been my time to go and Death had been on standby to pick me up—that was frightening.

"It's never a sure thing, Zoey. I get sent to where there's a likelihood I'll be needed. There are plenty of times I get there and Fate intercedes, or a Good Samaritan pushes my target out of the way of a bus. I'm there in case."

"Handy to have a day job that puts you close to dead bodies, I guess."

"It does help, yes."

I understood that he couldn't tell me everything. It's the afterlife. Knowing what comes next is a universal quest for humans. Nobody gets to know until they get there—at least not for normal people like me. Normal. That was sort of comforting. With everything that had been happening around me, this put me in league with the average Joe on the street. *Welcome back, Zoey. How's it feel to be like everybody else again?*

There was still one thing I had to know. I felt like it was my right, considering he seemed to be set on pursuing me.

"How did this happen? You said you used to be human."

His eyes went dark and he looked away, focused on something far off. "I was recruited, you might say."

I reached out and cradled his hand. "Doesn't sound like it was at a job fair."

He shook his head. "No. It was at a hospital. There was an accident. A train derailed after a bunch of kids drove around the crossing gate at the last minute. A lot of people died. A lot. My mother and sister were on that train."

My chest tightened, and I could feel his sorrow

throbbing up my arm, dull like an old toothache. "I'm so sorry. You don't have to talk about this if you don't want to."

He squeezed my hand. "It's okay. My mom died instantly, but my little sister hung in there. The hospital was packed with injured people from the accident. They didn't have room for them all. They did what they could for Izzy and parked her in the hallway with some of the other patients. She looked so tiny with all those tubes in her. She was only fourteen." He stopped and closed his eyes for a moment before he could continue. "I was sitting with her, watching all the activity around us, holding her hand, and hoping she'd wake up. Three men came down the hall toward me. They stopped from time to time over the patients in the worst shape. Nobody else noticed the men. I saw them taking souls. I didn't know at the time exactly what they were doing, but I knew it wasn't good for Izzy if they came to her."

"Did they?"

He nodded. "Yeah. They tried." His smile was weak. "I punched one of them."

I smiled back at him. "Good for you."

"They tried to convince me to let them take her, that it was a mercy."

"I thought you guys only took people who were already dead? Izzy wasn't dead, right?"

"No, she wasn't. But sometimes, we take the souls before death. Sometimes it's kinder than letting someone suffer."

I stifled my shudder. No wonder my Hidden family feared him. He could take any one of us on a whim. If his eyes had been a little less compelling and his smell had been a little less intoxicating, I might've reconsidered dating His Grim Hotness. Who was I kidding? I was already too far gone.

My voice was as gentle as I could make it. "Did they take her?"

He shook his head. "Nope. I won that fight, three against one. But not without a price. They brought in a healer, a necrofoil with the power to heal people near death—enough power to get people out of danger, anyway. In exchange, here I am. I'm on their payroll, so to speak, until I've paid off my debt." Sadness flickered across his face. "They didn't specify how long that would be, but the board reviews me every so often."

I frowned and eyed him with suspicion. "How old are you, really?" It would be just my luck to have a three-hundred-year-old Grim Reaper trying to date me. He looked to be around my age, maybe a little older. But there was a deep-seated ickiness to dating somebody who, regardless of appearances, could be my great-great-great-grandfather. If the words *pilgrim, Civil War* or *pioneer* came out of his mouth, I was done. Thank you, have a nice evening, your secret is safe with me, there's the door. I didn't care how dreamy he smelled.

He took my hand from my lap and squeezed it, smiling. "In human years, I am thirty-two. In dog years, I think that's, what? About six?"

I fixed him with my angry schoolmarm look for

evading the question and making fun of me. "And in reaper years?"

He rolled his eyes up to the ceiling, appearing to think about it. "Let's see, if you subtract my upcoming birthday, since it's not here yet, add the years I've been alive, take away the life sucked out of me by this long conversation, that would make me…"

*Here it comes. 287, I just know it.*

"Thirty-two," he finished. "Yes, that sounds right. Thirty-two."

I tried to recover my dignity. His lips twitched a little with suppressed laughter. "That's pretty old," I said. "Ever so much older than I am." I looked away at the abstract painting above my mantel. My attempt to appear nonchalant didn't impress him in the slightest.

"True. At least a good year or two on you."

My eyes flashed to his face. "Hey, I'm only twenty-eight!"

He grinned at me. "I know. I looked up your DMV records."

I made a face. "I look awful in that picture."

He shrugged. "They have special filters on the cameras to make everyone look their worst. It's the law."

"Stalker."

"I had to get your address. You wouldn't talk to me."

"Can you blame me?"

"I suppose not. At least I didn't have any ex-wives banging on the window."

I palmed my face with the hand he wasn't holding. "I am so humiliated."

R.L. NAQUIN 267

"I figure it makes us even. We'll start fresh next time and have a second first date. Deal?"

"I think I can do that." I could feel my face getting hot. Maybe the worst date ever wasn't turning out so bad after all.

"Good. Now I have some questions for you."

"Oh? Like what?"

"For instance, was that a closet monster serving us lemonade?"

WE TALKED FOR hours. Once I explained what had been going on with me, he was a little offended by my reaction to his oddness.

"You have to understand," I said, "up until a few weeks ago, déjà vu was about the most supernatural thing I'd ever experienced. I may look like I'm taking it all in stride, but inside I'm patting myself on the head and expecting a doctor to bring me meds. I can either drown in the unbelievable, or swan-dive into it."

It was a little after one a.m. when I walked him out to his car. Through a stand of trees off to the side, Iris's face poked out through the leaves. He winked at me and withdrew. Riley looked startled.

"No wonder you didn't want me to pick you up," he said.

I gave him a wry grin. "Takes a special guy to see past a girl's skunk-ape, especially on the first date."

"Takes a special girl to fight with Death and win."

"Did I win, then?" My stomach fluttered. He'd taken a step closer and was staring at me in that indecisive way guys have while they decide whether to kiss you or bolt.

"I think we both win. Let's call it a draw."

"Seems fair."

His eyes flicked to the brush where Iris had disappeared, then at the house. He took a step back. I tried not to look disappointed. He pulled his keys from his pocket and unlocked his car.

*Do it, Zoey. For once in your life, take what you want instead of backing down and waiting. Two steps. Kiss him.* I ignored my inner voice. If he didn't want to kiss me, I sure as hell wasn't going to beg for it.

"Thanks for, you know, explaining everything," I said. It came out stuttered and weak. "And for the flowers. They were really pretty."

He covered the two steps to me in one long stride. It happened so fast, I had no time to react. He stooped, kissed me on the cheek, and was back to his car door.

"Thank you for letting me in," he said, sliding into his seat. "I'll call you, and we'll try it again, if that's all right."

My cheek was hot where his lips had burned their imprint on my skin. I wanted to touch my face, to see if it was as hot as I imagined it to be, but I kept my arm down. "Sure. No ex-husband stalkers and no dead bodies."

He waved at me out his window, and pulled out of the driveway.

After his taillights disappeared, I turned and

sprinted up the porch steps—not an easy trick in three-and-a-half-inch heels. I blew through the door and hugged a wide-eyed Maurice.

"I think that went very well," I said, once I caught my breath.

Maurice was less enthusiastic. "I can't believe you're still going to see him."

My giddy high was instantly slapped down. "Why wouldn't I see him?"

"Because he's a *reaper*."

"So? He explained it. It's a job."

"He's a reaper, Zoey. He collects souls. He's the guy monster moms threaten their kids with to get them to stay under the bed at night."

"For a supernatural creature, you sure are superstitious."

He took a deep breath, held it, then let it out in a long whoosh. "If I'd known what he was, I wouldn't have let you out in the first place. I guess it's too late now." He ran his hand over the sparse hair on his head, making it stand up. "I'm sorry. You're right. I want you to be happy. Maybe having a reaper around where I can't protect you will keep you safer. I don't know."

"If I can adjust to my greatest childhood fear becoming my friend, maybe you can look past your worst nightmare being a nice guy?"

He grimaced. "Point taken."

"Should I assume Molly has the same problem? You both cleared out of here pretty fast."

"Reapers are scary dudes."

What the hell did I get myself into? All around me were some of the scariest creatures in urban legends, horror stories and fairy tales. And this sweet, unbelievably gorgeous guy I met out in the real world was the thing that kept *them* up at night.

My life kept getting weirder and weirder.

# TWENTY-TWO

ONCE I WOUND down enough to go to bed, I crashed into the pillow and was out like a coma patient. One second I was thinking of Riley's smile, the next I was gone. When I opened my eyes again, the sun was up and I could smell coffee.

My little family ate pancakes with me at the table, but refused to meet my eyes whenever I said anything about Riley. I was sure they'd get accustomed to him. For now, I was content to have them surrounding me, being supportive, if still wary.

With a full belly, I prepared to spend the rest of the day poring through some of my mother's books and practicing some of what I'd learned. I had a dim idea for dealing with Sebastian, but there were snags to work out.

The situation was a catch-22—I had to take my shields down to pummel Sebastian with an overload of energy that would, theoretically, send him back where he came from. But I couldn't get near him without my walls well fortified. There had to be a way around the problem. On top of that, I needed to avoid physical contact with him at all costs.

After hours of digging in dusty books, all I had to show for it was a crick in my neck, dusty fingers and an in-depth knowledge of third-tier scat demons. I had no intention of knowing anything about something so disgusting. There's no need to discuss it here. It's enough to say they're not at all pretty.

I spent some time on the beach practicing focus techniques, getting nowhere. I could easily build up my walls, tear them down and create windows. But now I needed someone to center on. I had new things to learn, and I wasn't going to learn them sitting on a rock by myself.

I looked over my shoulder. Iris was lurking at the tree line, watching. I had Maurice and the brownies at home. I had fairies.

What I needed was humans.

I drove to a park in Muir Beach and found a comfortable spot at a picnic table. I avoided Sausalito. There was no way I was ready for a face-off with Sebastian yet. The likelihood of being rescued a second time by a reaper who was scheduled to take my soul was slim.

People milled around in the grass, reading books, eating, talking. One or two flew kites, a few tossed a Frisbee back and forth. Kids climbed and swung in a play area, and moms chatted with each other, one eye on their little ones.

I focused my attention on a guy kicking a Hacky Sack. I watched it bounce and spin, landing on the top or the side of his foot. He was good. He was so focused on what he was doing, he didn't notice me scrutinizing him.

I opened the shutter over my thin, mental win-

dow and willed in only what he was feeling. It wasn't
easy. I had to block out the ruthless gossip of the
mothers, the exuberance of the kids and the love ra-
diating off a couple having a picnic. The minute my
window was open, their emotions came floating toward me as if I were a magnet.

I pushed out everything else and focused on
Hacky Sack guy. I pictured a beam of light connecting us, thin and tight.

The world narrowed. There was nothing but me
and the athletic guy tossing a bean bag on his foot.

I couldn't hear his thoughts, of course. I didn't
know if anyone could do that, but I certainly couldn't.
Still, I could feel him. He was worried about something. The random patterns of the sack pounding
against his foot were soothing to him. There was
guilt, too. Whatever he was worried about, he felt
like it was his fault.

I wasn't overwhelmed by what I was receiving. It
was hard for me to tell whether that was because he
wasn't feeling it intensely, or whether I was somehow learning to tamp it down into more manage-
able doses.

I turned off my emotional laser beam and let him
go. There were others around me to try, and I picked
one at random. A young mother by the play area
drew my attention.

She stood up from her park bench gossiping and
marched over to her son. Her outfit captured my interest almost as much as the odd emotions she was
giving off.

I like my comfy sweats. They're thick cotton in subdued shades of blue or gray. I lounge around the house in them. I wear them for working out or hanging out at the beach when it's a little chilly. I was almost jealous of this woman. I was quirky, but she had balls. I would never have the guts to wear a lime-green velour track suit. Kudos to her.

"Joshua! Get down from there!" She barreled down on some kid in a bulky cardigan. He stood at the top of the handrail above the slide. "You're going to fall and break your neck! I am sick and tired of telling you over and over. Get down now!"

To my surprise, Joshua laughed and climbed higher.

I focused on the waddling, irate mother. Nothing else existed for me but her. I let her in full force. *Irritation.* For all her blustering and yelling, all I could get from her was a mild annoyance tinged with a bit of dislike.

Joshua stood tall on the top of the jungle gym handrail and let out a raucous belch. He turned his back on his mother, waggled his butt, made a heart-stopping leap and slid down the slide, laughing.

Truth be told, I didn't much care for Joshua either. *Embarrassment.*

Well, that was no surprise. I'd be embarrassed too if he were my kid. I didn't much blame track-suit lady for being less than fond of her own son. He was a little shit.

She turned in resignation and waddled to her seat on the bench. Her emotions petered out and weren't worth following anymore. I had a feeling her life was difficult and she hid inside herself. I think maybe she didn't feel much of anything anymore.

The couple in the grass was making out. The idea of opening myself to that felt like voyeurism. I'd had enough of feeling other people's sexual urges, thank you very much. My skin crawled when I thought about it.

I scanned the crowd. A young girl was sitting by herself on a swing, scooching her feet in the tanbark, kicking up dirt. She seemed preoccupied and a little sad. I liked this. It was like a game I was playing with myself. Body language alone was hard for me to read, since I'd gone my whole life not depending on it like everyone else. I focused on her.

The beam was easier to create the third time. I fine-tuned it and surrounded her with it. I blocked out everything around me and reached for her.

*Sorrow.*

*Fear.*

*Loneliness.*

I had underestimated what her body language was saying by a mile. Unfortunately, all I could determine was something terrible had happened to this girl. Maybe someone had died or her parents were getting divorced. There was no way to tell what the cause was without asking her directly. For all my gifts, I was almost as clueless as the rest of world. I wanted to put my arms around her and tell her whatever it was would be all right.

This is what I'd come for. This was what I needed to learn.

I reversed the flow of emotion, concentrating on comfort, love and contentment. It trickled into her, pushing away the negative emotions and giving her something more positive in its place. I shared what I could with her, taking away a little of the hurt.

She straightened in the swing, and while she didn't exactly smile, her lips turned up a touch at the edges, and her eyes lost some of their dullness. She stopped scraping her feet in small patterns in the bark, stepped back and lifted her legs. The swing moved forward and back in a gentle motion, the girl's hair ruffling in the breeze.

Sometimes we all need a hug and a heart full of lies, even if the relief won't last.

MONDAY WAS THE first day of Hell Week. Alma Dickson called three times with changes to the music program, and Gail called twice crying about a lack of RSVPs and then changing the music program back to the original list.

The agency we used for extra help called to tell us they only had two girls to send us to help out on Saturday. Charlie, who usually took care of deliveries, slipped a disc and was stuck in bed for the duration.

Through it all, Sebastian's parting words hung over me like a cloud of dread. This wedding was important—it could make or break our business. I had to be there. And even if I could quit and remove myself from the proceedings, Sebastian might still show up. I couldn't bear the thought of him taking a single life more than he already had. How many bridesmaids, mothers and guests might fall victim? Two? Five? More? It could be a massacre.

I didn't know if I had the strength to defeat him, but I was the only one who could try.

Sara ran her hand through her hair leaving it in uncharacteristic disarray. "This one's huge. We'll need everybody we can call in to help." She stopped pacing and narrowed her eyes at me. "Probably wouldn't be a bad idea to call in Brad, you know."

I groaned and palmed my face. "Wonderful."

"Hey, I'm just saying we could use the help for coordinating and deliveries."

"He's pretty high on my shit list right now, but if we need him, we need him."

"Something new or same old Brad stuff?"

"He barged into the middle of my date Friday night."

Sara banged her cup on her desk, and coffee slopped over the side. "A date? Why am I only hearing this now? Tell me."

I felt guilty. I used to tell Sara everything. She'd been so tired, and we'd been so busy. I hadn't wanted to bother her. That wasn't really it though, and I knew it. Recently, my near-loner life had acquired a complete set of new family members—and then some. And nothing about any of them was something I could openly share with my reality-based best friend.

But that wasn't a good excuse. I couldn't tell her about closet monsters and grim reapers, but I sure as hell should have mentioned a date with the gorgeous paramedic I'd babbled about two weeks before.

I was a horrible friend.

I gave her the rundown on what she had missed, minus monsters, soul collecting and magical security systems. It made my week sound almost quiet.

"He sounds really sweet. I'm happy for you," she said, blowing on her coffee. She did sound happy, but not as excited and gossipy as she usually was when we talked about guys.

"Well, we'll see where it goes. We're from two different worlds. It was only a first date." Two different worlds was an understatement.

"Sure. Paramedics and wedding planners. It could never work out." Sara's eyes were cloudy and distant, as if she'd already lost interest. I resisted the urge to feel her forehead again. It was a nice gesture, but it wasn't telling me anything useful.

"Maybe you should see a doctor," I said.

She frowned. "So he can take my temperature and tell me to get some rest? In case you haven't noticed, there's no place in the schedule this week to pencil it in. Besides, it's just exhaustion. Let's get through this week. Once Councilwoman Bitchmistress is out of our lives, I'll sleep like a baby and be good as new."

I was doubtful, but I couldn't force her to go. She was probably right. I wasn't feeling too perky myself. One more week and we could relax.

I put off the phone call to Brad as long as I could, but there was no way around it. I was going to have to call him.

For once, he was mercifully cooperative. This, of course, put me on edge. It meant he was coming in for the sales pitch.

"Of course I'll help you out, Zoeygirl. You know me. I'm Mr. Reliable in a pinch."

Sure he was. "Seriously, Brad, if you can't make it, please say so now. I'm up to my armpits in problems, and I really need you not to be one of them."

"I'll be there, baby. Don't you worry. Put me to work. I want to show you how useful I can be."

That didn't sound good. I was going to owe him for this. "Thanks, Brad. You've got the address? Eleven a.m. Please don't forget. I need you on time."

"Of course. Don't worry. And maybe afterwards, we can go out for dinner or something?"

"Probably not, but thanks." Crap. That's what I needed. A date with my ex-husband.

"Sure, sure. Some other time. Soon though, okay? I want to run some ideas past you, see what you think."

I stifled a groan. There it was. The pitch. At least he was being considerate enough to give me a rain check. "When all this is over, we'll talk."

"Okay, doll. I'm looking forward to it."

All in all, the phone call had been painless. Despite the fact I'd be paying Brad for his time, it still came under the heading of "doing Zoey a favor." I knew he'd collect on it eventually.

With the two temps I had lined up, Adrianne and Frankie, I had one errand boy and two assistants. A little more manpower would have been nice, but it would do.

Sara left around four-thirty, promising to go straight to bed. I was wrapping up to go home when the phone rang. I was both delighted and relieved to see it was Andrew—one more crisis might have done me in. Andrew was a much-needed reprieve.

"How's our favorite supernatural rock star?" I could feel some of the tension in me dissipating at the sound of his voice.

It's good to have friends you don't have to keep secrets from. That used to be Sara. The strain of keeping things from her was wearing on me.

"Oh, I'm good. The world is falling down around my ears and I'm likely to be killed anytime I go outside, but I'm coping."

"I have just the thing, my darling. I whipped up a batch of bath salts guaranteed to banish the most trying of mystical problems."

"Do they smell like Christmas sweat socks?"

"Absolutely not. Christmas is not in the least bit relaxing."

"True that. I was on my way out the door. Are you at the shop?"

"I am, but don't you dare walk over here alone. Can't have you running into any hungry demons. Milo needs to stretch his legs anyway, and I could use a little exercise to work off those muffins you brought last week. We'll be over in five minutes."

He hung up without saying goodbye. Andrew was cool that way.

True to his word, it was under five minutes before the boys came through the door. "Ready to go?" he asked. He looked around. "Hey, this is nice. Very swank. If I ever get married, I'll hang out here in luxury while you do all the work."

"You wouldn't do that if it were a dump?"

"Sure, but I wouldn't enjoy it as much. You should get a cappuccino machine. That would up the swank-level."

"I'll take it into consideration."

I locked up, and we walked down the street to his shop in a cloud of companionable chatter. I told him about my date with Riley, including the big reveal about his true nature. I knew it was probably against the rules to divulge reaper secrets, but screw that. I had to keep everything from Sara, and she was in mortal danger. With Andrew, I didn't have to hold anything back. If it was a supernatural faux pas, shoot me. I had enough problems.

The bath salts smelled more like vanilla and gardenias than sweat socks, for which I was grateful. Andrew tried to give them to me, but I insisted on paying.

"You already gave me miracle tea," I said. "If I start coming in here and taking everything I need, I'll run you out of business."

I told him everything—the dreams, Spider's death, the confrontation with Sebastian under the dock, Riley's heroic rescue. I told him about training in the park, and I told him about my ideas on how to take out an incubus. By the time I finished going over everything, I was drained, but feeling less alone.

"Hell of a week," he said.

Milo licked my hand in commiseration.

"Can you, you know, check me?" I said.

It was a weird question, but Andrew understood and became still and quiet. After a few minutes, he nodded his head.

"The cord's gone," he said. "You severed it. There's a small, blackened knot where it used to be, but you're good."

"Do auras get scars?"

"Sometimes, they do, but I wouldn't worry about this. When you do your housecleaning, send some healing juice to it for a while. I bet it drops off like an umbilical cord."

"That's gross. Kind of gives me the willies thinking I'm trailing it."

He shrugged. "It's better than having him trace you and your relationships all over town."

I dropped my hands in my lap and stared at them. "So, I'm free of him. I don't feel any better, though. Nearly every woman in town is now tagged because of me." I rubbed my tired eyes with my fingertips. "He won't stop killing until he leaves."

Andrew put his arm around me and squeezed my shoulders. "It's not your fault, Zoey. We'll figure something out."

"If he shows up at the wedding, it may be my only shot to do something. I have to try. No more deaths, Andrew. I can't let him kill anyone else." I paused, pulling together the courage to say what I couldn't tell anyone else. "You know, if I die, I think he has to go back."

Andrew narrowed his eyes. "Let's try other avenues before we jump to self-sacrifice, shall we?" He patted the little fox's head. "What time do we need to be there on Saturday?"

"What?"

"I clean up pretty nice. I can shut down the shop for the day and come help."

"I couldn't ask you to do that."

"You're not asking, I'm insisting. I'll come as backup manpower, but mostly I can't let you go into battle alone."

Relief spread from my scalp down to my toes. I didn't realize how frightened I was. And how alone. And Andrew was a man, so I wasn't putting him in danger.

"I'm not sure how I managed to survive all these years without you."

"You kept out of trouble, that's how. Now that you've stepped in it, it's taking an entire team to keep an eye on you. Milo's not going to be very happy stuck at home without you, though."

Milo yipped in agreement and I rubbed his ears. "Let's hope trouble goes away after this weekend. I'd kind of like my life to get back to normal."

"Honey, I don't know what you think normal is, but I doubt you'll ever see it again."

# TWENTY-THREE

TUESDAY, ALMA DEMANDED two additional tables be set up at the reception for last-minute guests. This required calls to the florist, the caterers, the venue and the company providing the linens. They were out of the silver pattern the Dicksons had chosen, so we'd have to go with a similar pattern and keep our fingers crossed the old biddy wouldn't notice.

Sara was holding up pretty well, though there were smudges under her eyes like faint bruises.

"Are you sleeping at all?" I asked, setting a third cup of coffee in front of her.

She yawned, not bothering to cover her mouth. "I'm sleeping. I started taking something to help. Puts me right out. It's not very restful though. I get up in the morning feeling like a slug, and I find clothes strewn around and dishes in the sink. Apparently, I've started sleepwalking."

I frowned. "Honey, that sounds dangerous. Do you want me to come over for a few nights? Keep an eye on you?"

She waved her hand at me, dismissing the idea. "I'll live. Give me through the weekend and I'll be back to normal. Don't worry so much. We have enough problems."

She wasn't wrong about that.

Wednesday, two of Gail's bridesmaids, having reached their limits with the fragile, over-sensitive bride and the pushy, demanding mother, quit the bridal party.

No amount of begging, cajoling or bargaining could get them to change their minds. But I don't give up so easily, and I was going to make this wedding a success if it killed me.

I picked up Erin and Samantha and took them out to lunch. Sara stayed behind to put out other fires. The girls were wary, at first, but I said I wouldn't force them into anything. I wanted to talk, nothing more.

We ate burgers and fries, and they both looked like they were in heaven. Their eyelids fluttered with each bite. Grievance number one: Mama Dickson had everyone on strict diets so they'd be prettier for the wedding.

I let them vent. Lord knows, I could have participated. I had a list of grievances of my own a mile long. But that would hardly be professional, and it wouldn't help my cause in the slightest.

"She showed up at my house with a tape measure last night," Samantha said. She slurped her chocolate shake. "It was humiliating."

Erin popped a fry in her mouth and licked the salt from her fingers. "She told me my hair was too blond. She tried to make me dye it darker so I wouldn't outshine her precious flower."

I wanted to laugh. Instead, I nodded my head in

sympathy. "Weddings are stressful," I said. "For everyone involved. Not everybody understands that."

They groused. They gorged. And I listened. Their frustration took up more room on the table than the steaming plates of food. It weighed heavy between them, pulling me into their circle. Their anger buzzed in my ears like dragonflies trapped in a gourd.

I inhaled and thought of the people I loved. Sara. Maurice. Andrew. My father. I let the calm and comfort wash over me, then sent it toward the girls down a tight beam of light.

Their conversation was instantly less hostile, less hurt. It turned to Gail and things they loved about her. The things that made them friends.

"When Jeremy cheated on me, she keyed his car," Erin said. "Did I ever tell you about that?"

Samantha laughed. "No, but I can believe it. I once got a D on a test in Mr. Gardener's algebra class back in high school. That was when I was really sick and we found out later it was mono. She harassed him for a week until he let me retake the test."

I kept the positive feelings flowing, letting them talk it out. Was it a skeevy thing to do? I was using my gift to manipulate people into feeling what I wanted them to feel, so they'd do what I wanted them to do. Yeah. It felt skeevy. But not enough to stop.

By the time they'd finished their brownie sundaes, there wasn't a chance in hell they would desert their friend.

Another crisis averted.

Thursday was Gail's final fitting, and she called

in a panic because her veil was the wrong shade of tulle. I calmed her over the phone while the consultant went in the back to check on it. Somehow they'd switched veils with someone else's dress. Gail's dress was perfect and so was the veil.

Through the whole wretched week of harassment and emergencies, I watched Sara grow slower and more exhausted. While I was dealing with vendors and wayward bridesmaids, she was spending most of her time dealing with Mrs. Dickson.

The rest of my attention was spent worrying about Sebastian.

I scoured the papers every night. There were no unexplained deaths. I worried that someone would die at any minute. I worried that someone had died and I didn't know about it.

I worried that Sebastian was so quiet.

Friday, I couldn't take not knowing anymore. I was jumping at shadows, and I was so filled with dread that tomorrow's wedding would become a feeding frenzy that I steeled my resolve, quelled my feelings of foolishness and impending doom, and walked down to the dock to face him.

I knew it was a stupid risk to take. But Sara could handle things without me now. I was prepared to die if it came to that. I'd learned to reverse the emotional flow. If nothing else, maybe I could debilitate him.

My thoughts were dark and my feet fell heavy on the rocks as I clambered down to his lair. Goose bumps covered my bare arms in the breeze.

I stood peering into the blackness for some time,

allowing my eyes to adjust. Every shadow could be him, hunkered down in wait. I shivered. I was alone. The place was deserted. The tides had washed away every sign of him, including his cloying scent. He hadn't been there for a while.

My amulet lay warm against my skin. This was no longer a place of danger. I had no way to find him. I had to wait for him to come to me.

IN THEATER, THEY say "Bad dress rehearsal, good performance." I hoped the same was true for weddings, because the rehearsal Friday night definitely came under the heading of "Bad."

For starters, the minister failed to show. Not a huge problem. These things happened sometimes. A bigger problem was the absence of one of the five bridesmaids and two of the groomsmen.

A wedding rehearsal should be a quick procedure from start to finish. We group everybody with their escorts, run through the processional and recessional once or twice, they all go off to dinner, and Sara and I go home. An hour, tops.

Sara needed to be on top of things with me the next day, so I'd talked her into letting me handle things. No problem.

The minute I walked through the door, Councilwoman Mama accosted me. She put her beaked nose and shrewish face as close to mine as she could get it without smearing her makeup. I liked my personal space to remain personal. I didn't care for people breathing my air. I took a step back, knowing while I did it that she would count it as a personal victory of domination.

She puffed up her scrawny, ruffle-enhanced bosom like an African bird in mating season. "Why isn't Reverend Conrad here? I specifically asked you to be sure he was here for this. I won't have this ruined because of your inept management."

She tried to poke me with a taloned finger, but I moved too fast. I smiled in my most professional, plastered-on expression. "Have a seat, Mrs. Dickson. I'm sure he's just delayed. I'll take care of it, and we'll get started."

I handed her off to her husband, a mousy man with a down-trodden look to him. I couldn't imagine what it would be like married to that woman, but he took her arm and led her away.

Samantha and Erin helped me track down the missing party members while I called the minister. His presence wasn't strictly necessary for the rehearsal, but he was kind of a central figure in the actual ceremony. I couldn't take a chance that he wouldn't show for final curtain on Saturday.

When I reached him, Reverend Conrad told me he would most certainly be there on time the next day. He apologized for missing the rehearsal, but he'd had an emergency to attend to.

"Sometimes," he said, "God calls me to less joyful events."

With that cryptic line, he hung up.

A half hour later, the missing party members walked in, having started the festivities early.

They burst through the door, laughing, weaving and slurring.

I might have reprimanded them, or at least pulled them in line, but Alma Dickson got there first.

She scurried over in a flurry of polyester, her tightly curled gray hair poking out around her head. She fixed them with her steely eyes and they froze.

"This is unacceptable behavior," she said. Her lips were squeezed so tight I thought they might meld together that way. We should be so lucky. "You were given your schedules and were expected to be here on time. I will not have this. Get over there so we can get started. You've wasted everyone's time with your lack of consideration." She waggled a talon and herded them into the crowd.

For a brief moment, I admired her.

I paired off the attendants and showed them where to stand at the front of the church. Gail was more quiet than usual, with none of her usual hysterics, though she had the look of a bunny ready to bolt into a hedge at the slightest provocation. Her fiancé wasn't taking the proceedings at all seriously, and loped beside her like a clumsy baby giraffe with a learning disability.

They practiced the recessional. It went well until Aidan tripped on his own flip-flop and went sprawling, which caused the best man behind him to stumble and take the maid of honor down with him.

I despise flip-flops. Outside of the pool or the beach, they're tacky. I squelched the urge to yank one off his foot and beat him about the head and shoulders with it.

Instead, I made them practice the recessional again.

Half the group was talking and missed their cues. They did it again.

The fourth time was the charm, and they all made it up the aisle with flawless grace and timing.

"Now," I said, "we reverse the process. Everybody line up in the foyer so we can practice the processional. Groomsmen first, then Aidan. Gail, you'll be last with your parents on either side to give you away."

The groomsmen groaned and looked at each other.

The best man stepped forward. "It's the same thing, only the other way, right? Can't we just call it good? We're starving."

I looked at the clock on my cell phone. We were already almost an hour over schedule, and they had reservations. I opened my mouth and stopped. My amulet burned ice cold against my chest.

*He's here. Do something, Zoey. Do something to stop him.*

"Five-minute break, then we'll do one quick run up the aisle. I'll be right back."

I ran out the front door into the darkness. I had no plan.

Lanterns lit the garden surrounding the chapel. I saw no one moving in the shadows, and Sebastian didn't step out in the light. In fact, my amulet felt warm again. The chill might have been my imagination.

*Paranoia. Very professional.*

I went back and sent the bridal party up the aisle. They performed admirably, and I had a suspicion that Mama Dickson had yelled at them while I was gone. When I gave them the okay to leave, it was a stampede to the exit.

When they were all gone, I gave the chapel a final inspection for loose papers, forgotten purses or beer bottles that might have been smuggled in. It was all clear and ready for the next day.

I flipped off the light and walked along the paving stones toward my car. My amulet cooled, though not to the same sub-zero temperature as before. I touched it with my fingertips and turned back to look at the chapel.

Sebastian sat cross-legged on the roof beneath the steeple.

Moonlight glinted off the white of his grin. He waved, then scurried over the roof and disappeared.

# TWENTY-FOUR

SATURDAY WAS A traditional Bay Area overcast, which did not bode well for an outdoor reception. They were holding the whole thing at a gorgeous, restored Colonial Revival complex overlooking the Bay. The wedding would be inside the chapel where we'd rehearsed, then move outside to the gardens for the reception.

The venue offered everything a bride could want—catering, setup, linens, crystal. However, Alma Dickson had declined all the in-house services and preferred to have us use outside vendors instead. Financially good for us, but a logistical nightmare, since the location coordinator did not approve of our meddling and made it clear we were on our own.

I arrived an hour earlier than I was expected, and this put a wild hair up her ass from the start.

She pursed her lips and gave me a once-over. At the end of her perusal, I wasn't sure if my nose was on backward or if she disapproved of my eye color.

She sniffed. "I suppose we can accommodate you with a space to work for the time being. In the future, please be aware of appointment times. Yours may not be the only event planned for the day, and we must give priority to those who retain their given schedule."

Bitch. I knew damn well they never scheduled more than one event in an entire weekend. What a load of crap. "Thank you, Margaret. I appreciate your assistance." I ducked my head and followed her. *Play nice, Zo. Let's get through this day with our reputation and our temper intact.*

She dropped me in a corner of the delivery area in back. I don't know if she meant it as a slight, but it was exactly where I needed to be. It was a good thing I was early. Vendors started showing up about a half hour later.

There was a minor difficulty with the cake when it arrived. Somehow, they'd managed to leave the top tier at the bakery. I sent them scurrying home to retrieve it, while I paced. This is what happens when a client doesn't use my vendors. Moira never would have made a mistake like that. If I hadn't stood over them and made them assemble the cake right then, we might not have known in time.

Of course, screw-ups like that look bad for the coordinator. Brides and their tyrannical mothers don't care who made the mistake. It was me they paid to catch it.

Right on time, Brad sauntered in, with Adrianne and Frankie giggling on his arms. I rolled my eyes. Now there was a problem I hadn't considered. Brad the Charmer needed to stay away from my temps, or nobody was going to get any work done.

I set the three of them to work on table settings. Boxes of linens, crystal, flowers and place settings were piled up in the delivery area. Much of it had arrived in the days previous, but some had to wait till the last minute. According to my super-functional dinosaur of a clipboard, everything was present and accounted for.

With the setup underway, I went in search of the bride. Knowing her, she was probably either throwing up or breathing into a paper bag.

On the way to Gail's room, I shot off a text to Sara. She should have been there already and I was getting nervous.

Sara may not have been in her pre-arranged spot, but Gail was right where I expected. Five bridesmaids flittered around her, all in different stages of undress. Mrs. Dickson was uncharacteristically quiet, hovering in front of a mirror with her cheeks sucked in, trying to apply fake eyelashes to her already over-made-up face.

Gail was in sweatpants, her hair pinned and hanging in ringlets. She was sitting on the edge of a bed, professionally painted eyes getting ready to overflow with tears. When she saw me walk through the door, she blinked and the first tears plopped in her lap.

"Zoey, it's ruined. I can't do this." Someone handed her a tissue and she blotted at her face with a dainty motion.

"Everything's perfect, Gail. We're setting up for the reception as we speak. Everything is exactly what you wanted." I knelt down next to her and dabbed at a wet cheek. "Tell me what's wrong so I can fix it."

"Everything's wrong!" I swear, her voice sounded like a moaning banshee. If I hadn't known she was an accountant, I'd have pegged her for a B-movie actress. "I haven't seen or heard from Aidan since he went off to his bachelor party last night. I don't know where he is. Karen's dress has a rip in it. Tammy's got a run in her hose with no spares, and look at this!"

She shoved a monogrammed, lavender hand towel into my hand. I didn't understand what she wanted me to see, at first. The towel was clean. Then I noticed the monograms: AsS & GaS. The letters were in gold and quite elegant.

"What are your middle names?" I asked, trying not to smirk.

"Stephen and Alison. My Aunt Charlotte had these made for us. We're Ass and Gas!"

There was absolutely nothing I could say to fix this one. The best I could do was not laugh. "Honey, this is a problem for another day. Let's focus on today, okay?"

She nodded and reached for the offensive hand towel, rubbing at the letters with her fingers.

As part of our on-site coordination, I carried a large leather satchel filled with every imaginable damage-control item. I reached into my bag of tricks and took control of the room.

"Tammy. Where's Tammy?" The girls were milling around, paying little attention. Wedding-planner-voice kicked in. "Ladies, I need your attention. Where's Tammy?"

A mousy girl with dirty-blond hair stepped forward in her bra and pantyhose. "Me. That's me."

"Where's the run?"

She pointed to a spot mid-thigh where a small nick in the threads was running upward. Good. Not a bad spot. The dresses were at knee level. If we acted quickly, no one need know.

I pulled out my bottle of clear nail polish and dabbed it around the run. "Don't touch it until it's dry," I said. "Otherwise, it'll keep growing." I capped the polish and dropped it in the bag. "Now. Where's Karen?"

It always amazed me when people didn't bring essential emergency items to a wedding—especially when the party was as big as this one. I found it hard to believe nobody had thought to bring spare hose, nail polish, safety pins or a sewing kit.

Amateurs.

Karen's problem was a little bigger. Somehow she'd managed to snag the waistline, and part of it had unraveled from the bodice. If it had been one of the seams at her bust line, I might have understood. Karen was a girl blessed with boobs. This, however, was the sign of inferior sewing. How nice for Alma to spend an outrageous sum on an extravagant location, a planner and vendors she didn't need, yet cheap-out on the bridesmaid dresses. It was a nice gesture for her to pay for all the dresses, but I was betting Gail's friends would have been happy to take over the expense if it meant dresses that wouldn't split open and expose them in the middle of the chicken dance at the reception.

No wonder they didn't bother helping her with

anything. I needed something to eat. I was getting cranky.

Out of my emergency kit, I pulled a hand sewing machine. I wasn't able to match the thread exactly, but it was close enough. Once Karen was out of her dress, I had it fixed in three minutes.

I'm so organized.

Having dealt with the first round of catastrophes, I ran out the door promising to check on Aidan. Gail wasn't exactly perky, but her eyes were dry and she was making progress toward getting dressed.

In the hallway, I ran into Andrew. I wanted to stop and hug him, but I had no time.

"Walk with me," I said. I checked my texts while we sprinted to the groom's quarters. Sara was running late but should be there any minute. "For the time being, will you be me? I need you to run down to the reception area and direct traffic. I have a horrible feeling work has stopped while I'm up here. Brad's alone with two giggly females. Can you crack a whip over them?"

"That's my dream job." He gave my shoulders a squeeze and disappeared into the elevator.

Aidan and his boys were, of course, hung over and self-medicating with the proverbial hair of the dog. They were obnoxious as hell, and one of them actually grabbed my butt, but they were getting ready.

On my way out the door, I pointed at the stubble-faced guy in the corner. "Somebody get the ass-man a razor. No grizzly bears in the wedding photos."

I trekked to the bride's room and stuck my head

through the door. "Aidan's fine, Gail. Everybody's getting ready. No worries. Do you need anything else before I go?"

She looked much more relaxed than she had a half hour before. "I'm kind of thirsty."

I scowled at the women lounging around the room. "Ladies, room service. Get her a drink. Your job today is to get yourselves ready and to wait on her. She should not have to be thirsty. Not with all these people here to take care of her."

The women looked startled and stopped chattering. Erin picked up the phone and dialed. Externally, I smiled my brightest smile. Inside, I was rolling my eyes. These women were in their mid- to late-twenties. They were behaving like teenagers. I was going to have to make several more trips up there before the ceremony.

By the time I reached the parking lot, Sara was pulling herself out from behind the steering wheel. Her skin was pale and papery, her eyes ringed with dark puffiness. But she was dressed nicely, if slightly wrinkled by her standards (not mine), and her hair was tidy. I knew at a glance she would be lagging behind.

"I'm sorry I'm late," she said. "My alarm didn't go off."

I almost pointed out that it was well after noon, but it didn't seem worth the effort. First thing Monday morning, I was taking her to a doctor whether she agreed to it or not. Possibly sooner.

Normally at a wedding this size, she'd be running

as hard as I was. She was far too out of it for that this time. I got her set up folding napkins and passing them over to Brad and his mini-harem.

"Just keep an eye on them and keep things going, okay?"

She smiled at me in an absent way and started humming while she folded.

I snagged Andrew by the arm and pulled him aside.

"She looks like hell," he said.

I nodded. "I'll take care of her. The sooner we get through today, the sooner I can get her to a doctor."

"Zoey, what's wrong with her? I've never seen an aura like that. It looks so thin and brittle."

I watched her for a moment, frowning with worry. "She hasn't been sleeping. Should we take her to the emergency room?"

Andrew squinted at her. "It doesn't look like she's sick, exactly. Just worn out. I think she can make it through the wedding. I'll keep an eye on her, then we'll take her in tonight."

I nodded, relieved to have him there. Sara was okay for the moment. We just had to get through this afternoon.

Andrew and I stepped into the chapel for a quick once-over. "Where the hell are the decorations? The extra chairs are here, but the runner and the flowers haven't been set up."

I dashed out the door with Andrew trailing behind me. We located the chapel decorations and pulled Frankie in to help us haul them over and set up. Halfway through, I left them to it, ran back to check on Sara, then tore up to the bride's room to look in on her.

If I'd had time for my mind to wander, I'd have been daydreaming about the upcoming vacation I hadn't realized I needed.

Alma Dickson had given up on her false eyelashes and was now harassing her daughter.

"This wouldn't have happened if you had a tighter rein on your fiancé," she said. "I have two hundred and fifty people waiting to see my daughter get married, and you let him and his no-good friends go out drinking last night." She paced the floor, shooting eyeball darts at each of the women in the room before returning to her daughter. "I can't have anything go wrong today."

Gail huddled on the bed in a sea of white satin, lace and tulle, her face pink, tears threatening to spill.

I stood in the doorway, fuming. I'd had enough of this hateful woman.

My smile was fierce. "Mrs. Dickson, I need to see you in the hallway, please."

She waved me off. "In a minute. I'm speaking to my daughter."

"Now."

The chill in my voice broke through to her, and her head swiveled in my direction.

"Excuse me?" Her painted eyebrows shot up into her hairline.

"I need to see you in the hall. Now." I pushed the door open the rest of the way and stepped aside.

She was fuming by the time I got her outside the room and closed the door behind us. "You do not speak to me that way," she said. "You work for me, and I…"

I raised my hand to stop her. "This is not your day. This is hers. You are not the main event today, Mrs. Dickson, and browbeating the bride is unacceptable behavior from anyone, even you. Making the bride cry on her happy day is something you wouldn't allow anyone else to do. I don't know why you think it's okay for you."

I could feel her anger pounding against my defenses like a drummer in a middle school band.

She sputtered, but didn't find any words. She probably didn't have enough experience with people standing up to her to know what an appropriate response might be.

"Now," I said. "You hired us to coordinate all this. Everyone has a job to do, and I need you to do what you do best." I gave her my most professional smile. "I have members of the press downstairs needing direction. Would you be so kind as to answer their questions and show them where they need to be, Councilwoman Dickson?"

Her entire demeanor changed. Her professional smile matched mine, she straightened the jacket on her pantsuit and stalked to the elevator without another word.

Frankly, I didn't care anymore if she dropped a truck full of dead sea bass into my office. *Shut us down, I dare you. I'll run for city council myself and kick your ass to the street, you old bat.*

Forty-five minutes later, I had the bridal party in their places and ready for the ceremony. I'm not sure how I pulled it off.

Sara should have been helping me herd the wedding party, but I hadn't seen her since planting her at the reception tables with the napkins. I could only hope she was busy arranging centerpieces and overseeing the catering staff. The groom and his half of the party were at the front of the chapel. I sent the bridesmaids down at regular intervals, Gail and her parents went through the door, and I was free. My shoulders had been up around my ears, but with the bride sailing down the aisle with a smile on her face, I relaxed in tiny increments. Round one was complete.

"Psst."

I jumped. Maybe I was still tenser than I thought. I was alone in the foyer. I had to have been hearing things.

"Psst. Zoey!" The whisper was not my imagination. I made a circle, looking around the empty room. Nobody was there.

From a dark cloakroom, a familiar, chalk-white hand fluttered at me. "In here!"

"Maurice?" I went into the cloakroom and flipped on the light.

Maurice was pressed up against the back wall, his eyes larger than usual, peering over my shoulder in agitation.

"What the hell are you doing here? How did you get in here?"

"Technically, it's a closet." He said this as if it explained everything.

"Kind of busy here. What's wrong?"

His hands were splayed out and gesturing like an Italian on six cups of espresso. "She's gone. Nobody's seen her since this morning. I don't know what to do, Zoey. I know you're busy, but she could be hurt or worse, and the longer she's gone the more scared the kids are, and I'm just not equipped for this kind of problem. I don't know what to do."

"Hold on, deep breath. Who's missing? Molly?"

"Yes, Molly, who else would I be talking about?" He sounded exasperated. "She went out this morning saying she had errands to run and she'd be back in a little while. That was seven hours ago. I've looked everywhere."

"Who's watching the kids?"

"Iris is keeping an eye on them. I told him not to let them out of his sight, in case, you know, their dad tries to come for them, too."

"You think he has Molly?"

"Where else could she be?"

For a moment, I worried that Sebastian had planted the idea of his appearance at this wedding as a decoy so he could get to Molly. But no. I had to trust the Demon Handbook that my house was outside his territory. Sausalito was as far as he could go. Molly might be dealing with her jerk of a husband, but she was safe from the incubus.

This was so not part of my plan for the day. "I can't leave here right now, Maurice. I'm worried, too, but I have to see this through first. I'll come home as soon as I can, but it's going to be several hours. Keep looking for her. She can't be far. Tell Aggie. Maybe she's got a way to track her."

Maurice looked disappointed, as if he thought I could fix this. I'd grown to depend on him so much, I hadn't realized how much he depended on me, as well.

I felt terrible. Guilt seemed to be my most often-used emotion these days. "Listen," I said, "keep the kids inside. Get everyone searching. We'll find her, and she *will* be fine. I need a few more hours, and I'll come home and help."

Maurice looked doubtful. "She's part of our family, Zo."

"I know she is." I wanted to cry. I was as worried as he was, but I couldn't show it or we'd both fall apart. "We'll find her."

"What are you doing in the coat closet?" Andrew's appearance made both of us jump. "Hey, Maurice. What's up?"

The closet monster looked cornered, as if he were fighting off a panic attack. "Molly's missing."

"Well, shit," Andrew said. He looked from Maurice to me, his face serious. "Sara's missing, too."

I groaned and smacked my forehead with my palm. It hurt. *Deep breaths, Zoey. You can handle this. Delegate. Breathe and delegate.*

"Maurice, you have to find Molly. I'm sorry I can't help right now. And I swear, it's killing me. But I have to find Sara and see this reception through

till it's running on its own steam. I'm trusting you
to handle this. You can do it. You're the one with all
the resources. If she's in trouble, you're the one who
can get her out of it."

Maurice nodded his head, his face solemn. "I've
got it, Zoey."

I was looking right at him, but my eyes refused to
focus. It was the oddest sensation. He was there, and
then he wasn't. I was staring at shadows and blem-
ishes on the wall that looked like him. It was as if
his presence had been in my imagination, a trick of
the light. If I hadn't talked to him, I might have believed he'd never existed.

"Weird," Andrew said, reaching forward and patting the wall.

"Wish I had that skill right now," I said. "Where
did you see Sara last?"

"Last I saw her, she was lighting candles."

"You let her play with fire?"

"I didn't 'let' her do anything. She was wandering around humming and fussing with things. I figured it was best to leave her be so she didn't get into
any trouble."

We sprinted to the reception area. Frankie and
Adrianne were standing aside chatting while the caterers busied themselves with their setup. To my surprise, Brad was working hard, moving chairs around
and adjusting place settings. Sara was nowhere. The
girls didn't remember seeing her in the last half hour.
Andrew and I split up to cover more ground.

In the parking lot, I found her car still locked and

empty. I felt like an idiot poking my head around bushes, inside closets, under tables. I dialed her number. There was no response.

No one I talked to had seen her recently. I checked at the front desk to see if Sara had checked herself into a room for a nap. Nope.

I was in the hotel lobby and decided to check the parking lot one more time. I spun around toward the door and smacked into a man walking in.

Riley grabbed me to keep me upright.

My heart leaped at seeing him again. And then it sank. His beautiful gray eyes were filled with sadness.

When your best friend has gone missing and the Grim Reaper shows up, it doesn't much matter how long his eyelashes are.

Sara was in serious trouble.

# TWENTY-FIVE

I HAD TO take a breath and assess the situation. The bridal party was due to come out of the chapel and head for the reception area any second, with no one from my office there to direct them. Molly was missing, possibly bleeding somewhere at the hands of her abusive husband. Sara was on her last legs, now missing and maybe dying in a back room somewhere. I was afraid my new squeeze had come to collect her soul.

That about summed it up, and my brain was shutting down.

Riley was holding me up by the elbows while I stood in place, trying to sort it all out. I needed a minute, that was all. Sure. If I could have a moment to reorganize, I could get back into action.

I didn't have a minute.

Brad came barreling into the lobby like Paul Revere announcing the arrival of the British. In this case, it was the bridal party and guests he was heralding.

"Zoey, I don't know what to do. They're flooding out of the chapel and milling around. I've never done this part before. I'm lifting and carrying, not hosting and directing."

*Ah, but what I've always wanted to do is direct! Shut up, Zoey.*

As if a light switch had been thrown, I snapped out of my dazed confusion. "It's like herding cattle. Tell the wedding party I had an emergency and direct everyone to the reception area. As long as they think someone is in charge, they should be fine."

He flicked his eyes to Riley and back to me. "Zoey, what are you doing out here? You have to come do this. I'm not capable."

"Brad, trust me. You're capable. I need you to do this for me. Schmoozing is your thing. Sara's sick and I have to find her."

Brad did not look happy. Truthfully, he looked a little shaken up. If I'd had time to ponder it, I might have enjoyed his lack of self-confidence. It was a rare sight.

"Please, Brad," I said. I knew my voice sounded desperate. "You wanted to prove to me you were reliable. I'm relying on you now. I'm trusting you with my business and my reputation. Please tell me I can count on you."

He straightened his shoulders and his face firmed with resolve. He nodded once, looked at Riley with narrowed eyes, then trotted off.

I was so going to owe him after this.

I returned my attention to Riley. His fingers were digging into the flesh in my arms—or maybe that was my imagination, since I was distracted by the physical contact between us.

"Where is she?" I said.

He didn't answer me right away. I could see he

was worried, but I could also see the resolve on his face. "I can't interfere, Zoey."

I jerked away from his grasp. "So don't. But you got a text with my best friend's name and location, correct? You're here to make a pickup."

His head moved up and down once.

"Then go find her. I'll follow. But you are not taking her, I guarantee that."

His hand rose to touch my face and I took a step back. "You have to stay here," he said.

"No."

"You can't follow me. I can't have you there."

"The hell you can't. I'm the only one who has a chance of saving her, and you can't stop me." I was yelling now, right in the middle of a posh hotel lobby. People were beginning to stare.

Riley grabbed my shoulders before I could step out of reach again. His face was inches from mine. "You are staying here."

I twisted free. "No. I'm not."

He reached for me again and I pulled away. His exasperation was palpable, even with my walls sealed up tight. "Dammit, Zoey, stay out of the way. Sara's wasn't the only name in the text."

I felt the blood drain from my face. "He's really here then."

"I don't have those details."

"Take me there. Now." I know I sounded bossy, but I felt more like a death-row inmate about to take the long walk. "I'm not arguing, and I'm not asking, Riley. Let's get this over with."

Riley's face sank, his head drooping in defeat.

He took a deep breath and squared his shoulders. "I hate this job," he said. He reached out and stroked my cheek, then turned away.

I followed him to the reception area. I could see the guests outside talking, locating tables, admiring the breathtaking view of the Golden Gate Bridge below. I loved that view. Shame I might never see it again.

I thought he would take us out there, but before we hit the glass doors, he made a left into a side room I hadn't noticed. Andrew came around the corner, saw where I was headed and fell into step without a word.

I didn't make it through the door before my amulet shot ice down my shirt and nearly freezer-burned my chest with a permanent mark. I yanked it out and tucked it over my collar while it bit at my fingers. Any last hope I had that Sebastian wasn't in the next room was gone. The metal was so cold it gave off wisps of condensation from the front of my blouse.

The scene inside the little room made me want to vomit. It was probably a good thing I hadn't had time to eat since breakfast.

Sara was pressed up against the wall in the far corner, her legs wrapped around Sebastian's waist. Her once-perfect hair was soaked with sweat and stuck to the sides of her face. She was ashen and her blue eyes were unfocused, staring off at some vague point on the opposite wall. One shoe lay on the floor, forgotten, and the other hung from a bobbing foot. Tears burned my eyes, and my breath caught in my chest.

Somehow, I'd come to the mistaken conclusion

he didn't have physical intercourse with his victims. I'd assumed wrong. What was going on in that small, stuffy room was not what I'd witnessed in my dreams. He wasn't relegating himself to stroking her thigh or kissing her neck, though there was plenty of that going on as well.

His prissy, ironed jeans were down around his ankles. I wanted to avert my eyes, but I couldn't look away. It wasn't any kind of sex I'd ever had, that was for sure.

He was lit up like a road flare, and she was gray and barely moving. Her eyelids fluttered, and if he hadn't been holding her legs around him, I doubt she would have had the strength to keep them there.

Fortunately, we were spared the sight of his scrawny ass pumping into my friend. He hadn't bothered to remove his coat and it hung down to his thighs.

Andrew put his hand on my shoulder. "She doesn't have long, Zoey. There's barely a spark left in her aura. It's so close to her body there isn't much left of it."

Riley glanced at his watch and stepped aside. "I'm sorry," he said. "I can't help."

There was no sign that Sebastian had noticed he had company.

"Hey, asshat," I said.

His rhythmic hip movements stopped. He looked over his shoulder at me and grinned. "Dream Girl, how wonderful! I was just finishing up here."

"You're finished now. Get off her."

"I do hate to leave food on my plate when there are starving orphans all over the world. This will only take a second. I tried to make her last longer, but it seems I'm a bit of a glutton. I've enjoyed her so much over the last few weeks. She has so much of you in her, I can't help myself." He made an attempt at looking contrite before resuming his motions.

So he was the reason she was so exhausted. She wasn't sick at all. He'd been killing her a little at a time for weeks. My fists clenched at my sides.

Sara's eyes flashed open and a weak moan escaped from her lips.

*Come on, Zoey. Pull your head out. You've learned things. You have tools. Use them, and use them quick.*

A picture of Molly's irate husband danced across my vision. That was something I could use.

In my mind, I formed a solid glass bell and dropped it over Sara. I sealed it tight, cutting her off from all external contact. It wasn't an easy thing to create with him touching her. Determined, I focused on separating them with my barrier. I shoved the glass between them and willed it to conform around her, pushing him away.

Sara needed me. I had to be stronger than Sebastian. The glass bell was my construct, and I held my concentration to keep it from shattering at his touch. He'd have to come after me first to reach her again.

"Oh, now that's just unfair," Sebastian said. His hips twitched a few last times for good measure, perhaps testing the strength of the barrier I'd put up. He gave a dramatic sigh and bent over, pulling up his pants. I looked away as he did it. His dangly bits were not a memory I wanted seared into my consciousness.

He turned to face me. His jeans were buttoned up, but his fancy pirate shirt flapped in the breeze. The lyrics to "Blowin' in the Wind" ran through my mind and I had to squelch them.

Fear often sends my mind to babbling.

For the first time, Sebastian noticed I wasn't the only intruder in the room. He dropped his head to Riley in an archaic show of respect. "Grave digger. Glad to see you're on the job. I trust you won't be interfering again today."

Riley said nothing. He looked at his watch and waited.

The demon turned his attention to Andrew. His brows rose in surprise. "Oh my. You brought me someone new to play with. How thoughtful. Normally, I prefer women, but at the end of the day, they all taste the same. They taste like you, Dream Girl."

I was confused. I looked from Sebastian to Andrew and my breath caught in my throat. I'd forgotten that Andrew was gay. His eyes were already glassy as Sebastian approached him.

"Oh, hell no," I said, stepping in front of my friend. I heard the breath whoosh out of Andrew from behind me. Apparently, I'd broken the connection for the moment.

That was the last straw. I was small and weak. I felt so terrified in that moment I was afraid my bladder would let go, and I'd pee all over the floor. But more importantly, I was furious.

I threw open my mental shutters and opened myself up to Sebastian's emotions.

*Hunger.*

*Need.*

*Hunger.*

He moved toward me. I focused a beam of his own emotions at him with all the mental force I could muster. He took a step backward, confusion lining his face.

"That's a new trick," he said. "A little disconcerting, actually." He stepped forward. "What else do you have?"

I gathered my fear and worry, and most of all, my anger, and hurled it into the beam, willing it to punch him in his smarmy face.

He stopped moving and closed his eyes. His body shuddered, as if in ecstasy. "Oh, Dream Girl, that was incredible." He ran his fingers down his chest and to his stomach. "I had no idea you could do that. Do it again." His eyes opened and the green had turned crimson. "I'm starving."

It wasn't enough. No matter how emotional I was at that moment, all I was doing was feeding him. I reached out to Andrew and grasped for any emotions he could give me. Andrew, unlike the rest of the world, kept himself sealed. There was nothing in him I could reach.

I stretched my mind toward Riley. I wasn't sure I wanted to know what he had, and honestly, as detached as he had to be, I wasn't sure there'd be any emotion there at all. I was wrong. Underneath the cold veneer of Death, he was as big a wreck as I was.

*Fear. Hatred. Worry.*

I gathered them up, added them to mine and let them fly. Sebastian jerked and smiled. I kept the stream connecting me to Riley open.

*Fury. Love.* Love? I did not want to know about that right now.

Everything I collected channeled through me and out at Sebastian. But his smile widened, and his hands skimmed over his chest. He was enjoying it. All I was doing was keeping him distracted.

Andrew's hand was on my shoulder again. "I'm open," he said. "Take what you need."

Andrew's emotions were much the same as mine and Riley's. I opened up a line connecting Andrew to the flow, and it knocked Sebastian back another step.

Still, it wasn't enough.

Sara was out cold on the floor underneath my protective barrier. Besides, she had nothing to offer that wouldn't kill her. I turned my head toward Andrew without taking my eyes off Sebastian. "Open the doors," I said in a low voice. "The ones outside, too."

I heard the door open behind me and he was gone. In his absence, I lost my concentration and my stream of Andrew-energy.

Sebastian regained momentum and came for me, his hand outstretched. My skin crawled at the idea of his flesh touching me. I stepped away, but I was too slow. His fingers brushed my arm.

I moaned and fell to my knees. Watching him touch those women, seeing with my eyes the effect he had on them, in no way prepared me for what really happened when he was serious about feeding.

When he'd touched me under the pier, he'd been toying with me.

There was heat and moisture between my legs before my brain had time to process it. The orgasm that slammed into me was nothing like anything anyone should ever experience. There was no lead-up, and it was not as pleasurable as one might expect. It burned—not like acid, but more like an acetylene torch had been ignited inside of me. This, while every nerve ending in my body fired, and every muscle contracted. The orgasm was there, but so was the pain. God help me, I liked it. And I craved more.

There was a part of my brain whispering, frantic to be heard through the blood pumping in my ears. The chill of my amulet seared through my blouse, yet it was so far removed from my attention, it might have been the sound of the ocean in the distance. I couldn't imagine why I'd been fighting this for so long. I should have let him have me the day I met him. Sebastian loved me. At that moment, I would have given him every ounce of myself.

It stopped as quickly as it had started.

I was on the floor and I didn't remember how I got there. Sebastian was holding my arm and looking irritated.

Riley held my other arm.

"Come on, Reaper," Sebastian said, pulling his hand away. "You know better than to interfere. I'll have you up on charges. I cry foul!"

Riley ignored him and pulled me to my feet. His

eyes clouded with worry, and he pulled me closer, his arm around my waist.

It was a nice place to be. If only I could have a chance to enjoy it.

Andrew reappeared on my other side. "It's all open out to the gardens," he said. He noted the possessive way Riley held on to me. "Glad you decided to join the game," he said.

Sebastian stretched his arms out to me, as if willing me to run into them like a scared child. His ego did not give up. "Dream Girl, why do you play with boys when you can have a real man? They don't appreciate you like I do."

I wanted to have a snappy retort, really I did. I was going to have to accept who I was and quit wishing I were someone else. I was not a kick-ass judo chick with guns, knives and crossbows. On the other hand, I was not the clumsy, love-struck heroine who sat around waiting for someone else to finish off the bad guy for her.

And I wasn't the wise-cracking comedienne who always had a witty last word before plunging a knife into the villain's chest.

We do what we can with what we're given.

I reconnected my channels to the two men by my side, but I kept the emotions inside myself. Feeling outward to the crowd of revelers, I gathered up the flood of good feelings pooling in the gardens. The energy of the guests collected in one enormous river and poured into me. I let it all swirl and crash together, mixing with Andrew and Riley and with me.

I was overflowing with emotional energy, but I

owned it. I could feel myself expanding to hold it all. I felt like the sun, a bright beacon glowing from the inside.

At long last, Sebastian looked nervous. I looked down at my hands and saw it wasn't in my imagination—my body was throbbing with white light.

Here was my chance for that witty closing retort. I gathered all that energy and light into a solid ball.

Nope. I wasn't going to get to be the witty heroine.

"Asshole," I said.

I hurled everything I had at him in one enormous wave. It spattered over him like bacon grease and absorbed into his chest. His face convulsed in pain. He flung his arms out to the sides and bellowed. Light consumed him and he shattered into thousands of prismatic shards.

And then he was gone.

The three of us stood like that for several minutes. I was out of breath, my head hurt, and I wasn't entirely sure he was gone for good.

"You know," I said, "I really didn't think that was going to work."

There was a burnt spot on the carpet where Sebastian had been standing. I wondered if snooty Margaret would make me pay for it.

Riley moved first. Despite being in shock, I felt like a horrible friend. Sara lay collapsed on the floor, unconscious. Riley knelt beside her and felt for a pulse.

"It's weak," he said. "But she's still here for the moment."

"I'll call an ambulance," I said. By some miracle,

I had my bag with me. I dug around for my phone, my hands shaking. I cursed myself for not bringing the purse Molly had made for me.

Riley shook his head. "It's not physical. There isn't much they'd be able to do."

I supposed he would know that better than anybody.

Andrew touched my arm. "You're running hot, Zoey."

He was right. I hadn't shut off the channels I was bringing in from the party guests. I snapped it off at the source. I could still feel the energy I'd collected surging inside of me.

I moved to her side.

"Guys, can you turn your backs for a sec?" They shifted for me, and I straightened Sara's skirt, tucking her ruined underwear into my bag for later disposal.

I closed my eyes and lifted the mental wall of protection I'd dropped over her. I didn't know if it would help, but she was drained, and I was overflowing. I prodded at her with a gentle touch of my mind. I made the beam small and tight; I didn't want to overwhelm her. She felt so weak.

I fed her in a slow, steady stream.

"Andrew, I can't see. You have to be my eyes."

It trickled into her, and Andrew watched. "It's like watching a fishbowl fill up," he said. "I think it's working."

It was a slow, agonizing process. I once owned a waterbed when I was in my early twenties. That took forever to fill, too.

After about a half hour, the color in Sara's cheeks was more to my liking—more like a human and less like a bowl of oatmeal. I had no idea what I was going to say to her if—when—she woke up.

I didn't have long to contemplate it. Not long after I started to worry about an explanation, she stirred, and her eyes fluttered open.

"Shit," she said, sitting up and patting at her hair. "This doesn't look very professional. I have got to get more sleep."

# TWENTY-SIX

THE MIND IS a resilient thing. Self-preservation is its top priority.

Sara was mortified to have fallen asleep during the Dickson-Strauss wedding. I used her embarrassment to convince her to take a vacation and get some much-needed rest.

The incubus had been robbing her of psychic energy, but there was a physical toll, too. Her eyes were still bloodshot with dark bags beneath them, and she was moving slower than the Sara I knew.

She had no memory of the dark lover who had been keeping her up nights. There's no way to know if that was more parlor tricks of the human mind or the supernatural erasing of all signs of Sebastian's visit to our world. Frankly, I didn't care, as long as Sara wasn't going to need therapy—or explanations.

The reception had gone well in our absence. Brad had stepped up and performed like the professional schmoozer he was. The toasts were performed in the right order, the DJ was set up properly and, apparently, Brad had a previously undiscovered talent at cake cutting. I still owed him a big one. So far, he'd left me alone about it, but I knew I'd have to pay up soon. I certainly couldn't afford to send my ex-husband to college, or wherever it was he had in mind, but when he finally got around to telling me his plans, I'd help him. After all—helping was kind of my thing.

The only thing that had gone wrong had me slapping myself in the forehead. Those stupid birdseed favors, the bane of my existence for the past two weeks, had been left in the storage room without being passed out.

Gail hadn't even noticed.

We made it out alive with our reputations intact and our fees paid in full. That was far more than I could have hoped for. The photos in the paper were gorgeous, and Alma was even quoted, praising Happily Ever After for creating and coordinating her daughter's flawless day.

The minute I could get away from the reception, I sped home and flew through the front door.

Maurice was sitting on the couch, feet up, reading the paper. He glanced up at me. "Hey, how'd it go?"

"Could have been worse," I said. "You're not looking for Molly. Where are the kids?"

"Molly came and got them."

"And went where? Please tell me she didn't go back to her husband." My heart would break if he said yes.

"She's been talking to him. But no, she didn't go back to him." He folded up the paper and stood up. "Come see."

He led me out the front door and around the side till we were behind the house. Toward the back of the property, but still well within the invisible fairy line, was the most enormous mushroom I'd ever seen. It came up to my hip and was a bright green trimmed with yellow.

Molly must've seen us approach through a window, because she came flying out a small door in the stem.

"Welcome home, Zoey. Surprise!"

"Surprise?"

"You have been so kind to us. I could not take advantage of you forever. I have a house now. Surprise!"

"It's lovely," I said. And it was. "You know, you were welcome to stay as long as you wanted, Molly."

"I know that. This is best. We are nearby but not underfoot."

"Well, welcome home, then." I would have to think of some sort of housewarming gift for her. "We should have a party."

"That is very kind of you."

"What about your husband?"

"We are talking. A little. When he stops drinking, we will talk more."

I nodded. "All right then. If you need anything at all, I'm here." I was proud of her and happy. But I was also sad. I'd grown used to having Molly and her children in my home. At least she hadn't gone far.

That night, it was Maurice and I at the table alone. At least I still had him with me.

"Zoey," he said after pushing his plate away. His face was serious. "I know I barged in on you, but now that Molly moved out, it got me to thinking."

I wanted to cry. Whatever he said next was not

something I wanted to hear. I considered reaching for a leftover breadstick and shoving into his mouth to stop him from saying it.

"Don't think, Maurice. Eat." I pushed the basket toward him.

"No, I'm serious. I should find my own way and stop leeching off of you."

I looked at my plate of homemade spaghetti and meat sauce and snorted. The pots and pans in the sink, the crumbs on the table, the peach cobbler I'd seen in the fridge—none of this was stuff I had to worry about anymore. If anything, I was leeching off of him.

"I won't keep you here, Maurice. But I do wish you'd stay."

"You do?"

I swallowed. I was having a hard time keeping calm and not bursting into tears. I wanted to grab him and shake him. "Please stay? You don't have to do so much work around here, you know. You're not on salary."

"I like cooking and cleaning. I like taking care of you."

"Then why would you leave?"

"I thought you liked living alone."

"I did. But I'm obviously incapable of taking proper care of myself. What if another incubus shows up?"

"Then you'll vanquish him with all your smit-eyness."

"What if a dragon shows up at my door demanding room service?"

"You'll feed him ice cubes and give him your dinner."

"What if I can't sleep at night?"

He grinned. "You can't make your own hot chocolate?"

"Nope. I'll poison myself with instant chocolate milk mix."

He got up and started clearing the plates. "Fine, I'll stay. But only because you're so pathetic in the kitchen."

"I could have made spaghetti, you know."

He sniffed and put the plates in the sink. "Sure. From a jar."

The peach cobbler was, as expected, exquisite.

I tossed and turned that night for all of five seconds. The events of the previous weeks had drained me of every ounce of physical strength I had. I dreamed of seashells and talking fish, dancing bears in tutus, and Riley. There was no black wedding dress, and no one died. It was peaceful.

I was up by eight and ready for my first stress-free day in what felt like a decade. The smell of coffee woke me and I said a little prayer of gratitude to a god who made gourmet-chef closet monsters.

I padded into the kitchen, planning my day of absolute nothing.

Maurice was at the table, tented by the morning paper, with nothing of him showing but his checkered sneakers and bony fingers. He was not alone.

The fingers clutching another section of the paper were different. They were thick and gray with spots of green in the joints. Under the table I could see a pair of enormous, black work boots. I braced myself.

"Good morning?"

Both papers went down and Maurice was grinning from ear to ear. "Zoey, good morning! Sit-sit-sit! I'll get you some coffee, and then I'll whip up some waffles."

I sat, obedient. "Hello," I said to the mountain in front of me.

The face staring at me was like a chiseled chunk of stone. Bits of moss were caught between moving parts and flaked as he moved his jaw. I might have been alarmed but for the warm brown eyes that stared out at me from his craggy eye sockets.

"Oh, this is Phillip," Maurice said. He slid coffee across the table to me. "He's my brother-in-law, and he needs a place to stay for a few days."

"Oh," I said. I took a sip and scalded my tongue. "All right. It's nice to meet you, Phillip."

Words rumbled out of him. They sounded like a quiet avalanche. "My bread fell asleep in the toaster," he said.

I nodded my head, as if this made perfect sense to me. "Well, you're welcome here until it wakes up."

"Phillip is a gargoyle," Maurice said. His tone implied this should explain everything. It did not.

Breakfast was disconcerting, but somehow still pleasant. Phillip made weird grinding sounds when he ate, and pieces of moss had a tendency to break away into his plate, unnoticed.

He liked syrup very much. Phillip had quite the

sweet tooth for someone with no real teeth. "Mice make excellent painters," he said by way of asking for the butter.

I smiled and passed it to him. Phillip was going to make for an interesting weekend.

My phone rang and I excused myself.

"What's for breakfast?" It was Riley.

"You know, proper etiquette requires you to say hello first."

"Hello. What's for breakfast?"

"Gargoyle surprise."

He laughed. "New houseguest?"

"Indeed."

"Do you have to stay home and entertain him tonight or can you sneak out so I can feed you pasta and make fun of you?"

"I suppose I can make time for you."

"You're a giver, Zoey. Always thinking of others."

"That's me." I paused. "All joking aside, how much trouble are you in for helping me?"

"Don't worry about it."

"I'm worried about it."

He sighed. "Some trouble. I can work it out. Really. Nothing for you to worry over."

"I have nothing else to worry over right now. I'm between problems. I thought I'd choose you to rebuild my waning stress levels."

"We'll discuss it tonight. Wear a white shirt. I want to make sure I can point and laugh when you drop food on yourself."

"You need to get a hobby."

"You are my new hobby. I'll pick you up at seven."

After we hung up, I did a little dance in the living room. Maurice popped his head out and watched. "Another date with the reaper?"

"Does it show?"

"It shows. Can you come in here a minute?"

He had a worried look on his face and pulled me toward the window facing into the backyard.

"What am I looking at?"

"The pool."

I squinted. The water rippled and slopped over the sides. "What's going on out there? What am I missing?"

A slick rope of dull-green flesh slid across the water and disappeared under the surface.

I gasped. "Tell me we don't have a mermaid in the pool."

Maurice grinned his toothiest. "We don't have a mermaid in the swimming pool."

"Then, what?" My imagination was on full blast. I waited, shivering, for the Creature from the Black Lagoon to climb out covered in seaweed. Swamp Thing might drag himself to my back door any second, stringing moss behind him.

"Sea serpent," Maurice said. He looked positively thrilled at the idea. "Do you know how rare they are these days?"

I nodded my head as if, of course, I knew how rare sea serpents were these days. "It's kind of puny."

"The world gets smaller every day. But there's more of her in the pool than you can see."

"So. What do we do about it?" I reached for a sweater. It looked cold out there, and I knew I was about to get splashed.

"I guess you'd better buy some fish today at the market," Maurice said. "Lots and lots of fish."

\* \* \* \* \*